BLOOD MONEY

Arlene Hunt is originally from Wicklow and now lives in Dublin with her husband, daughter and mêlée of useless, overweight animals. *Blood Money* is her sixth novel.

Also by Arlene Hunt
Vicious Circle
False Intentions
Black Sheep
Missing Presumed Dead
Undertow

ARLENE HUNT

BLOOD MONEY

LEABHARLANN CHONTAE
L215,715
Longfoirt
AFP

HACHETTE
BOOKS
IRELAND

First published in 2010 by Hachette Books Ireland
First published in paperback in 2010 by Hachette Books Ireland
A division of Hachette UK Ltd

1

Copyright © 2010 Arlene Hunt

The right of Arlene Hunt to be identified as the Author of the Work has
been asserted by her in accordance with the Copyright, Designs and
Patents Act 1988.

All rights reserved. No part of this publication may be reproduced, stored
in a retrieval system, or transmitted, in any form or by any means without
the prior written permission of the publisher, nor be otherwise circulated
in any form of binding or cover other than that in which it is published and
without a similar condition being imposed on the subsequent purchaser.

A CIP catalogue record for this title is available from the British Library

ISBN 978 0 340 97731 6

All characters in this publication are fictitious and any resemblance to real
persons, living or dead, is purely coincidental.

Typeset in Sabon MT by Hachette Books Ireland
Printed and bound in the UK by
CPI Mackays, Chatham ME5 8TD

Hachette Books Ireland policy is to use papers that are natural, renewable
and recyclable products and made from wood grown in sustainable forests.
The logging and manufacturing processes are expected to conform to the
environmental regulations of the country of origin.

Hachette Books Ireland
8 Castlecourt Centre, Castleknock, Dublin 15, Ireland
A division of Hachette UK Ltd, 338 Euston Road,
London NW1 3BH, England

To Tim. Keep on running.

Acknowledgements

My father-in-law Terry Mangan had a heart transplant over a decade ago. This vibrant, funny, loving man lived because some other person lost their life, some other family grieved, some other family said goodbye to a loved one. It is a measure of great compassion that people can look beyond their grief to those who still suffer. A simple gesture, like that of carrying a donor card, can mean the difference between life and death. On that day, that donor and their family gave us back a hugely important member of ours and we are eternally grateful.

I thought of that unknown family often over the years and, in time, the basis of an idea developed. What would you do if you could avail of an organ by more nefarious measures? Would you wait? Would you risk time elapsing? Could you stand by and watch a loved family member grow weaker while they waited on a transplant list? I do not know the answer. I deal in the realms of fiction and I am happy enough to stay there for a while longer. But *Blood Money* is a fiction based on the actions of those who do not wait, who attempt to circumnavigate lists and waiting times. It is based on those most human emotions: fear and greed.

My thanks as always go to Faith O'Grady, my agent. To Ciara Considine, my most excellent editor. To Breda and all the staff at Hachette. No man is an island, nor is any woman, so to this end I must say a hearty hello and thank you to Anna, Antonia, Corrina, Madeline, Megan, Sarah and Tara, my beautiful ladies who drag me kicking and screaming from my office into the open air. To my friend Bryan for being fabulous and for park walks, and to Billy for putting up with us all. A special thank you to John Connolly for taking the time to read this novel and for being an all-round peach. To Kriss for being brave and an inspiration, you did it Melvin. To Megan and Sam for being soundboards in more ways than one, valued opinion is a wonderful pool to dip into and yours runs deep. To my family Terry and Tim, and finally to Andrew and Jordan, love always, unconditional and true.

I swear by Apollo Physician and Asclepius and Hygieia and Panaceia and all the gods, and goddesses, making them my witnesses, that I will fulfil according to my ability and judgement this oath and this covenant:

To hold him who has taught me this art as equal to my parents and to live my life in partnership with him, and if he is in need of money to give him a share of mine, and to regard his offspring as equal to my brothers in male lineage and to teach them this art – if they desire to learn it – without fee and covenant; to give a share of precepts and oral instruction and all the other learning to my sons and to the sons of him who has instructed me and to pupils who have signed the covenant and have taken the oath according to medical law, but to no one else.

I will apply dietetic measures for the benefit of the sick according to my ability and judgement; I will keep them from harm and injustice.

I will neither give a deadly drug to anybody if asked for it, nor will I make a suggestion to this effect. Similarly I will not give to a woman an abortive remedy. In purity and holiness I will guard my life and my art.

I will not use the knife, not even on sufferers from stone, but will withdraw in favour of such men as are engaged in this work.

Whatever houses I may visit, I will come for the benefit of the sick, remaining free of all intentional injustice, of all mischief and in particular of sexual relations with both female and male persons, be they free or slaves.

What I may see or hear in the course of treatment or even outside of the treatment in regard to the life of men, which on no account one must spread abroad, I will keep myself holding such things shameful to be spoken about.

If I fulfil this oath and do not violate it, may it be granted to me to enjoy life and art, being honoured with fame among all men for all time to come; if I transgress it and swear falsely, may the opposite of all this be my lot.

Hippocratic Oath

1

When the buzzer sounded and the doors rolled back Pavel Sunic stepped from the cell he shared with three others and moved down the walkway towards the metal stairs at the end of the level. He knew as he descended to the floor below that his every step was being tracked by Minsk's number-one lookout, Amor. Pavel did not glance up. He would not give Amor the satisfaction of seeing his searching eyes. This was the day they would attempt to take him out. He had heard it the night before from the snitch, Dabic.

He glanced at the guards, standing with their rifles held across their massive chests. They sensed something too. There was a definite vibe in the air, that invisible scent of trouble. They could feel it but were powerless to prevent what was coming.

It amused Pavel to see them so nervous. Every single guard in Zenica looked like a steroid-filled gym bunny. They were loud and abrasive and liked to throw their weight about. What fools they were. Pavel despised them. He had learned long before that muscle did not equal might, certainly not in this place, filled as it was with thieves, murderers and psychotic madmen. Or outside on the streets where crooks and men made inhumane by the war would slit your throat for making the wrong kind of eye contact. Pavel Sunic had long ago learned that *all* eye contact was the wrong kind.

Pavel should have been frightened but instead he was strangely calm. What did fear offer a man like him – or any man for that matter? What was the point of it? He had tasted fear, had choked on it and been paralysed by it. He had smelt it on his father during the early days of the war, when neighbour had turned on neighbour and people had disappeared from their homes never to be seen again. He would not forget how useless fear had made people. Now he understood that fear was a weakness: it sucked the strength from a person and left them shaking and vulnerable, like a child. It did not prevent anything.

He would fear no man. He would fear no one.

Pavel entered the mess hall, falling into line near the kitchen. Zenica was the largest of the Bosnian prisons and could house 464 inmates. Because of a fire in another prison, it was currently holding 620. Overcrowding caused tempers to flare and emotions to run high as rival factions snapped and snarled over space and rations like junkyard dogs over a spilled bin. The week before, two Muslim hustlers had beaten a Croat thief into a coma. There was no telling where a fuse waited to be lit.

Pavel collected his food and turned to find a seat. He immediately caught sight of Minsk and his crew sitting at a table to the right of the hall. No one looked directly at him, but he knew they had noted his presence. Their studious refusal to glance his way was a clear indication of their interest. Stupid though they were, they were also cunning. There were five of them, a tight-knit group originally from Sarajevo, and they had been transferred to Zenica from the city a month before. Within the first week, Minsk, their leader, had found Pavel in the exercise yard and thrown a friendly arm around his shoulders. He had ordered Pavel either to cease trading cigarettes and weed or to cough up a percentage. Pavel had declined to take his 'advice', offering instead to cut off Minsk's head and rip out his spine if he laid a hand on him again. The resulting fight had seen both Minsk and Pavel spend twenty days in solitary.

It had been a mistake. Pavel had let his emotions rule his head. He was a hard man. At twenty-eight he had spent almost a decade living on the fringe of society – a drifter, a freelance criminal, cold, hungry and beholden to no one but a younger sister to whom he sent money every week. But ever since that fight he had felt the eyes of the wolves watching him in the mess hall and the yard. His days were numbered. As a lone operator, what little support he might have garnered had trickled away while he had been holed up in isolation. Minsk's men had taken over his trade by force. Now Pavel had nothing left to offer, no free pass to call on. His card was well and truly marked.

After breakfast they went to the showers. Two men started a fight just beyond the toilets. As the guards went to break them up, Pavel found himself surrounded by Minsk's crew. He put up a good fight but, outnumbered as he was, it did not take them long to overpower him. Once he went down he was savagely beaten, shanked and left for dead. He crawled along the tiles to the main drying area and watched as his blood streamed across the wet tiles like pink ribbons. The inmates ignored him or drifted away, like steam. He was unconscious when the guards found him and raced him to the infirmary.

He lived. The doctor stitched him up, dressed his wounds and left him in the ward for two weeks. The pain medication confused him and left him irritable and frightened. He had hallucinations. His sister Ana was contacted and came to see him. He thought he remembered her being there, but it might have been a dream. He thought he remembered her crying, begging him to hold on, that she would have him released. Pavel lay shivering on his bed and watched the shadows move across the walls as day turned to night and night to day again. His fever broke, but he barely slept and could hardly bring himself to eat. He thought of the man who had put him inside, a corrupt policeman called Ademi; he thought of the stash Ademi had confiscated. He thought of the beatings he had received before, during and after his incarceration. He thought of death.

It was hard not to think about death when he had seen so much of it already. He felt as though he knew Death personally, recognised him as part of his life. In his half-sleep he dreamed that Death was a black-eyed spectre, tall and emaciated with hands like talons and hooves for feet. Death whispered to him in his dreams. He tried not to listen, to turn his head away, but Death would not be ignored. Death knew him. Death waited for him. His father had met Death, his mother too. Only his sister remained, and it was because of her that Pavel did not tie his sheets into a noose and rid himself of his agony. He had practically raised her and she needed him. He would not abandon her, would not leave her alone in the world.

There would be no suicide.

To occupy himself, he thought instead of Ademi. He thought of the cop's greasy face. He thought of his smell, the way the man had beaten him with a two-pound sap, making sure not to break his skin, to leave the bruises hidden and evenly spread.

Pavel thought of Ademi and vowed to stay alive.

Four days after he was released from the infirmary Pavel was summoned to the warder's office. He limped there between two smartly dressed guards. The one on his right with the pockmarked face was called Kruskey. Pavel had learned that he had found him lying, bleeding, on the floor. Pavel thought to thank him, but the older man's jaw was set in such a way that he did not bother. The guards did their jobs, but they did not care for people like him. He was Roma, worthless to them, but less trouble and paperwork if he remained alive.

Stolvat, the warder, was seated behind his desk when Pavel and the guards arrived. He was an impressive hulk of a man with a handlebar moustache and a five o'clock shadow twenty-four hours a day. Stolvat was old school. He ran the prison with a steel fist. It was said that the highly polished wooden baton he carried on his customised belt had dented the head of many a rabble-rouser. It was said that more than one crushed head was buried behind the sandpits to the rear of the prison. It was said that as a young man he had worked within the shadows of the ruling party. It was said that he was untouchable. Stolvat would neither confirm nor deny any rumour.

'Sit.'

Before Pavel had a chance to comply Kruskey's hand clamped on his shoulder and he was shoved into a chair. He winced. His stitches had only been out a few days.

Stolvat leaned on his desk and linked his hands together. 'I thought you were an orphan.'

Pavel tried to work up some saliva. It dawned on him that he had not spoken in many days. 'Yes, I have only my sister.'

Stolvat looked at him as though Pavel was something unpleasant he had stepped in.

'You must have great friends, then. Important friends.'

'I have no friends.'

Stolvat and Kruskey exchanged a look that Pavel did not like.

'Your sister is married?'

'A widow.'

'What does she do?'

'She cuts hair.'

'Where?'

13

'All over.'

'Your father, what was his occupation?'

'He repaired cars.'

'Did he work "all over" too?'

'No,' Pavel said, narrowing his eyes. 'He had a shop.'

'A Roma with an occupation,' Stolvat sneered. 'What happened to it?'

'During the war the landlord sold it to another man. He had put up the rent and my father could no longer afford it.'

'So he decided to become a criminal instead.'

'My father was no criminal.'

'Just you, huh?'

Pavel shrugged. 'I did what I had to do to support my sister and my mother when she was alive.'

'I think you are a troublemaker.'

'You are free to think what you like.'

'I know that,' Stolvat said, more forcefully. 'I think you have many irons in the fire.'

Pavel did not reply.

Stolvat stared at him for a long time. He gave a half-smile when he noticed Pavel's hands were bunched tight on his lap. Finally he reached for a piece of paper on his desk and slid it across to Pavel. 'Can you read?'

'Yes.'

'Then read that.'

Pavel picked up the page and scanned it quickly. He read it once more and put it back on the desk. The charges against him had been withdrawn: new evidence had come to light exonerating him of owning the drugs found in his car. Ademi had signed it. 'I don't understand.'

'Neither do I. But I know Ademi. He is not a man who admits many *mistakes.*'

'I don't know why he has changed his mind.'

Stolvat narrowed his eyes. 'Perhaps it's because someone put the squeeze on him.'

'I have no one to do such things,' Pavel said, genuinely bewildered.

'Well, someone convinced him to issue a retraction,' Stolvat said, his gaze never wavering. 'Something persuaded him.'

Pavel thought of his sister and, for the first time in many years, he tasted fear.

2

'Dad!'

'Just a minute, I'll be right with you.' Tom Cooper grabbed a dishcloth from the sink and lifted a pan of boiling potatoes onto a different ring.

'Dad! Sean's picking his nose at the table! Tell him to stop.'

'I am *not*!'

'You were, and that's *gross*.'

'I wasn't!'

'I *saw* you.'

Tom took a smaller saucepan from the rack and emptied a tin of baked beans into it. He glanced at the kitchen clock and wondered when his wife would get home from work. Alison spent more and more time at the hospital, these days. 'Sean, what did we say about nose-picking at the table?'

'But, Dad, I wasn't—'

'You *were so*. Don't lie, Sean, you'll only make things worser.'

16

'Worse,' Tom corrected automatically, rolling his eyes at Maggie's tone of outrage. If there was one thing Maggie couldn't abide it was to be challenged. He bent down and checked that the fish fingers in the oven hadn't burst into flames.

He swirled the beans, opened the press over the sink, grabbed the ketchup and the malt vinegar, then carried them next door into the dinner nook. 'Maggie, I asked you to stop feeding Toby from the table.'

'I'm not.'

Tom lifted the flap of the oil-cloth table cover. The spaniel was sitting between the children's legs. His tail thumped on the ground twice. He was still chewing the crusty bread that Maggie had lovingly smeared with about an inch of butter. Tom wondered if dogs ever suffered from high cholesterol. 'Now who's telling fibs?'

'But, Daddy—'

'He'll have his food after dinner. Come on, Toby, out of there.'

Toby slunk out and climbed into his bed.

'Do you think it'll be *very* scary?' Sean asked his older sister.

'It might be, but I won't be scared,' Maggie said, raising her chin in defiance.

'Me neither. I was only asking.'

Tom ruffled Sean's hair. 'Don't worry – Harry Potter's not scary.'

'*He*'s not, but Voldemort is,' Maggie said. 'Daddy, did you not see his head on the posters?'

'Well, yes.'

'Then how can you say it's not scary? Think about his face. If you met him on the road, wouldn't you be scared?'

Tom retreated to the kitchen. There was no use arguing with that sort of logic.

At twelve Maggie was already a mini Alison. She had his

wife's dark curly hair, her pale skin and her luminous grey eyes. She had also inherited her preference for the last word.

'Dad, I can smell burning,' Maggie called.

'Shit – the fish fingers!'

'Dad!'

'Oops, sorry. You didn't hear that.'

'We did,' Maggie said.

'We did,' Sean agreed.

Tom was scraping the fish fingers from the tinfoil onto the chopping board when the kitchen phone rang. He grabbed it and shoved it under his chin. 'Hello?'

'You sound frazzled – is everything okay?'

'Fine. All under control,' Tom replied, wondering how Alison could tell he was frazzled from one word. Maybe it was a doctor thing; maybe they just sensed when things were off kilter. 'I'm about to dish up. Are you nearly home? Did you remember to pick up the popcorn?'

'I'm sorry, Tom, I won't be able make it. I've been asked to hang on for a few hours.'

Tom noticed Maggie was watching him. He winked at her and moved deeper into the kitchen until he was out of view. 'Hold on, Alison, we're watching *Harry Potter*, remember? The kids are expecting you home.'

'Tom, please,' Alison said. 'You know we're short-staffed with that bloody virus doing the rounds. There's no need for you to take that tone with me.'

'Jesus,' Tom kicked a cupboard door shut with his heel, 'we've hardly seen you this week and the kids were really looking forward to seeing that damn film with both of us.'

'You can still go ahead with dvd night.'

'Can't you get someone else to do it?'

'Like who? Edward is sick and Maura is still on maternity

18

leave. Beth and I are both pulling extra shifts. It's not like I can be selective about when I work.'

'What's that supposed to mean?'

'It means the hospital is running on a skeleton crew and we're swamped. There are people blocking up the corridors in A and E.' She sighed. 'I don't want to fight with you.'

'I don't want to fight with you either.'

'I'll be home as soon as I can. Tell the kids I'm sorry.' She hung up.

Tom dropped the phone onto the counter, drained the water and tumbled the potatoes into a large bowl. Next he scraped the beans – the ones that weren't stuck to the bottom of the saucepan – onto the plates with the fish fingers. He put everything on a tray and took it to the dining area.

'Who was on the phone?' Maggie asked immediately.

'Mammy – she got held up in work and she can't make it in time for the film.'

Maggie pulled a disapproving face in a disturbingly adult fashion. It was as though she had predicted it. Sean, however, looked crushed. 'Will we see her later?'

'I don't know, kiddo. She said to give you a big kiss and a hug in case you fall asleep before she gets home.'

Maggie lifted the lid of the bowl and wrinkled her nose. 'These are not mashed.'

'They're new potatoes. You're not supposed to mash them.'

'I like them mashed.'

'You'll like these too.'

'I won't.'

'I'm going to stay awake until Mammy gets home,' Sean said.

'There's skin on them!' Maggie said.

'It's just potato.' Tom could feel a headache building behind his eyes. 'It peels off.'

'But—'

'Maggie! Don't start – please.'

She puckered her mouth, but jabbed a potato with her fork and lifted it onto her plate. 'How many do you want, Sean?'

'One, please.'

'Daddy, will you get me the milk?'

'There's water in the jug, Maggie.'

'Please, I'd prefer milk.' She glanced at him slyly. 'And you always say calcium is good for bones.'

Tom sighed, went back into the kitchen and got the milk from the fridge. He returned and placed it on the table. 'Okay, now – hey! Where's your potato gone?'

'I ate it.' Maggie pointed to her stomach.

Tom glanced down. There was the tiniest piece of skin on her plate but nothing else. He glanced at Sean, but his son was suddenly engrossed in his own dinner. He checked the bowl, then tilted and looked under the table.

Toby was finishing off his daughter's potato.

Tom straightened. He said nothing, but got another from the bowl – a bigger one this time – and dropped it onto her plate. 'Eat.'

'But, Daddy—'

'But nothing. If you don't eat it, you can forget about the film.'

'That's not fair.'

'Your choice, potato or *Harry Potter*.'

Maggie's pupils seemed to darken, as if a sudden squall had raced across the iris of each eye.

'The choice is yours, Maggie,' Tom said softly.

In sullen silence she began to hack pieces of skin from her potato. She smothered it in ketchup and began to eat.

Sean picked at his food listlessly. 'I don't like them like this either,' he said, more to himself than to Tom. 'I like Mammy's ones.'

'Well, I like them too, but Mammy's not here so eat up.'

They shared a silent dinner before both children asked to be excused and slipped off into the sitting room.

By the time the film was over and he had harried and harassed them into their pyjamas, Tom Cooper was exhausted and cross. He opened a bottle of red wine and headed to the living room. He drank, listened to Bowie's *Diamond Dogs* and tried not to think of how trapped he felt in his marriage.

3

John Quigley signalled to the barman for another two drinks. He fumbled some money onto the counter and watched somewhat blearily as the little man free-poured at least a double into his glass.

'How's business, John?' he asked.

'Ticketyboo,' John said in his head, but it came out as 'isytiboo'.

The barman laughed and hopped off to chat up two kids who looked as if they ought to be at home studying for the Leaving Cert.

John was in Solas, only a few doors from his office. It was Friday evening so the place was packed with people who hadn't been home yet and others on their way out. He was among the former and beginning to feel it. He glanced up the bar. The DJ, his trilby pulled low over his eyes, blended one tune seamlessly into the next. Or did they all sound the same? Maybe it was just one long tune. He thought he might be a bit drunk. In fact, there was no denying it.

John took up his change, and dropped it into his shirt pocket. He tipped his head to his right and tried to concentrate on what Michelle, his date, was saying. That turned out to be easier said than done. Had she noticed he was a bit tipsy? She was glaring at him. Had she said something? Had she? Shit, she must have. She was looking at him in the irritated way people did when they were expecting him to reply.

'It's very loud in here,' he shouted, spraying her face with saliva. 'Sorry 'bout that. Don't you think it's very loud?'

Michelle Parks was twenty-six and gorgeous. She worked as a receptionist for Vantage Advertising, which had hired John to do a spot of work. He had asked her out on the day he was finishing and she had surprised him by saying yes. Perhaps she had thought a private investigator would be more interesting than one of the tedious dweebs from accounts or sales. She had been wrong. By now she'd be sorry she'd even asked him about his business, he thought, especially since he'd made it obvious to her that he was pining for someone else.

QuicK, the detective agency he owned, had been a two-man show, he had explained twice to the uninterested Michelle, until Sarah Kenny, his former partner, had hightailed it four months before, leaving him to run things alone. It had been, he kept repeating, something of a surprise.

'She never even had the balls to say it to my face. Left me a note. Not even a call since. Howdja like them apples?'

'I think I might go.'

'That's what women do,' John told his drink. 'They go. They come and they go. And we're supposed to just sit there, waiting, like dogs.'

Michelle said something. John missed it. He turned on his stool and squinted at her. 'Huh?'

Her lipstick was shiny, he noticed. He squinted some more. Her lips reminded him of wet tyres. He blinked and drained his rum. It burned its way down the back of this throat. He shook his head and picked up his fresh drink. He peered at Michelle. 'I can't really hear you.'

'I think,' Michelle Parks picked up her handbag and leaned in close, 'you're a complete fucking tool. Don't ever call me again.'

While John was thinking of a response, his date stalked out of the bar without a backward glance. He consulted his watch – twenty past ten. He'd met Michelle at nine. One hour and twenty minutes. Surely this was a new record. His friend Stevie would laugh when he heard about this one.

He signalled to the barman for another rum.

'Just one?' the grinning Lothario said, when he managed to drag himself away from the young ones at the end of the bar.

'Yep, just the one.'

'Where'd she go?'

'Beats me.' John shrugged. 'She's evampur … evampue … vanished.'

A short while later, he decided he might as well call it a night. He said his goodbyes and ambled up towards Zaytoon, on Camden Street, where he ordered a kebab and chips and sat at one of the square wooden tables to eat it.

A tool. A *complete fucking tool*, no less. Well, so what? What did *that* have to do with the price of tomatoes? Tools were useful: what was wrong with being useful?

He chewed his food mechanically, turned his head and caught a glimpse of his reflection in the window. Hello there, Tramp Face. He saw a slouched sandy-haired man, grouchy and hostile-looking, with grease smeared on his chin and sauce on his fingers.

A complete fucking tool. Maybe *that* was why Sarah had left.

24

Maybe that was why he was sitting alone on a Friday evening with grease on his chin feeling sorry for himself.

He set down the last of his food and left.

He walked the mile and half to the two-bedroomed cottage he owned off the main drag in Ranelagh. He had bought it with money his parents had left him before the property boom and bust, and it was his oasis of calm. He gazed at the dark windows and realised he had sobered up enough to feel totally down in the dumps.

Dating – why did he even bother with the pretence? Who was he trying to kid? He wasn't interested in any of the women who might be interested in him. He didn't want to sit around making small-talk. He didn't want to discuss films or books or preferred holiday destinations. It was all a load of old bollocks. He was a thirty-eight-year-old private detective, with bugger-all money, few prospects and no real will to alter either.

He let himself into the house, walked to the back door, unlocked it and was almost mown down by Sumo, his wolfhound-German shepherd cross, who came bounding up to greet him. 'Whoa – whoa there, big fella!' He scratched the top of Sumo's wiry head affectionately.

Sumo gave him the customary half-wag of his fanned tail. For Sumo this was a greeting and a half.

'Who loves ya baby?'

When John had rescued Sumo – then a small, growling, flea-ridden mutt pup with plate-sized paws – he hadn't realised it would turn out to be one of the best decisions he was ever likely to make. Life was like that: anything he planned turned to crap, anything he didn't was hunky-dory. Maybe he should be more 'random', as the kids seemed to say.

He shucked off his jacket and draped it over a chair in the kitchen. He checked his answering machine and poured himself another drink – Jameson this time. He knew his head wouldn't thank him in the morning.

He carried his drink into the sitting room, put on a lamp and collapsed onto the cord sofa. He switched on the television, but muted the sound when he saw it was *House*: he couldn't cope with Hugh Laurie's ridiculous mid-Atlantic grumble as he played the eponymous doctor. John didn't understand the appeal of *House*: the man was a pig-ignorant rude junkie who played with people's lives to amuse himself. Yet even his sister Carrie – usually a smart cookie – went into spasms of delight whenever it was on.

'Now that's a complete fucking tool,' he said to Sumo.

Sumo cocked his head.

John took another sip of his drink and set it on the floor next to him. He crawled across the floor and flicked through his CDs. He found a Soulsavers album and put it on. As Mark Lanegan's deep voice rumbled from the speakers, he sat back in the sofa, removed his wallet from his jeans and opened it. His thumb traced the piece of folded paper that peeped out from behind his credit card.

It was Sarah's note. He didn't need to read it. He knew by heart the message she had left for him when she had walked out of his life without so much as a by-your-leave.

Gone.

He wondered where she was and what she was doing right at that moment. Was she listening to music? Was she sleeping? Was she reading? Was she thinking of him? Was she with someone else? Was she watching *House*?

He thumbed the paper, and watched as House made snarky faces at the good-looking black doctor. He wondered how come none of House's colleagues punched him in the face. He would if he could.

When Sarah had left he had been worried, frantically making calls and chasing down people he thought might have some idea of where she was. But no one had offered him any clue, and as the weeks had passed and she still hadn't called he had grown angry. He was still angry.

God, he missed her.

There had been no contact now for nearly four months. Her flat on Patrick Street had just been sold through an agent arranged by Sarah's eldest sister, Helen. What little money the sale had generated after the mortgage had been paid was forwarded to an account in the UK. It had been emptied and closed two days later and that was the last anyone had heard of Sarah Kenny.

Or so they said. Maybe it wasn't. What the hell did he know? Helen had never liked him and had been vehemently against Sarah working with him from the outset. She blamed him for Sarah leaving to work in England all those years before. Sarah and John had been childhood sweethearts until John had betrayed her – a stupid drunken fumble with a barmaid. Sarah had decided he was a cheating dog and gone to England where she had lived for years. But that had been another lifetime.

When she had come back and sought him out, he had assumed she had forgiven him, that one day they might get back together again. She had wanted them to be business partners and that was okay with him too. John took a sip of his drink and scowled at the television. When he thought about it, everything had always been on Sarah's terms. She had wandered back into his life just as he was thinking of setting up a detective agency and he had offered her a job immediately. It had been serendipitous timing, fate, even – if you believed in that sort of thing.

Now she was gone again. And he was supposed to – what? Sit around and be okay with it? Be grateful she had left a note this time?

What had he done wrong?

Even if Helen knew something she might keep it from him. But Jackie, the middle sister, knew how much John was hurting – she would let him know if Sarah got in contact.

Wouldn't she?

He couldn't understand Sarah leaving the way she had. Couldn't understand why or how she could just cut him out of her life. He hated that he needed her. That he had made himself vulnerable to her.

Despite her initial coolness there had been an unmistakable spark between them. They had shared a kiss just before John had gone to England in October to work on a missing-person case, but when he had returned a few days later Sarah had changed. It was as if someone had thrown a switch. The sardonic good-hearted woman he loved had been replaced by someone who balked at shadows and looked hunted when she thought no one was watching.

And then there had been the bruises on her face. She had been mugged, she claimed. She had been walking Sumo and someone had jumped her.

He had never bought that story. It had made no sense to him then and it made none now.

Someone had done a number on her – that had been his interpretation of it – but when he had pressed her she had refused to talk. And now she was gone.

He threw his wallet onto the coffee table and picked up his drink. On screen Dr Gregory House was throwing a ball into the air, his leg on his desk. In the background Mark Lanegan sang a pleading refrain to Jesus, asking Him not to let him die alone.

'A complete fucking tool,' John said, and drained his glass.

4

As soon as he was released Pavel had one driving thought and one alone. He had to find his sister. From the moment he had seen Ademi's signature on his release form he had known she had been behind it and now he needed to know how.

The car he had been using at the time of his arrest had been stolen and was impounded so he caught a bus into the city centre, his few belongings in a grey holdall slung over his shoulder. From there, he took two more buses and eventually reached the village of Susanj, west of Zenica, and from there made his way to the run-down bullet-strafed tenements where Ana shared a two-room flat with her friend, Julia.

But Julia had no idea where Ana was – she had not seen her for almost a fortnight. She told Pavel she was worried for her friend. Ana had been upset after she had gone to see Pavel in the infirmary and had told Julia she would do everything in her power to secure her brother's release. She had gone to see the policeman, and then a lawyer. Julia thought the latter must have said something useful because Ana had come back excited, sure that she could persuade Ademi to make the retraction. She had said she would be away for a few days and that had been the last Julia had heard from her. 'She must have said something more,' Pavel said.

'Only that she would get you out – and here you are.'

Pavel sat forward on the threadbare sofa. 'Give me the name of the lawyer.'

Julia wrote it down and passed it to him with a shaking hand. She did not ask what he was going to do. She wished he would leave the apartment. She knew many stories about Pavel, about his exploits. She loved Ana, but Pavel terrified her.

Pavel thanked her and folded the address into his pocket. When he stood, she remained seated until he had closed the apartment door behind him.

Later that afternoon Pavel stood across the street from the building in Zenica that housed the lawyer's office. He was smoking and eating an apple at the same time. The block was old, standing ugly and squat between two newer commercial developments. This had been a residential area in his younger days, but now it had gained a reputation as a professional area. Around him men and women strode along in sensible shoes and mid-priced suits. He watched them, pitying them, the lives they thought they lived. Rats on a treadmill.

They made no eye contact with Pavel, as he knew they would not. He had long been invisible to the world of legitimacy.

Pavel finished his apple, tossed the core over his shoulder and crossed the street. He read the plaques outside the main door. The lawyer's office was on the fifth floor. He pretended to read the many notices stuck to the wall until someone came out. Then he slipped inside before the door could close behind them.

The building was poorly maintained. The foyer was grubby and dated and the metal lift did not work. Pavel climbed the stairs quickly and, on the fifth landing, found himself facing two massive mahogany doors. The lawyer's office was on the right.

He bent forward to listen, and heard typing from inside. He tapped and the typing stopped. The door buzzed and he pushed it open.

The office consisted of one large room with a single window. It was divided into two by a partition of wood and frosted glass. The woman who now regarded him with bored detachment was obviously a secretary. She was thin and brittle-looking, with glasses dangling from her wrinkled neck on a gold chain.

'Yes?'

'I'm here to speak with Igor Travnic.'

'Do you have an appointment?'

'No.'

'You need an appointment.'

Pavel waited. The woman frowned at him.

'I must see him.'

'What is it in connection with?'

Pavel could see the shape of another person seated at a desk behind the frosted glass. 'I was given his name. My business with him is for his ears only.'

'As I told you, Mr Travnic is busy. You must make an appointment if you wish to see him.'

'Tell him I'm looking for my sister. Her name is Ana Sunic.'

The woman opened a large ledger on her desk. 'I can give you an appointment for . . .' she ran a finger down the page '. . . next Tuesday, the nineteenth.'

Pavel shook his head. 'No. I must speak with him now.'

She locked eyes with him. 'Must I ring the police?'

Behind the frosted glass the figure pushed back a chair and stood up. Igor Travnic appeared from behind the partition. 'It's all right, Vana.' He was a small man, birdlike, wearing an ill-fitting blue suit that looked twenty years out of date. His hair was a dirty grey and thin. There was dandruff on his shoulders. 'Please, how can I help you?' he asked.

'I am looking for my sister.'

'I heard. But why are you here?'

Pavel tilted his head. 'I was told she came here to talk to you two weeks ago.'

'What was her name again?'

'Ana Sunic.'

'I don't recognise it.'

Pavel could tell Travnic was lying to him. He described his sister, but he knew he was wasting his time.

'I'm sorry.' Travnic spread his hands. 'I cannot help you.'

'Maybe I have the wrong information.'

'It would seem so,' Travnic said. 'I wish you luck with your search.'

Pavel left and closed the door. He walked down the stairs and stood outside in the sunshine. Travnic had lied, which meant he had something to hide. The lawyer would soon learn that luck had very little to do with the way in which Pavel operated.

5

On Monday morning a grumpy and mildly dishevelled John Quigley let himself into a ramshackle Victorian building on Wexford Street. He collected his mail and climbed the rickety stairs to the fourth flour, where his office nestled under the eaves. It was a small room, with two desks, a cupboard, a filing cabinet, two wicker chairs for clients and two sash windows that let in the cold air during winter.

He put on the kettle and sat at his desk to open his mail.

The first envelope contained the cheque from Vantage Advertising. For some reason the money did little to cheer him – it was great and he needed it, but it reminded him of their receptionist's summation of his character. 'A complete fucking tool,' he muttered.

The contents of the second envelope sent him from grumpy to foul-tempered. The vulture-run management committee that owned the building, and numerous others in the area, was demanding that he and the other tenants paid an additional sum to improve the 'distressing state of the communal area'.

John read the letter again, balled it up and tossed it into the bin. They could bloody well sing for it. He doubted any of the motley crew who shared the building would think any differently. Rodney Mitchell, an alcoholic solicitor who kept an office on the floor below John, was permanently broke. Freak FM, a pirate radio station owned by John's pal Mike Brannigan, was in crisis because Mike was on enforced R&R in Mountjoy Prison: he had been caught driving across the city one night with sixty thousand black-market cigarettes in the boot of his car. Upon being presented with the evidence he had expressed surprise, claiming he had loaned the vehicle to a number of people the day before and hadn't checked it thoroughly when he'd got it back. Because this was blameless Mike's third such 'surprise', Justice Carmel Healy decided she'd soften his cough by sticking him inside for a few months.

John had learned this from DJ Clique, one of the more amenable youths who worked at Freak. Clique was a multi-pierced, softly spoken, intelligent Gothy-emo kid, who did a daily show. He often did odd jobs for John, and everyone was fond of the young man, even the vicious-tongued harpy who ran the dusty grocery shop on the ground floor.

Bloody gentrification, John thought, flicking through the rest of his post. That was one thing the recession had going for it: it was killing off the boho bollocks. At one point you couldn't swing a cat in Dublin without bouncing it off high-end boutique coffee shops and overpriced wholefood outlets. It had been downright tiresome.

John was reading the *Sun* when the office phone rang. ''Lo?'

No one spoke but he could hear a television or radio in the background.

'Speak now or forever hold your peace,' John said, and

turned a page. Kerry Katona was on another diet and gurning for the camera. How was that news?

'Am I through to the detective agency?'

It was an older woman's voice, high and uncertain.

'You sure are.'

'I need … I need you to help me.'

'Why don't you fill me in and I'll see what I can do?'

'My name is Rose Butler. My daughter Alison is … She was a doctor at Mercy Hospital. She died on Friday.'

John sat up straighter. 'I'm very sorry for your loss.'

'I've read about you and your agency in the papers. Can I come and see you? I just need to talk to someone.'

'Of course. I'm free this morning.'

Shortly before noon John Quigley made a cup of tea and handed it to Rose Butler, a smartly dressed lady in her late sixties. She wore a grey woollen skirt, matching jacket, brown tights and sturdy shoes. She was holding her emotions in check as best as she could, but her eyes were red-rimmed and she looked washed out under her face powder. She reminded John a little of his own mother, old-school Dublin: there would be no nonsense and no dramatics.

'So, your daughter was a doctor at the Mercy,' John said, handing her the cup and saucer, then taking a seat behind his desk.

'Yes, she was always a clever girl, Mr Quigley. When she was little she was reading books I couldn't make head or tail of. Her father – may the Lord have mercy on him – used to say she was a walking encyclopedia.'

John smiled.

'I don't know what to think,' Rose said, and for a moment her resolve threatened to break. 'Alison was a gentle, kind person. She wouldn't have done this to us, or to her children.'

'Can you tell me what happened the day she died?' John wished he had a box of tissues to offer her, but it had been Sarah who had thought of such simple touches.

'She went to work on Friday as normal. She was in work and, as far as anyone knows, she was fine. Then she went out for lunch and when she came back she said she had to go. The next time she was seen was when a maid found her in a room at the Hill Crest Hotel early on Saturday morning.'

'Where's that? Out near Stillorgan?'

'Yes.'

'Was she alone?'

'She was when they found her.'

'Do you know who hired the room?'

'She did. At least, they think she did. The receptionist says it was a woman.'

'Was this an unusual thing for your daughter to have done? Take a hotel room like that?'

'Yes, I believe so.' Her voice was shaking now. 'Although she might have done it before.'

'Mrs Butler, I'm so sorry but I have to ask this. Was there any sign that Alison had been with somebody?'

'Not that I know of.' Tears glistened in Rose Butler's eyes. 'She was just there in the bath, with her poor wrists torn to ribbons.'

'I know how hard this is for you.'

'Of course, he has them convinced she was suicidal.'

'He?'

'Her husband. He was the one to call me on Saturday. I knew something was wrong when I heard him on the line. I knew right away something bad had happened. You just do, don't you?'

John made a mental note of the 'he'. Rose Butler had not used her son-in-law's name during the entire time she had been in his office.

'I don't understand any of this. Alison had everything to live for. She was a great girl, well respected, she had her children and her work.' She looked out of the window, her eyes blank. 'She loved those kids – she wouldn't have done this to them.'

'Was there any indication that she was depressed or anxious about anything?'

'She was always running herself ragged. Couldn't do enough for people, so she couldn't.'

'And you don't believe she was seeing anyone else?'

'Indeed and she was not. Alison was not that type of woman. I didn't rear her that way.'

'People have complicated lives, Mrs Butler. None of us ever really knows what's going on in another person's life.'

'There's nothing complicated about being a cheat, Mr Quigley,' she said, her voice rising in anger, 'and my girl was no cheat. She hadn't the inclination and she certainly hadn't the time. Sure didn't she work all the hours God sent?'

'Was she always at the Mercy?'

'She lived in Canada for years after she graduated and worked in a hospital there. Fifteen years ago she came home, when her father was unwell. Alison was very caring.'

'She married when she came home?'

'She did, fourteen years ago. Her wedding anniversary was last month.'

'And what does her husband do?'

Her mouth drew into a tight line. 'Not much of anything, these days.'

'Excuse me?'

'He's a painter and decorator. Only he's been out of work since he had an accident a few months ago.'

'So it would it be fair to say Alison was the family's main breadwinner?'

'Yes.'

John nodded. The doctor had been under considerable pressure, then. 'You say there are children?'

'Two, a boy and girl.'

'Do you know if your daughter had made a will?'

'She did.' Rose blinked. 'The house was in her name, and everything goes to him.'

'Okay. But you don't think he was involved in her death – am I correct?'

'I don't know. I wish she'd never got involved with that man. He was a bad egg from the word go.'

'Mrs Butler, being a bad egg does not make a man a murderer. If you have suspicions that he had something to do with your daughter's death you need to talk to the gardaí.'

She put her cup down and clasped her hands. 'I have spoken to them – a number of times – but they're not interested in what I have to say.'

'What do you need from me, Mrs Butler?

She looked around her helplessly. 'I don't know – I just want you to do something. I want you to find out what really happened to her. I need to make sense of this. I need answers. The guards won't help me. Will you do that for me?'

It was hard to imagine what she was going through – her husband dead, her daughter dead, alone with only a 'he' and the two grandchildren she might get to see if 'he' allowed it.

'I'll need Alison's home address and any contact numbers you can give me.'

6

It had been easy to follow Travnic, so easy that Pavel suspected the lawyer was on to him and leading him into some kind of trap. But after half an hour of tailing he began to relax. The old fool was clearly preoccupied by more than Pavel.

The evening air was cold yet curiously stagnant, fumes from the crawling traffic held trapped to the roof-tops by a dense bank of pewter-coloured clouds. Pavel moved easily, keeping half a street between them. He was comfortable now, in his element.

They walked to a shop where Travnic bought tobacco and a newspaper, then on to a major junction and left, moving deeper and deeper into older, narrow streets, moving from commercial to residential, from new to old, where the buildings carried the visual wounds and memories of war, where neighbours and friends still eyed one another with suspicion and mistrust. Muslim, Croat and Serb lived side by side, going about their business, but always aware of the history, always aware that the future was unstable, that peace lay over a volatile fuse that could easily be lit.

Not that he gave a shit. His people had long been the butt of every unkind word and hostile action. They were considered garbage – worse, vermin. It stuck in his craw to see the tears of outsiders over the state of the country, the so-called atrocities. Where were the tears for his people when they were hounded from one place to the next, when families scrabbled around filthy camps with no running water and no sanitation, when babies routinely died before their first birthday? Where was the worldwide condemnation then? He remembered how people had treated his family, contemptuous even as his own father tried to better himself. War, *pfft*! Pavel had been fighting his own war from birth.

Pavel followed Travnic down a hill, then across a cobbled square and here Travnic paused. Pavel slipped into a doorway and watched as the lawyer patted his pockets and fumbled for his keys. Travnic opened the door of a narrow townhouse and shut it behind him. As Pavel watched, lights came on in the hall, then, moments later, on the second floor.

He could see Travnic removing his coat, disappearing from view and reappearing to close the curtains with a tumbler in his hand.

Pavel smoked a cigarette and waited until darkness was complete, then crossed the cobbles. It took him no time to undo the main door. He went inside, dumped his holdall and climbed the stone stairs, his rubber-soled shoes silent to everyone but him.

There was only one door per floor. Outside Travnic's apartment, Pavel could hear music, classical crap. He cocked his head, recognising what his father used to play when he was in his cups. Rachmaninov. 'Music of heaven,' his old man used to

40

say. 'Heaven': a luxury for the simple-minded. Pavel had long ago thrown off the notions of heaven and God.

He picked the locks quickly and slipped inside. He inched across the hallway. There were two doors before him. He waited, standing silently in the shadows where the air was thick with old cooking smells. His eyes became accustomed to the gloom. The lawyer was not a rich man, it seemed: the carpet was threadbare in places, the paintwork on the doors peeling and yellowed with age. Strange how such a man could have helped his sister get her hands on enough money to release him.

On the music played.

Near the end of the track, Pavel pushed open the door to his immediate right and glanced into a long, narrow room with two narrow floor-to-ceiling windows. He knew they led to the metal balcony overlooking the square. A single lamp burned, barely illuminating the darkness within.

Travnic was squatting beside a shelf filled with vinyl records. An old-fashioned record-player sat on a trestle table. It was from this that the music filled the room.

Pavel stepped lightly towards Travnic. He waited until the old man stood up and turned, then drew back his fist and cold-cocked him. The needle scratched over the surface of the record as Travnic fell against the table. It jumped wildly when Pavel grabbed the front of his shirt. 'Look at me.'

'Please!' Travnic flinched and held up his hands before his face. 'I have nothing.'

'I said look at me.'

Travnic peered through his fingers.

'Remember me?'

'You were at the office.'

'Good. Now, let's try again,' Pavel said. 'Ana Sunic, where is she?'

'I don't know.' Travnic's cheek was bleeding profusely from

41

where he had struck his head against the table on the way down. 'Please … I—'

Pavel punched him in the side of the head.

Travnic keened. 'Please, I am an old man.'

Pavel smiled. 'Age,' he said, standing to his full height. 'At your age you should know better than to use it as an excuse.'

'Don't hurt me.'

'Don't *make* me hurt you.'

Pavel sat on the arm of a chair and prodded Travnic with his foot. 'Ana Sunic. Talk.'

'All right. She came to see me. She was upset, very upset about her brother. About you.'

'Go on.'

'She wanted me to act on her behalf.'

'For what?'

'She wanted – she needed money.' The old man licked his lips. 'She had heard I might be able to help her get it.'

'How?'

'Look, I can't tell you this – they will kill me.'

'What do you think I'm going to do to you if you don't talk?'

'None of this is *my fault*!'

'None of what?'

'Can I have a cigarette, please? I can't think.'

Pavel passed him one and lit it for him. 'Okay, now talk.'

'I don't really know much. She came to see me about raising some money and—'

'Why?'

'What?'

'Why would she go to see you? How does she even know who you are?'

Travnic swallowed. 'I got to know her some time ago.'

'How?'

'She used to cut the hair of a client.'

'What client?'

'She is dead now.'

'So, you got to know my sister.' Pavel removed his jacket and rolled up his sleeves. His forearms were covered with prison tattoos, the cheap blue ink standing out against his pale skin. 'Why did she think you could get her money? You live like a tramp.'

'I gave her my card, told her if she ever needed help to contact me.'

'So you met her and she came to you. How were you going to get money for her? What was the deal?'

'Deal?'

'You live in this shit-hole.' Pavel jerked his head, indicating the room behind him. 'What money were you going to give my sister? And why?'

'No, not me, I wasn't – please, you must believe me, I never meant for anything to happen. It was just an introduction.'

'Who did you introduce to my sister?' Pavel leaned in. 'Was the money for prostitution?'

'No! I swear. Nothing like that. Your sister is an honourable woman. I introduced her to a friend, a colleague. A doctor.'

'Why would you introduce Ana to a doctor? She wasn't sick. If she needed money why—'

Pavel's eyes widened. Travnic looked terrified.

'Please—'

Pavel grabbed the front of his shirt and yanked him close. 'What kind of doctor?'

'A surgeon.'

'Why?'

'Oh, please – I can give you money! Don't hurt me – please.'

'Money? *O lov tai o bebg nashti beshen patshasa.*'

The old man cringed. He did not speak Romi, but

43

understood enough to know that Pavel had said something about money, and the devil being restless.

'Give me this man's name.'

Pavel hit him, only once but hard. When he hit Travnic the second time the old man began to talk. When he had finished he pleaded for mercy.

But Pavel had heard enough. Disgusted, he stood and raised his foot. He smashed the heel of his shoe on the old man's head, mashing it against the floor, again and again until Igor Travnic was dead.

Pavel cleaned his footwear in the bathroom and stared at his reflection in the mirror over the basin. His face was ghostly white and covered with blood spatters. He dampened a cloth and wiped it away. He patted his face dry on a clean towel and returned to the living room. Travnic's blood fanned out beneath him, snaking slowly across the floor like black wings.

Pavel ignored the body. He began systematically to search the apartment. After an hour he had located what he wanted and was on his way back down the stairs. Out on the square he paused and looked up into the starless sky. But he had no God to call on and presently he moved off into the night, trying not to think of the fate that had befallen his sister.

7

Late on Monday afternoon John Quigley was perched on a three-legged stool in the cluttered kitchen of a large red-brick house just off the North Circular Road. He was drinking a cup of instant coffee and eating a stale biscuit. The kitchen was littered with unwashed dishes and mounds of teabags, drying like brown pyramids in various shallow saucers. The spaniel who had greeted him on arrival was at his feet.

Tom Cooper, husband of the deceased, the 'he' to whom Rose Butler had referred, eyed John with unease. John thought he looked as if he hadn't slept in days. He was pale and hollow-eyed. His own coffee remained untouched and cooling by his elbow.

'I should have known Rose would do something like this.'

'She didn't tell you she was coming to see me?'

'No. Why would she?'

'Well, I thought maybe she might have discussed it with you

first,' John said awkwardly. 'She's very upset. People don't always—'

'She's *upset*? I'm upset – I've just lost my wife, my kids have lost their mother … I have people picking over my life, asking me all sorts of fucking questions, and now you … Jesus.' He picked up his cup and set it down again. 'I'm fucking upset.'

'Mr Cooper—'

'Did Alison do this? Did I do that? Was she depressed, worried about anything? My daughter won't stop crying, my son won't talk, everyone's all over the place.' He shook his head. 'Don't talk to me about upset.'

'I know this is hard and that you're going through a rough time. You're angry, you're raw, but it's normal for people to ask questions when someone dies so suddenly. It's normal to feel angry and upset. Mrs Butler doesn't know whether she's coming or going. She's searching for answers – same as you, I imagine.'

'Answers to what? What is there to question? My wife killed herself.'

'I suppose Mrs Butler is trying to understand why.'

Cooper looked at him hard. 'I'm pretty sure she's already got some notion racketing around in her head.'

'What do you mean?'

'Look, I don't know what she told you, but Rose never made it any secret she doesn't think much of me. I was never good enough for Alison.'

'I know how that one goes, believe me.'

'She thought Alison should marry another doctor. She couldn't believe it when she hitched her wagon to a down-at-heel scrubber.'

'A scrubber?'

'That how me and Alison met. I was working for a catering firm that supplied the hospital canteen.'

'I thought you worked as a painter and decorator.'

'I did, for ten years. Then I had a fall last year on a job and I've been off since then. No doubt she told you that.'

'She mentioned you'd been hurt.'

'Yeah, well, with the downturn things had slowed down in my line of work anyway. I worked hard and made good money for years before the accident, but it suits Rose to gloss over that. When I met Alison I was on my uppers – hadn't two cents to rub together. Didn't matter to Alison, though. When she had her heart set on something it was all or nothing.' He lowered his head and his voice softened. 'She didn't care what people said or thought.'

'So what can you tell me about your wife? Was she on any medication? Something that might have affected her moods?'

'No, she wasn't a pill-popper. Funny thing about doctors, they're usually the most sickly bunch. They work long hours, drink too much and chew pills like Smarties. But not Alison.'

'How did she seem when you spoke to her on Friday?'

'I can only tell you what I told Rose and the cops. I picked the kids up from school at three and took them swimming, then back here. We had a family film night planned. I made dinner, then Alison called and said she'd been asked to work late. Next thing I know it's morning and the cops are at the door telling me she's dead.'

He ran his hands through his hair, leaving it sticking up in many different directions. As he did so, his sleeve moved up along his arm, exposing a tattoo. It was a dark Rorschach shape, like an image of two men standing back to back.

'Interesting tattoo,' John said.

Tom Cooper glanced at him. 'What?'

'The tattoo.' John indicated it with his thumb. 'I seem to remember seeing one like it back in the day.'

'You recognise it?'

'I've seen a few before.'

'Like you say, it's from back in the day, long ago.' Tom rolled his sleeve down. 'Stupid shit. I got it done before I had a lick of sense.'

'You ever keep in touch with that crew?'

'No. Half that lot are dead now anyway.'

'Or inside.'

'Or that.'

John was surprised. The tattoo meant Tom Cooper had once belonged to a group of thugs who for a spell had terrorised a certain Dublin area. Not exactly the sort of group men usually walked away from.

'You ever spend time inside, Tom?'

'Why do you want to know? You think that's going to make any difference to what happened?'

'Just curious.'

'A few months, not long, but enough to straighten my head out and make me see what direction I *didn't* want to take with my life.'

'Fair enough. Lot of people never learn that lesson.'

'Lot of people are stupid. I learned and I learned it hard.'

They sat in silence. John took another sip of his coffee.

Tom looked at his watch. John knew he was wearing out his welcome. 'Have you any idea why Alison was at the Hill Crest Hotel?'

'No.'

'She didn't mention anything to you about meeting anyone?'

'No, she didn't.' Cooper's Adam's apple bobbed as he swallowed.

'Do they have any idea of time of death yet?'

'They think between eleven and three. They're only exact on TV.'

'Okay.' John wrote briefly in his notebook. 'Can you give me anything else? Maybe something the guards might have said?'

'They haven't *said* anything else, but they *implied* Alison might have been seeing someone. They *implied* that maybe she was upset over a break-up and killed herself. They *implied* that maybe she was at the end of her tether providing for her family. They *implied* that doctors get depressed, drink a lot and die by their own hands more than we know.'

'Subtle, as always.'

'Yeah, fuckers.'

'You didn't bring up the idea that Alison might be seeing someone?'

'No, I didn't. They asked me was it possible and I said I didn't think so. But then I said that Alison had been acting a little off lately. Course they jumped on that one. Stupid. I wasn't trying to blacken her. I'm telling you that.'

'How do you mean she seemed off?'

'I don't know . . . distracted, working longer hours, always on the phone … things like that.' He shook his head. 'She just wasn't herself. She always got too bloody involved with that place. It wasn't work to Alison, it was a calling.'

'Why do you think she lied to you that day? Why call you and say she had to work?'

The muscles in Tom's jaw bunched. 'I can't give you an answer to that.'

John said nothing. It was his experience that no one ever wanted to confront the possibility that their loved ones could betray them with another or that they were taking the road less travelled.

'Look, I don't know what to tell you or Rose. Something was going on with Alison lately. She was worried about something . . . she seemed anxious and distracted.' Tom looked at him. 'She couldn't sleep. I'd get up and find her sitting in her office or here in the kitchen.'

'Did you talk to her about it?'

'I tried, but she kept telling me there was nothing to worry about.'

'Were you having problems?'

'Doesn't everyone have problems?'

'I guess so.'

'Why are you asking that anyway?'

'My job is to ask awkward questions.'

'Rose thinks I know something too, does she?' He laughed bitterly. 'Fuck me.'

'She wants answers, same as you.'

'Yeah, right.'

John glanced at his notebook. Everything this man was describing spoke of secrets and lies, which usually indicated an affair or a troubled mind. Tom Cooper was in denial. And why wouldn't he be? 'Can you give me the names of Alison's friends and maybe some of her co-workers? I have a few but it would be good to compare.'

'Sure.' Tom stood and rubbed his eyes with the heels of his hands. 'That'll be easy since they were pretty much one and the same. Alison didn't know a lot of people outside her work. She didn't have a lot of anything outside her work.'

'Can I see her office?'

'Sure.'

He led John along the hall to a small box room. Alison's desk was littered with photos and mementoes, notebooks and pieces of chocolate.

Tom leaned against the door jamb. 'Her diary is sitting somewhere under that pile of rubbish and you'll find the names of her friends in it. Take your time, and give me a shout when you're through.'

John sat at Alison's desk. He looked around the tiny room. The shelves were stacked with medical books interspersed with novels. She had stuck her children's drawings and paintings on the yellow walls.

A book lay on the desk. John turned it over. Bill Bryson. He opened it. It was inscribed: 'To Alison, It is only when the storm clouds break we can see the wonder of the sky, Love, Ivan.'

John put it down and dug out her agenda from under the papers. It was stuffed with business cards, Post-its and receipts. He flipped it open to the phone-numbers page and scanned them, then returned to the daily planner.

There was a hastily scrawled line on the Friday Alison had died: 'Ask about Corrigan.' It was encircled in black marker.

John closed the agenda. He looked through her desk, but aside from medical journals, envelopes, more junk, more books and an ancient tin of mints, there was little for him to go on.

He stood, and as he did so he saw a photo on one of the shelves. He picked it up. It was of Alison with another woman, clinking cocktail glasses. They looked brown and happy, young and carefree. He turned it over. 'Alison and Beth, Florida, 1990'.

He put the picture into the agenda.

He found Tom at the kitchen sink, staring out across the ragged garden at a clothes-line laden with wet laundry. 'Would you mind if I hang on to this for a day or two?'

'No.'

'Do you have a recent photo of your wife I could borrow?'

Tom walked to the fridge and took one from under a duck fridge magnet. He handed it to John. It showed Alison sitting on the steps of the house, with the dog between her legs. She was smiling for the camera, but her eyes were sad. 'I took that last September. Just before I had my fall.'

'She was very lovely.'

'Yes, she was,' Tom said, and went back to staring out of the window.

8

The exterior of the apartment building was crumbling and many of the ground-floor flats were boarded up. Pavel climbed over debris and broken rubble, walked past burned-out cars, soiled mattresses and junk that had been picked clean for anything of value. It had been a few years since he had been in this area of Zenica and he had forgotten just how bad it was.

Inside it was no better: the lift was broken and the stairs were littered with broken glass, syringes and human waste. Old women hung out washing between the air shafts and scores of filthy children ran around shrieking and cat-calling. The air stank of urine and excrement, of decay and death. Pavel took the steps in leaps, passing a wino collapsed on the return to the fifth floor. He doubted the drunk would ever rise again. Looking at the swollen feet and mottled skin, he thought maybe it was better that way.

He consulted the piece of paper he carried and knocked on the door of a flat on the seventh floor. A wire mesh covered a square partition cut into the door at eye level, and at his second knock it was slid to the side. A rheumy eye peered through the wire. 'Yes?'

'Open the door. I'm Pavel, Ana's brother.'

'Who?'

'The girl, you stupid fuck, I'm her brother.'

The man looked him over carefully before he closed the partition. Pavel heard the sound of many bolts being scraped back.

The man who opened the door was short and toothless. He wore striped trousers like a circus performer's and a leather singlet. He might have been forty, he might have been sixty. His clothes hung on his gaunt frame as though from a coat-hanger and his face was weathered, deeply lined.

'Where is she?'

'The lawyer sent you?'

'Yes. Where is she?'

'What is his name?'

'Travnic.'

The man nodded. 'Look, kid, you tell him this. We had a bad situation here. He can't blame us for this one.'

'Where is Ana?'

'She's sick, man. We're doing our best, but she's real sick. I don't know what else we can do. You've got to understand – we did everything, yeah? I mean, sometimes these things don't go the way they're planned. She knew the risk, she knew what was involved. You've got to tell Travnic we did everything, man.'

Pavel dropped his bag and shoved the man hard in the chest, sending him sprawling in the hall. He kicked the door closed behind him and went to grab the man, who was scuttling away as fast as he could.

A woman came into the hall from a room to his right. She wiped her hands on a dishcloth. If she was surprised to see the short man on the floor it did not show. She was about Ana's age, with short, peroxide-streaked hair. She was heavily tattooed and wore a nose-ring.

'Where is Ana?' Pavel said. 'I am her brother.'

'You're too late. There was nothing more we could do.'

'I asked you a question.'

The woman jerked her head towards the end of the hall. Pavel moved past her. He pushed open the last door and peered inside. The room was dark and cold, the wallpaper peeling and riddled with damp. One weak lamp illuminated the squalor. Though the window was closed, a draught stirred the light curtains. The air was heavy with the smell of sickness.

His sister lay crumpled on a cot in the corner. Despite the chill her sheets had been kicked off. She wore a stained nightdress and her long dark hair was matted to her head.

Pavel went to her and knelt beside her. He lifted her head gently, turning her face towards him. 'Ana, it's me.'

At the sound of his voice she opened her eyes. They were sunken, and her lips were dry and cracked. Her skin had a dull yellow tinge. 'Pavel?'

'Ana, it's okay now. I'm here.'

'Then … they let you go.'

Her voice was barely a whisper. Pavel laid her head down and took her hand in his. Her skin felt clammy and cold. 'Ademi withdrew the statement.'

'Good.' She tried to lift her head again, but a spasm of pain rocked through her.

'Ana, please, what did you do?'

'It is okay,' she said, but her voice was fading. Her eyelids fluttered and began to close. 'You will be okay now. You are safe. I will go to my father and you will be safe.'

The tattooed woman came up behind him. 'She's got an infection. It's very bad. We had medicine but it's gone now.'

'We've got to get her to a hospital – we've got to get her help.'

Ana's hand slipped from his.

'No.' Pavel glanced behind him to where the man stood watching from the doorway. His eyes were darting between Pavel and the woman. 'I told him this wasn't our fault. We did everything we could. We gave her what we had, what she paid for.'

'It's too late now.' The woman stepped closer. She lifted Ana's nightdress.

Pavel stared at his sister's body, horrified. The gauze was clean but the skin around it was livid and beginning to decay. The smell was of rotting meat and he reeled back in shock. The rest of sister's skin was jaundiced, dying.

He knew immediately it was too late, but he could not sit there and do nothing. 'I need to get her to a hospital.'

'Please, we cannot.' The woman shook her head. 'Her blood is poisoned, it is too late.'

'She's dying – she's going to die.'

'If you go there, they will report this to the police. Please, you must understand. You'll be sent back to prison, we'll go to prison – that's if we live long enough to be arrested. You don't know the people she spoke to who arranged this. The policeman who changed his words, he will be questioned, he will seek you out.' The woman pressed her hands together, her face racked with anguish. 'If people find out you got the police involved it will be bad for all of us.'

'So you have a car?'

'You must listen to me. You are too late to save her. You *cannot* do this.'

Pavel jumped to his feet, grabbed the woman by the throat, spun her around, walked her across the floor and smashed the back of her head through the window. The curtain ripped free of the rail and glass tinkled as it bounced off the concrete wall of the narrow shaft outside. 'Listen to *me*. You will help me or you will die right now. I swear it.'

The woman gasped in pain and fear. The man lunged forward and grabbed Pavel's arm. 'Please, don't hurt her!'

'I will not mention your name to anyone, but if you do not help me, I will kill her and then you. Do you have a car?'

'Yes. In the garages at the back.'

Pavel dragged the woman inside and flung her down. Her hair was wet with blood from where the glass had lacerated her scalp. He turned to the man. 'Get it.'

The man bolted. Pavel bent and brushed Ana's hair off her face. He glanced at the woman who had crawled away from him. 'You, over here.'

She struggled to her feet and came to his side. Pavel gathered Ana to him and lifted her off the bed. He was alarmed at how light she felt in his arms. 'Get me a blanket.'

The woman did as she was told.

Pavel carried his sister to the hall. 'Pick up my bag.'

She did so.

'What is that old man to you?'

'He is my uncle.'

'Your uncle is going to drive us to a hospital. We'll leave her there. They'll help her – they'll know what to do. We won't sign or say anything. No identification. Take my bag downstairs for me. Hurry.'

The woman slumped, the weight of the world seemed to rest on her shoulders, but she did as he said.

The man brought the car around. It was an old battered Ford, more rust than paint. Pavel placed Ana on the back seat. Her eyes remained closed and her breathing was shallow and laboured. The skin around her mouth was pale and faintly bluish. Pavel wrapped the blanket tightly around her.

'You must be careful,' the woman said, handing the man her keys. 'If you are caught we will all pay the price.'

He nodded. Pavel climbed in and put Ana's head on his lap. They drove off.

They had not even reached the outskirts of the flat complex when Ana convulsed.

'Stop the car,' Pavel said.

'What?' The man was looking at him in the rear-view mirror.

'Stop the car! She's being sick.'

The man careened across the road and pulled up outside a derelict hardware shop. Pavel tried to turn Ana onto her side to prevent her choking.

'Ana, hold on, stay with me.' He scraped the vomit from her mouth with his fingers. 'Ana, please . . .'

But she was too weak and ill to fight any longer. In her brother's arms, on the back seat of a battered brown Ford, Ana Sunic took her last struggling breath and died.

Pavel and the man buried Ana among the scrub bushes and rocky soil in the hilltop high above Zenica, using only the headlights of the Ford to see. Neither man spoke as they dug into the frozen earth with pickaxes and shovels. When they could dig no further Pavel laid his sister's body – wrapped in a tattered sheet – in the ground and placed an image of the Blessed Mother on her chest. '*Akana mukav tut le Devlesa*,' he whispered. I leave you now with God.

He wept silently as they covered her. While they filled in the remaining soil, a light snow began to fall, the flakes covering their handiwork like frosting on a chocolate cake.

The man offered to take him back to town but Pavel refused. The man shrugged and climbed into his car. He drove off, leaving Pavel in freezing darkness with only his grief for company.

As dawn approached Pavel left Ana's graveside and climbed up to the crest of the hill. Shivering in his thin jacket, he watched the first fingers of daylight creep across the valley. He glanced down at his hands. Tiny flecks of blood lay under his fingertips, the detritus of his day's work, the detritus of his life. He rubbed them together, watching the filth roll across his skin and crumble away like dust.

He could not reconcile himself to her death, to what she had sacrificed. He was not worth it; he was not worthy of her. A bubble of bile rose in his chest and he forced it back down.

They would pay, the monsters who had done this. They would all pay. If it took every last breath in his body he would find them and take his revenge.

He would start with the surgeon.

He slipped off the rock and wiped the tears from his face. He went back to Ana's grave and retrieved his bag. He said a short prayer, asking the God he did not believe in to guide her to heaven, and walked away. He went down the stony path into the woods. The deepening shadows embraced him as one of their own.

9

'You don't remember anything about her?' John said, in exasperation, to the aged crone behind the desk of the Hill Crest Hotel. She had just shown him Alison's signature in the register. It was unmistakably her handwriting.

'How am I supposed to remember the face of everyone who comes through the doors?'

'It was only Friday.'

'We were busy last weekend. The RDS had a house-and-home thing on and we were booked solid. I've been run off my feet.'

John sighed.

'Don't be puffing and blowing at me,' the old woman said, snatching back the register.

'Do you remember if she was on her own or not? If she was expecting anyone?'

She looked at John as if he had grown an extra head. 'This is a hotel,' she said. 'We don't grill our clients.'

John gave up. He left the run-down hotel and decided to try Alison's friend, Beth, and see if she could offer him any insight to the dead woman.

Beth Gold's eyes were as dry as her delivery. She expressed no emotion when she spoke of her friend other than to hesitate twice over the word 'gone'.

She's a cold fish, John thought at first, but the longer the interview went on and the longer he looked into her pinprick pupils, the more he found himself thinking of Tom Cooper's words. He found himself wondering just how much of the good shit doctors were able to prescribe to themselves before questions were asked.

'Did you say something?' Her brow furrowed slightly.

'I said it's a beautiful place you have.'

'Oh, yes.' She glanced away.

Beth Gold lived in a plush penthouse in Sutton. The apartment was bright and modern, complete with hard, uncomfortable furniture and large paintings John couldn't figure out. The one thing he did appreciate was the wraparound balcony overlooking the bay.

Though it was a cold day he wished Beth Gold would crack open a window. The heat was stifling in the living room, despite the high ceilings. It had to be more than thirty-five degrees in there.

John studied her profile. She was an attractive woman in her way, and he guessed her to be in her early or mid-forties. She wore a white shirt, open at the throat, dark green linen trousers and her feet were bare. Her blonde hair was natural and cut in a no-nonsense pageboy. Her accent was flat, Irish, but from no discernible region that John could pinpoint. She wore a diamond the size of a grape on her right hand and no wedding ring.

She had not been happy to have John call on her and, although not exactly rude, had made no effort to conceal her irritation with his questions.

'I know this is a very difficult time. You and Alison were close.'

'She was my best friend.'

'Did she seem depressed to you?'

'Depressed?'

'Well, out of sorts.'

'I'm sorry, I'm … You're a private detective? Really? I must say I am surprised. I don't know why Rose feels she has to do this. I mean, it's awful about Alison, it really is, but digging through her private life … It's so sordid. Alison would have hated it.'

'She's grieving and looking for answers as to why her daughter might have taken her own life.'

Beth looked away.

'How long have you known each other?'

'We were in college together. We graduated the same year. Why did you ask if Alison was depressed?'

'Tom Cooper told me she hadn't seemed herself lately, that she seemed distracted.'

'Did he now?'

'Did you notice anything amiss?'

'No. Maybe she was a little preoccupied but, then, she was incredibly busy.'

'Would Alison have confided in you if she was seeing someone?'

'What do you mean "seeing someone"?'

'Well, another man, perhaps.'

'She might have been.' Beth sat forward, her pale eyes fixed on John's face. 'But I can tell you right now Alison was not the sort of woman to go running around behind anyone's back. She

61

worked hard. Her whole life revolved around her job and her children.'

'Did she ever mention any problems between herself and Tom?'

'Like?'

'I don't know – anything out of the ordinary?'

Beth crossed one leg over the other, taking care not to crumple her trousers. 'Alison's only problem was making sure she brought in enough money to keep a roof over her children's heads.'

'You think the Coopers had money troubles?'

'Tom's an idealist and a dreamer with notions. Look at the house they live in. Do you think Alison wanted that big house? No, she didn't. She would have been happy in a semi-d, but Tom wanted the great life, the cute kids, the nice car. Ever since they've been married Alison's been doing the lion's share of the earning, even when Tom worked in the building trade during the supposed boom years. And when Tom was injured it was down to Alison to take up the slack.'

'I get the impression you're not a big fan of Tom.'

'I didn't say that. He's all right. But I don't have to live with him.'

'Did he and Alison fight much?'

'I wasn't privy to their marital business but I know he had an affair last year.'

John sat forward. 'Oh?'

'Yeah, I'll bet he didn't mention *that*.'

'No, he didn't.'

'Of course not.'

'When was this?'

'Alison found out in August. I don't know how long it had been going on.'

'How did she find out?'

'I have no idea.'

'Do you know who he was having an affair with?'

'Some solicitor who worked for an apartment complex Tom's crew was working on.'

'Do you have a name?'

'Karen Deloitte.'

'Is there any chance it's still going on?'

'Alison found out about it and made him end it. He told her he had.'

'You don't think so?'

Beth shrugged one shoulder. 'I don't know. All I do know is that I would have thought it was obvious to everyone that what Alison was doing went above and beyond the call of duty. As to her happiness or the state of her marriage, I really can't say.'

'Would anyone have reason to hurt Alison?'

'No, why would they?'

'I don't know. I'm just trying to get a feel for the lady.'

'She was a hard-working woman, a wife and a mother. She was a good friend. She liked chocolate and decent coffee. I don't know that there's much more I or anyone else can tell you.'

'She never said anything to you about someone else? It might have been a recent development. Maybe someone she might have mentioned more often than usual.'

'No, I keep telling you.'

'Did you ever hear her talk about a man called Ivan?'

'Ivan? You mean Ivan Colbert? He's works at the Alton, one of the most prestigious private clinics here in Dublin. He and Alison are friends. Ivan used to work in Toronto. He and Alison met there.'

'Maybe she and—'

'Before you continue that line, Mr Quigley—'

'John.'

'Mr Quigley, you don't get to sully Alison's name here. She

was my friend and she was a kind and gentle person. I don't know why she's dead. I don't know why she would do something like that to herself. I don't know why or if she was depressed. I should have, I was her friend, but here we are. You're asking the same questions I've asked myself a thousand times since I heard the news. Maybe she was sad, maybe she was hurting, maybe she felt it was too hard to go on in this goddamn world. But whatever she thought and whatever she felt, she didn't share it with me.'

John wanted to ask more, but Beth Gold's eyes were now over-bright and her mouth had a hard set to it that he had seen many times in many faces. 'I am sorry for your loss,' he said softly.

'If that's everything, Mr Quigley, I can show you out.'

John closed his notebook and stood up. 'Are you going to the funeral tomorrow?'

'Yes.'

At the door John paused. 'Did Alison ever mention anything to you about leaving Tom?'

Beth's skin looked waxy in the bright light of the hall. Taut, overstretched. 'Not in so many words.'

'Not in so many words?'

John waited for Beth to say something more, but she sighed. 'Dreams don't put food on the table, do they?'

'No,' John had to agree, 'they don't.'

10

Dr Andrei Flintov waited on the steps outside the front door of his townhouse. It was cold and, for the second time in a minute, he glanced impatiently at the Tag Heuer watch on his wrist. Where was Yuri? He was surprised at the tardiness. The Turk had been his driver for more than a year now and he had found him exemplary. He was smart, polite and almost never late.

Flintov tightened his overcoat around him and whistled tunelessly between his teeth. He could, he supposed, walk around the block to the garages at the rear, but he disliked being on the streets. He disliked feeling vulnerable.

He waited.

A few moments later his Audi cruised into view and slid to a stop before him. Flintov slipped down the steps, threw himself into the rear seat and slammed the door. 'You're late, Yuri. I've been standing in the cold like a stray dog.'

'I'm sorry, sir.' Yuri's black eyes sliced to the rear-view mirror. 'Some tramp was lying in the road in front of the garage door.

I had to drag him to the kerb. Disgusting, these drunks – they should be rounded up and sent away.'

'An Albanian, no doubt,' Flintov said, his lip curled.

'I believe so, sir,' Yuri replied.

Flintov blamed the Albanians for all the ills of the country. He had been confronted and attacked by an Albanian street gang two years before in an attempted carjacking and that was the reason he had hired Yuri.

'Well, next time just run him over. Come on, put your foot down and let's go.'

'Yes, sir.'

Yuri pressed his foot to the accelerator and they flew along with relative ease.

When they reached the hospital, where Flintov kept a suite of rooms, Yuri waved to a security guard at the gates and used an automatic button on the dashboard to allow them access to the underground car park. It was patrolled hourly by a heavily armed security man, but even so Yuri stopped the car by an interior lift and waited until Flintov had gathered up his paperwork before he released the locking mechanism. You could never be too careful.

'What does Mariana have planned for today?' She was Flintov's very young and very beautiful second wife. He was always highly concerned about her activities when he was working. She was thirty years his junior, flighty, high-spirited and easily bored. She had many male admirers, and she liked to remind Flintov of this and tell him how lucky he was to have her and how easy it would be for her to find another lover. It drove Flintov crazy, as she knew it would. Fortunately Mariana liked Yuri to ferry her about as she found one way or another to spend her husband's money. Yuri was not exactly the soul of discretion where Mariana was concerned since it was Flintov who paid his wages.

'I don't know, sir, only that she has asked that I be available at midday. I believe she has yoga today.'

'I need you here at three.'

'Yes, sir.'

'Don't be late.'

'No, sir.'

Flintov climbed out, got into the lift and pressed the button to take him to the fifteenth floor. Yoga, he thought, with that French ponce Marcus no doubt. He had met Marcus once and taken an instant dislike to him. Mariana had laughed and suggested he, too, should work on his flexibility, saying it was not nearly as powerful as his imagination. She liked to tease him, and it galled Flintov that he fell for it every time.

It had been a mistake to marry Mariana. He had regretted it almost as soon as the ink had dried on the marriage certificate. He should have kept her as a girlfriend but he had been thinking with his cock, not his head. He had pursued her and she had allowed herself to be caught. Or, at least, that was the impression she portrayed. As soon as they were legally bound she had quickly shown him another side of her. She was beautiful, true, but cold and coarse beneath the façade. She had a terrible temper and often sulked. She was rude at parties connected to his work and had yawned openly in the face of the faculty director earlier that year while he had regaled them with a story of his childhood. On top of that she went through his money like a hot knife through butter. But somehow she always knew when his patience was running out and would wind her way around him like a cat, charming him afresh, whispering in his ear, cajoling him back to bed until she had him right where she wanted him.

It sickened him that she could play him like an instrument. Some days he wondered if he didn't hate her a little.

He got out at the fifteenth floor and approached the smoked-glass doors that led to the reception area. The new girl made eyes at him from behind the desk. Another, Flintov thought, as he nodded curtly to her.

'Good morning, Doctor.'

He was a fool worrying about Mariana. He was fifty-four, a surgeon, a respected colleague with a beautiful wife, the envy of many. He smiled as he entered his office, thinking of how the world must view him. As always, his sense of self buoyed his mood to where he felt it ought to be.

He remained in relatively good form until he finished work and went downstairs to the car park. There was no sign of his car. He tried to call Yuri. The phone rang out and went to voicemail.

'Yuri! I told you to be ready. Where are you? I will be in my office. Ring me the moment you get here. This is unacceptable.' He rode the lift back upstairs, fuming.

But Yuri did not call and by three forty-five an irate Flintov ordered a cab to take him home, swearing that he would sack the Turkish driver the second he laid eyes on him. He was, no doubt, still acting as handmaiden to his damned wife.

The taxi dropped him outside his home. Flintov paid the driver and climbed the steps to his front door. He tried to open it but it was locked from the inside. He rang the bell and waited.

No one came.

He balled his hands. Mariana must have gone off with Yuri and left the door locked.

He made his way back down the steps. He glanced up and down the street, then hurried around the corner to the garage entrance to his home.

Using his personal alarm he opened it.

The Audi was parked beside his weekend car.

He looked at it for a moment. If it was here, where was Yuri? And why was the house locked? He stepped into the garage and went to the door at the rear. It was unlocked. He went through the walled garden, past Yuri's flat – the door was locked – and up the flagged steps to the kitchen and the larder at the rear of his property.

As he let himself into the house he realised his heart was beating rapidly.

The metal gate to the rear delivery hall was slightly ajar and when he turned the corner he found Yuri sitting against the wall, his hands upturned on his lap. He would have looked as though he was merely taking a break, were it not for his sightless eyes facing the opposite wall and the trickle of blood that had dried from his ear.

Flintov stepped over his driver and eased himself gingerly into the kitchen. He found Kora, his cook and housekeeper, lying under an overturned stool. The vegetables she had been preparing for lunch remained on the chopping board. Flintov felt a pang of sorrow for the old lady who had been with him many years. He did not touch her and hurried past her body. Mariana – where was she?

He moved out into the hall as quietly as he could. Then he heard footsteps on the lower stairs. He flattened himself to the right of the enormous grandfather clock he had imported from Vienna and fumbled his mobile from his bag. In his terror and haste he dropped it and it skittered across the polished tiles. He stepped away from the wall, bent down to grab it and, as he did so, glimpsed a dark blur heading for him at speed.

He tried to straighten, but hadn't a hope.

Somebody struck him across the side of the face with a heavy bronze ornament. Flintov went down and was out before he could raise a hand to defend himself.

11

After he had left Beth Gold, John drove across town to the Mercy Hospital. He wanted to speak to the staff, find out who might have known Alison best. But although a number of people were happy enough to talk about her, he learned no more than that she had been a devoted mother and an incredibly hard-working woman. In fact, it occurred to John, nobody seemed to have known Alison Cooper very well at all.

'You could try talking to Dr Elliot,' one of the nurses – a cute redhead, whose curvy body strained to stay within her uniform – said, noticing John's disappointment.

'Dr Elliot?'

'Yes, head of surgery. He and Dr Cooper were pretty friendly.'

'How friendly?'

She straightened her shoulders and the smile she had been wearing evaporated instantly. 'I meant they were friends.'

'I'm sorry, I shouldn't have said that.'

'No, you shouldn't. Dr Cooper was always professional.'

'Right. Of course. Where might I find Dr Elliot?'

'He came in earlier so he's probably in his office. It's up the stairs, third door on the left.'

John thanked her. Moments later, he knocked on the door of Dr Saul Elliot's office.

A voice bade him come in.

'Yes?' Saul Elliot peered at John over a pair of bifocals. He was a handsome man, outdoorsy-looking, wearing a faded blue shirt open at the throat under his white coat. A variety of cardboard folders lay on his desk before him. He exuded 'busy'.

'I'm John Quigley, a private investigator.'

'An investigator?'

'Yes. I've been hired by the family of Alison Cooper.'

'I see.' Elliot closed the folder he had been reading and linked his fingers before him on the desk. 'And how can I help you?'

'I understand you and she were friends. Good friends.'

'Yes, we were.'

'Just here in work or outside the office?'

'Excuse me?'

'I don't mean anything iffy. It's just that everyone I've spoken to so far really only seemed to know Dr Cooper in a professional capacity. It would be nice to talk to someone who socialised with her, knew a bit more about her as a woman.'

'I see. Well, I'm not sure I can help you there. I mean, Alison and I knew each other from before she went to Toronto. We got on very well, but we didn't really meet outside office hours.'

'So you go way back to before she was married.'

'We do.'

'How did she seem lately?'

'Very busy.'

'More so than usual?'

'I think so. There's a virus doing the rounds at the moment

71

and it's been affecting patients and staff alike. We're missing some very key people right now and everyone's had to pitch in to cover.'

'How was Alison coping with the extra workload?'

'Alison Cooper was a professional in every sense of the word. She just got on with it.'

'She ever talk to you about being overwhelmed or feeling depressed?'

'No.'

'Maybe she was … I don't know . . . struggling. Maybe her home life wasn't all she hoped.'

Elliot's expression hardened. 'If it wasn't, she kept it to herself. Look, maybe she'd seemed a little down in the dumps recently, but I cannot honestly say I ever thought Alison Cooper would take her own life.'

'She never spoke to you about her marriage?'

'No, and I didn't pry into her private affairs.'

John decided to step out on a limb. 'But you knew she and her husband were having problems, right? You knew there was talk of them separating.'

Elliot hesitated for a beat too long.

'It's okay,' John said. 'I get it. You're her friend and you don't want to speak ill of the dead.'

'Ill of her? I wouldn't speak ill of Alison. Him, maybe.'

'Another Tom fan.'

'He's an acquired taste.'

'You don't like him.'

'He doesn't like me. I've met him a few times, and he's always struck me as a man with a chip on his shoulder.'

'In what way?'

'Oh, Alison was well educated, academic, and he painted houses for a living. I never really understood what she saw in him.'

John thought if arrogance could be milked and sold in bottles Saul Elliot would have himself a fine cash cow. 'You're saying he was jealous of her.'

Elliot shrugged, but it was obvious he thought exactly that.

'He'd have been pretty cut up if she'd left him, then, wouldn't he?'

'I suppose so.'

'You know if she was seeing someone or not? Wouldn't blame her after what her husband did to her last year.'

A flush of colour rose in Elliot's cheeks. 'And if she was, I for one wouldn't blame her, but this is a ridiculous thing to speculate on. Alison hasn't even been buried yet and you're picking over her character like a carrion crow. For God's sake, the woman was a mother and a wife.'

'Mothers and wives have affairs.'

'Does Tom honestly think such a thing?'

'I don't know what he thinks – I doubt *he* knows what he thinks at the moment.'

'*I* think you should leave,' Elliot stated. He opened the folder again.

'Hey, look,' John said, 'I understand you wanting to be loyal to your friend but she's dead and I aim to find out why. To do that I've got to ask the questions people don't like to be asked.'

'I see that, Mr Quigley, but I feel I've answered your questions.'

'Did Dr Cooper have an office here in the hospital?'

'Of course.'

'Would there be any chance I could see it?'

'Absolutely not. It's hospital property. Unless you have a warrant or some other official sanction I can't let you go rummaging through Alison's private papers. I won't allow it.'

'All right, all right, relax. I had to ask. Will you be going to the funeral?'

'Of course. Look, I'm rather busy, as you can see. If you don't mind …'

John took a card from his jacket, and placed it on the desk. 'If anything occurs to you or if you remember anything out of the ordinary my numbers are on the card.' He stood. 'Sorry for your loss.'

Elliot nodded tersely.

John let himself out and hurried down to look for the cute red-haired nurse. He was in luck. She was just coming out of the nurses' station. She raised an eyebrow when she saw him. 'Did you get to speak with Dr Elliot?'

'I did. But, Jesus, I'm just terrible with directions. Dr Elliot's up to his eyes but he told me which way to Dr Cooper's office and somehow I've managed to get lost twice. I don't want to bother him again, he's very busy – he's got I don't know how many files on his desk.'

'Oh, he's always up to his eyes,' she said. She glanced at the watch pinned to her chest. 'I've got a minute. I'll show you how to get there.'

'Really? You're an angel – I hate to bother you.'

'Oh, it's not a problem,' she said, smiling her sunny smile again. 'Please, follow me.'

John was happy to do so.

12

When Flintov came round he found himself lying on the floor of his en-suite bathroom. He moved his head slightly and gasped at the pain. For a moment he felt sick and close to passing out again. He managed to roll onto his side. The room spun wildly and he had to blink a number of times to clear his vision.

He discovered his hands had been bound and taped to his feet, which were shackled to the radiator with some kind of chain. He shut his eyes.

'Nice of you to rejoin us.'

He opened his eyes again and turned his head to where the voice had come from. A man dressed in black was standing by the French bath. It stood on a raised level at the end of the room, surrounded by scented candles. Mariana was sitting in it. Her face was streaked with tears, her hair soaked and plastered to her head. She was naked, freezing and terrified. She shivered uncontrollably and her lips were blue. She looked at him beseechingly.

'Mariana—'

'She thought you were dead but, as I told her, I knew you would be back.'

'What do you want?'

'You have beautiful things,' the man said.

'Please …'

'My name is Pavel Sunic.'

'Do not tell me your name,' Flintov said, squeezing his eyes shut. 'I don't want to know who you are. Just take what you want and go.'

'Strange,' Pavel said. 'I would want to know the identity of the man who was going to kill me.'

Mariana began to cry.

'Open your eyes.'

'Please, for God's sake, I have money, I have jewels – there are drugs here, anything you need. You can take what you want.'

Pavel smiled. 'I intend to.'

Flintov swallowed hard. 'You killed my staff.'

'The old lady had a weak heart. I did not hurt her. The thug was a different story, but you already knew that.'

Flintov blinked in confusion. 'I don't understand.'

'I saw how he handled the drunk I put in front of your garage this morning.'

Flintov groaned. So that was how this beast had gained entry. Yuri had been distracted with the tramp and he had slipped inside. All the complicated alarms in the world had not saved them.

'You obviously liked having people such as him around you – he probably made you feel safe.' Pavel glanced down at the petrified Mariana. 'He make you feel safe?'

'Please, Mr Sunic, whatever you want, tell me. I can help you. There is no need for more bloodshed.'

'Unfortunately you can't give me what I really want.'

'I don't understand.'

Pavel bent down and grabbed Mariana by the ankles. Before she could stop him he yanked her legs up to his chest. She screamed once but was quickly silenced when her head disappeared under the water. He had earlier tied her hands together in front of her chest. She could not use them to gain purchase on the rim of the bath.

'No!' Flintov screamed. He flung himself against the chain but he could not advance more than a few inches from the radiator. 'Stop it!'

'How long do you think she can hold her breath?' Pavel said, his lips drawn back tightly over his teeth from the effort of holding her. 'Of course, panic makes it harder.'

Flintov could hear Mariana thrashing against the sides of the bath, see her feet flexing as Pavel held them pinned. 'Please, stop. Why are you doing this?'

'My sister Ana lasted almost four minutes before her lungs stopped working. I could see the pulse beating in her neck even after her lungs gave up. Believe me, four minutes is a long time.'

'I don't understand. Please, for the love of God, let her go – don't do this.'

Pavel released Mariana's feet and a second later her head appeared over the rim of the bath. She clung to the side with her bound hands, coughing and retching.

'My sister's name was Ana. Do you remember her?'

'What? No.'

Pavel reached for Mariana again. She screamed and tried to shy away from his touch.

'Wait! Stop. Ana, yes, I remember a girl called Ana.'

'You removed her kidney.'

'She … she donated it.'

Pavel looked at him. 'You removed it and you gave it to someone else. I want to know who has my sister's kidney.'

Flintov licked his lips. 'That's confidential information. What is this? She wants more money now? Is that it? A fucking shakedown? We're not thieves. She was paid handsomely for her contribution.'

'Her contribution?' Pavel sneered. 'Is that what you call it? A contribution?'

'Look, she approached us. She wanted money. She signed papers. She came to a lawyer called Travnic for money, she came to him ... of her own volition.'

'She's dead.'

'What? I don't understand.'

'And you call yourself a doctor. She's dead.'

Mariana let out a sob. 'Oh, Andrei, what have you done?'

'She died from an infection.' Pavel looked at Mariana and smiled until she closed her eyes and whimpered. 'Travnic is dead too.'

'Look, okay, I'm sorry about—'

'Don't be sorry. It's too late to be sorry.' Pavel traced his index finger across the bath edge. 'No, what you can do is tell me where this *contribution* went.'

'I'm sorry about your sister, but sometimes there are complications – it's the same in any surgery. But I swear to you we explained everything to her beforehand. You've got to believe me.'

'I believe you.'

'Of course I understand your anger. That's why I want to make it up to you. I can give you money, I can—'

Pavel raised his head. He was no longer smiling. Flintov looked into his dark eyes and grasped that he was facing a man who could not be bought or pleaded with. He shuddered.

'Do you know what it's like to lose someone you love?'

Flintov looked at Mariana. He had been wrong: he did not hate her, not even a little.

'Do you know what it's like to watch them die in front of you, to see them struggle and fight for every breath as their body shuts down around them? It is an ugly thing.' Pavel's eyes moved over Mariana. 'It made me wonder. Maybe God is not in death after all.'

'I have money, a lot of money – cash. See that desk in the next room?' Flintov gestured frantically with his chin. 'If you move it you will find a hidden door. Under the floorboards, there's money. It's yours, take it.'

Pavel did not look at him. 'Do you believe in God?' he asked Mariana.

She nodded.

'Good.'

He leaned down and grabbed her ankles. She tried to kick him away but he was too powerful.

'No – no! *Please, no!*'

'I won't hurt her. But we will watch her die, just as I watched my sister die. Be thankful that she is close to God. If He is merciful, He will take her quickly. If not …' He shrugged. Then he yanked Mariana's feet towards him and watched her disappear under the water again.

'*Mariana! Mariana!*' Flintov fought desperately to free his hands. The veins stood out on his neck like cords and he flung his body from side to side, thrashing hard against the chain that held him. He knew Mariana was fighting to survive with every fibre of her being. Over his cries he heard her break the surface and take a desperate breath. Then Pavel dragged her legs higher and she was gone.

It seemed a long time before his wife was still. But finally Pavel pushed her legs away and took a step back. There was water everywhere and he was sweating hard.

'You are an animal.' Flintov lay on the tiles, weeping. 'A filthy fucking animal.'

'My sister's kidney, where did it go? Who has her contribution?'

'Go fuck yourself. I know you're planning to kill me so do it and let's be done with this charade.'

Pavel lit a cigarette. 'You know, for a man who likes to play God, you have very little understanding of the world.'

'What are you talking about?'

'You will tell me what I want to know.'

'Fuck you.'

Pavel smiled. He wiped the sweat from his brow with a luxurious towel and quickly smoked his cigarette. He tossed the butt into the bath where it hissed on the water.

By the time he had finished with Flintov two more hours had passed.

He had been correct. Flintov had known very little of the world, and certainly nothing of real pain. But he had learned. Pavel had seen to that. And the surgeon had told Pavel everything he needed to know.

13

John had gleaned little from his search of Alison Cooper's desk, but he was surprised to find her work-space at the hospital incredibly neat. He was further surprised to discover a bottle of Xanax and another bottle of something called Cipramil nestled in her top drawer. He read the labels. Maybe Alison had done her pill-popping in private.

He also unearthed a notebook filled with curious handwriting he couldn't decipher. After a moment of flicking through it he decided to take it with him, as well as a bulging Filofax he had found in the second drawer.

He parked his car, an '85 Opel Manta Berlinetta, in a private car park on Pleasant Street just around the corner from his office. He locked it carefully and made sure the electronic gates were closed before he walked away. He loved his car and had practically built it from the ground up, carefully sourcing parts and replacements. Though the car park cost him a fair chunk every year it was better than replacing the windscreen on a regular basis or coming out to find all four tyres flat as pancakes. Why disgruntled folk thought his beloved car was fair game was beyond him, but it had taken its fair share of knocks and John was loath to allow anything else to happen to it.

He let himself into the building, unlocked his office door, removed his jacket and tossed it over his desk. He checked his answering machine. There were two new messages. One was from his sister Carrie asking him if he wanted to grab some dinner with her during the week. The second was a male voice, calm, friendly, with an English accent. The man identified himself as Detective Inspector Ian Floyd and said he wanted Sarah Kenny to call him back. He provided an Irish number and his extension.

John's curiosity got the better of him and he decided to call.

'Harcourt Terrace, how can I help you?'

'Put me through to extension four, please.'

He waited, and presently the phone was answered.

'Hello?'

'Hi, this is John Quigley, from QuicK Investigations. You called my office earlier today.'

'Hello, Detective. Thank you for getting back to me so soon.'

John was immediately suspicious. Usually whenever one of the boys in blue called him 'detective' he had to scrape the ooze of sarcasm off his face. Floyd was either a better actor, not a complete dickhead, or wanted him on side. 'What can I do for you?'

'I was actually looking for Sarah Kenny. I believe she works with you.'

'What is this in relation to?'

'I'm not at liberty to discuss that with anyone except Miss Kenny. Is she available? I had a mobile number for her but it seems to be unobtainable.'

'She quit. I haven't spoken to her for months.'

'I see.' Floyd didn't sound quite so amicable now. 'Did she leave a number where she could be reached?'

'Sorry, Bud, but I can't help you there.'

'You *can't* help me or you *won't* help me?'

'Can't.' He thought for a second. 'But won't works for me.'

'Did she happen to mention where she was going?'

'Nope.'

'Have you any idea how to get in contact with her?'

'Nope.'

'Will she be returning?'

'Couldn't tell you.'

Floyd sighed. 'I was warned you'd be like this.'

'Yeah? Who's besmirching my good reputation now?'

'Goodbye, Mr Quigley.' He hung up.

John replaced the receiver and thought briefly about what to do. He called Stevie Magher, the only cop he knew who wouldn't cheerfully run him over on sight.

Stevie answered on the third ring, his singsong Limerick accent as strong now as it had been on the day he had left the county all those years before. '*Cad a tharla*, Johnny boy? I hope you're offering to come by and break a sweat? I could use an extra pair of hands on the patio.'

'Morning, Stevie, how's it hanging?'

'To my knees, Johnny boy.'

'Heh, you wish.'

'If you're not offering to help, you must be after something so let's hear it. Ailbhe has me under orders. We're heading for Ikea.'

'Ikea?'

'Aye, she wants us to look at furniture and get a few bits and bobs for the new house.'

'She has you well trained.'

'I'm hanging up now.'

'Okay okay. Look, you know I hate bothering you on a day off, but I've had a weird call. Some English DI called Floyd rang here looking for Sarah. Wouldn't even hint at what it was about but got irked when I said I couldn't give him any information on her whereabouts.'

'No doubt,' Stevie said. 'I've never heard of him. Did he leave a number?'

'He's in Harcourt Street, with his own extension no less.'

'Shoot.'

John gave him the number.

'I'll see what I can find out, might take a while.'

'If you can give it your full attention between the soft furnishings and the wicker baskets I'd be much obliged.'

'I'll probably be at the garden section when I'm reminded of you.'

'Oh?'

'They might have a compost bin for the shit you spew.'

'Oh, Stevie, what sweet music we make.' John made kissy sounds down the line.

'Laugh it up, boyo. You know the deal – you're going to owe me some labour for this one.'

John sighed. 'I miss the good old days when you used to do stuff out of the goodness of your black heart. None of this quid pro quo shit.'

'It's the recession. It's wrung the free out of me.' Stevie hung up.

John replaced the receiver. But he was troubled by the development.

He glanced across the room to Sarah's empty desk, but that didn't offer him any answers.

He flicked through Alison's notebook. Why write like this? It was obviously code, but what was it supposed to mean?

Sighing, he stood up, started the photocopier and set about copying every page of the notebook. It was a pain in the backside, but he wasn't sure how long he'd have everything and one thing he had learned over the years was that copies were *always* a good idea.

When he had finished he locked the pages in the filing cabinet and set about looking up Karen Deloitte. That turned out to be surprisingly easy: a quick Google located her work address and numerous photos of her at various recent charity events on the arm of a brawny, over-tanned piece of meat called Matt Sayers.

Matt Sayers. John peered at him. He had owned a slew of overpriced gourmet joints dotted around the city until the recession bit, and had once driven his motorbike up a one-way street after a round of charity golf. When arrested, he had declared himself 'shocked and horrified' – not because he'd been stupid enough to drink and drive, but because the gardaí had nothing better to do than harass 'decent hard-working men' like himself. He'd even given an interview to some fawning sycophant on a newspaper and whinged about his treatment.

John printed off the most recent photo of the 'glamorous couple' and shoved it into his back pocket. He checked his watch. Coming up to midday. He had an hour to kill before the funeral. Assuming Karen Deloitte ate lunch it was as good a time as any to pay her a visit.

14

'I really do not appreciate your tone, Mr Quigley.'

'I must work on my voice because people tell me that a lot. Anyway, call me John.'

'I'd rather stick with Mr Quigley.'

They were in Karen Deloitte's office, a large corner room with windows covering three walls. Through one John could see the trees in Herbert Park. The building, only two streets away from the American embassy, was an old Georgian house that had been sympathetically and tastefully restored. When John had called in unannounced, a receptionist had asked him his business. He had simply said, 'I'm here looking for Karen Deloitte. Tell her I want to have a chat about Tom Cooper and he's burying his wife today.'

It was this that had caused the current frost.

Karen Deloitte was a handsome woman in her early thirties with shoulder-length ash-blonde hair and pale blue eyes with blonde lashes. She was slim to the point of angularity and the suit she wore was extremely fitted. It looked uncomfortable and very expensive. She wore high-heeled shoes, which John guessed she never took off or kicked under the desk when no one was around. She didn't strike him as the comfort-seeking type.

She was watching him from across the expanse of her wood and chrome desk. There was no clutter on it, just an iMac, a notebook and a brushed-silver pen-holder. The only sign of a personal life was a photo of her and Matt Sayers in a silver frame.

'Like I said, I'm not trying to annoy you, Miss Deloitte, but anything I can learn about Alison Cooper would be a great help.'

'I really don't see how Alison's death has anything to do with me.'

'Well, maybe it doesn't. I mean, you have stopped seeing her husband, right?'

Her hands gripped either side of her chair that little bit tighter.

'But I've noticed over the many years I've been a detective that all sorts of things you think don't matter might, and shit you thought was important turns out to be worthless.'

'How deeply profound.'

John smiled. 'Well, maybe that's guff – but if you'd answer a few questions I'd really appreciate it.'

'What is it you need to know?'

'About you and Tom Cooper.'

'What about me and Tom Cooper?'

'I know you two had an affair.'

'That was a long time ago.'

'Well and truly over?'

'Yes.'

'I was surprised to hear he'd been involved with someone. I had the impression he was a devoted family man.'

'Please.' She sighed and looked at her hands. 'I met him when my company was handling a problem with off-plan sales for an apartment complex in Tallaght. The original firm had sold only one-third of the apartments and some investors wanted to pull out. It was a mess, really.'

'And that was where you met Tom Cooper.'

'Yes.'

'How do a lawyer and a painter connect up?'

'I didn't realise he was a painter. I thought he was one of the architects.'

'Why did you think that?'

She arched an eyebrow. 'Well, he was very hands-on, always around the site. He just let me think he was more involved in the complex than he was.'

'He spun you a line, then.'

'Initially. He's extremely confident – I was a little taken in by him.'

'You must have been,' John said, with no hint of a grin.

She glowered at him. 'You need to understand, Mr Quigley, that I didn't know he was married when we met.'

'I'm not judging you.'

'I'm not proud of that time.'

'How long were you involved with him?'

'Six months maximum.'

'You didn't know he was married all that time?'

'I thought you weren't judging me.'

John spread his hands.

'Look, it was obvious after a while that he was. I mean, we could never meet on a Sunday, he hardly ever stayed over, I couldn't call him at his home, only on his mobile. I confronted him about it and he told me he was married but that they were pretty much living separate lives.'

'Only together for the kids, right?'

'I'm sure in your line of work you've heard all that before.'

'Once or twice.'

'Well, I've heard it all before too but somehow you can never quite be sure of anything in the middle of all that intensity.'

'So what happened?'

'She called me one day during the summer, completely out of the blue. I was sitting right here and it was a Monday. Tom and I had plans that evening to meet. She told me she knew about me and asked why I was so determined to destroy her family.'

'Ouch.'

She smiled, but only with her mouth. 'It sounds really stupid, but up until that point I hadn't ever thought of Tom as a family man. He had always been a single entity to me, with murky baggage stowed elsewhere – if that doesn't sound too cruel or blasé. I hadn't thought of him as, God help me, somebody's daddy.'

'She opened your eyes for you.'

'She certainly did. She didn't yell or shout or call me names … I think it was that which unsettled me the most. She was very sad, but ladylike about the whole thing. Certainly she was far more gracious than I would have been. And certainly more so than I deserved.'

John admired her candour.

'Naturally I spoke to Tom. He was really angry, which I thought was very strange. He wasn't ashamed to be caught or worried, just furious that his lies were so easily exposed. It opened my eyes. There Alison was, with every right in the world to be outraged and she wasn't, and there he was, with no right to be anything other than contrite and he was acting as if he was the victim.'

'So he took the break-up badly.'

'He did, and that was when I saw another side of Tom Cooper. One I really didn't like.'

John sat forward. 'Like what?'

'He wouldn't take no for an answer. He kept calling me. He waited for me outside here, demanding I speak to him. He practically stalked me at work, so much so I had to hand over the account to a different partner. It went on for weeks – until I met my fiancé. Once it became clear that I was involved with another man he backed off, but I'm telling you, Mr Quigley, Tom Cooper is not a man to take no for an answer and not a man to cross.'

She glanced at the photo on her desk. 'When I heard of Dr Cooper's death I thought only one thing.'

'What was that?'

'Maybe what she did was the only way she could get away from him.'

15

Pavel shouldered his bag, climbed from the embankment to the road and walked down the hill to the depot. After leaving Flintov's house he had caught a bus south, heading out of the city to a small town called Mostar. The following morning he planned to make his way to a private airfield he knew of, situated fourteen miles east of the town. He had the name of a man there who, he had been told, would be happy to fly him into a small airfield in the country of his choice for the right financial incentive. He had already contacted the man and settled on a price, although he knew it would be upped once he reached the airfield. That was how it worked: the needy coughed up, the takers took.

He had used some of the money he had taken from Flintov's vault to purchase a single room in a cheap truck-stop motel to rest for a few hours. He had locked the door securely, dragged a chair over and wedged it under the handle. He had removed his shoes and lain on scratchy sheets to read carefully through the documents and papers he had also taken from Flintov. After a while, he switched off the lamp, turned on his side, and drifted off to sleep.

When he woke it was still dark, but dawn was fast approaching. He got up, showered and left his key at reception. He walked to the large truck depot and watched the action. With luck he would find a driver going his way and offer him some money for his trouble. He didn't want to leave any more of a trail than he had to.

The depot was busy, with small fork-lifts and large rigs ranging back and forth across the asphalt, gusting fumes into the frigid morning air. The area was busy with workers too, he noticed, watching men in bright yellow hard hats as they barked orders and read clipboards.

He decided he needed food before he cadged a ride. Strapping his holdall close to his body, he made his way to a large diner overlooking the depot.

The heat and the smell as he pushed open the door made him feel weak and it dawned on him that, apart from an apple and a cheeseburger, he had eaten nothing in two days. He squeezed into a vacant booth and picked up a menu.

Before he'd had a chance to read down it someone appeared at his elbow. 'What can I get you?'

He glanced up. She was about fifty and as broad as she was tall, with wiry hair dyed a harsh, flat red and hastily drawn-on eyebrows. Her fingers were stained with nicotine and her uniform was crumpled and grubby. The plastic name-plate pinned to her chest read 'Jadranka'.

'Can you give me—'

'I need to see the money before you order something.'

'Why?'

'It's restaurant policy.'

Pavel frowned. He looked past her to the men seated at the counter. 'Did you ask everyone else to pay before they ordered?'

She dropped her hip and glanced back at the bar where a man wearing a dirty apron was cleaning glasses. He didn't let on but Pavel knew he was paying attention to the exchange. 'See that man?' she said.

'Yes.'

'That's the owner, and he says you got to pay up front.'

'Why?'

'No offence, but we've been done by your kind before, so that's the rule. You don't like it you can go.'

'My kind?' Despite himself, Pavel felt the colour rise to his cheeks. He lowered his eyes and tried hard not to let his hands shake in front of her.

'Look, I'm sorry, but that's what he said.'

His kind.

'I want to order a cheeseburger and a banana milkshake. I want chips with that, crinkle cut, not thick.'

The waitress sighed.

'And I want a cup of coffee. I would like that first.'

She leaned in close and lowered her voice. 'Listen, I know you're angry, but you don't want to cause trouble in here, trust me on that.'

Pavel glanced past her. He noticed one or two faces at the counter were now also watching him in the mirrored shelves. One man in particular, a huge tub of lard in a check shirt and a Motocross cap, looked particularly interested.

Pavel took Flintov's wallet from his bag and handed Jadranka some *marka*s. She took them from him, wrote out his order and gave him his docket.

'Is there a men's washroom I can use?'

'Sure – down the end, second door on the left.'

Pavel thanked her and slid out of his seat. He walked past the bar, his face impassive, feeling a lot of eyes on him.

Watching his *kind*.

He entered the washroom and made his way to the basins. He dropped his bag on the floor and looked at his reflection in the mirror. There were bags under his dark eyes, and his skin, normally as sallow as a Greek's, was pale and washed out. He wore a fresh T-shirt, also taken from Flintov's house. It was white, Lacoste, two sizes too big. He tucked it into his jeans and surveyed himself. He looked like the world's skinniest hustler. Maybe that was what his *kind* was supposed to look like.

By the time he made it back to the table his coffee had arrived. He slid into the booth and gulped it rapidly. He smoked a cigarette, his leg jiggling under the table. *His kind*.

Jadranka deposited his food and walked away.

He attacked it with gusto, like a starving wolf would a fresh carcass. He used a piece of bun to mop the plate. No sooner had he finished than Jadranka arrived to clear away. Pavel looked around. Plenty of other diners were sitting with empty plates before them.

'You must have been starving.'

'You didn't bring my change.'

'What's that?'

'My change. You owe me some change.'

'I thought that was my tip,' Jadranka said. 'I already put it in the tip jar. I can ask the owner to drop it over to you, if you like.'

Pavel wiped his mouth with a serviette and dropped it on the table. 'Sure, I'll wait.'

She hesitated for a moment. 'It's okay,' she said, her voice low and hostile. She fished in her pocket and dropped some coins on the table. 'I don't need your kind's money anyway.'

'No?' Pavel grabbed her wrist. She yelped, startled. She looked around but the owner was at the other end of the bar, talking to a customer. Pavel looked at her hand, noted the faint trace of nicotine on her fingers.

'Let me go.'

'Do you know something else about my kind?'

'What?'

'We can see things other people cannot.'

'What do you mean?'

Pavel released her. He spread his hand across the back of the booth. 'Do you cough much, Jadranka?'

She looked at him sharply. 'What are you saying?'

'Cough.' Pavel demonstrated what he meant by barking into his hand.

'Why are you asking me that?'

'I don't want to frighten you,' he shrugged, 'but I can only tell what I see.'

'Frighten me? How? What is it?'

'I see you have a dark shadow.'

'What?'

He waved in the general direction of her chest, then tapped his own. 'I can see it. Black and very heavy, like a storm cloud.'

'You can *see* that?'

'It's a gift my people have. My grandmother had it, and my father had it and I have it.'

She narrowed her eyes. 'You can see … *a shadow*? What do you mean? How can you see that? Is it … a spirit thing?'

'Yes, something like that.'

'What is it you can see? Can you describe it?'

'I am very sorry.' Pavel stood up. He grabbed the bag, scooped up the money Jadranka had dropped onto the table and pressed it into her hand. 'Keep this after all.'

'Why?' And now the colour had drained completely from her face. 'Why are you giving me this money?'

'You should enjoy it … while you can.'

Her eyes widened as the impact of his words hit home.

'*Dza Devlesa*.' Go with God. Pavel grabbed his bag, slipped past her and made his way to the door. When he stepped out into the cold air he did not look back and he did not feel sorry for the terror he had read in the woman's eyes. If she wanted to imbue 'his kind' with ridiculous power, who was he to refute it?

He crossed the street and made his way back to the truck depot. Within an hour he had found a Serbian happy to take his money and he was on his way.

16

John arrived late at the church for Alison Cooper's funeral. It had taken him ages to locate a parking space and in the end he had to leave his car three streets away, which meant by the time he slipped in through the side door he was drenched from the heavy rain that had been falling since he left Karen Deloitte's office.

He shook the drops from his jacket, ignoring the dirty looks from those nearest to him. He wiped the moisture from his face and edged to a spot where he could see the family.

Tom Cooper and Rose Butler shared the front pew, sitting stiffly upright with the two children between them. Though the gap was barely two feet, they might have been on different continents.

John scanned the congregation. He was fidgety and uncomfortable. He hated funerals, and always had. This one was no different. He read shock on some faces, grief on others and, as far as he could tell, nothing at all on Tom Cooper's.

The priest's voice was crackling and loud in the speakers. He spoke of loss, of love and of compassion. He intoned gravely that there would be a reunion for the faithful in heaven, that God called his best and brightest home and that the congregation should rejoice as Alison's earthly suffering was far behind her. John watched the children as the priest said something else about how people should rejoice in God's mercy. The son's head was bowed, but the daughter's was up, tears rolling down her cheek. How hard must it be to listen to this? The old priest seemed heartfelt, but how did a man explain to a child that it was no bad thing her mother had died, better that she went to God than stayed with her children?

When the choir began to sing, Rose Butler's composure broke. She dabbed her eyes with a pristine handkerchief.

Before the Mass finished John slipped out and had a smoke. The rain had finally stopped. He walked outside the churchyard and wandered among the parked cars, noting the number of MD plates. The church bell tolled and the hearse backed up to the main doors. Children – school friends of Alison's pair – lined up on either side of the church door and stood silently as the coffin was carried outside.

John hung back, watching.

People approached Tom to offer condolences. Some shook his hand and embraced him, but others were more reserved and stiff. An unconvinced crowd, John thought, watching as the same people hugged Rose tightly and rested palms on the children's heads. He recalled the priest's words and wondered what exactly a merciful God had in mind when He allowed such atrocities to happen. Despite himself he felt his lips curl. The priest had been right. Suffering was not the preserve of the dead. Suffering was always for those who were left behind.

Rose Butler was looking directly at him. He gave her a little nod and moved away through the crowd. To the rear of the mourners gathered on the steps behind the pillars he spotted Beth Gold. She was speaking to Saul Elliot and another man. She wore large black sunglasses and a sombre suit. She seemed pale and was clearly distraught. The man he didn't know was tall, in his fifties, with close-cropped grey hair. He wore a long black overcoat over a well-cut suit.

John hurried over to the group. 'Some turnout,' he said.

The trio turned to him as one.

John held out his hand to the tall man. 'We haven't met. I'm John Quigley.'

'Ivan Colbert,' the man said, and shook John's hand.

'This is the private detective Alison's mother asked to look into her death,' Elliot said, with an edge to his voice.

'We should have a chat when you have time,' John said. 'I know you and Alison were friends.'

Ivan Colbert slipped his hands into his pockets and rocked back on his heels. 'You're looking into Alison's death?'

'Yes.'

'But why? She took her own life.'

John shrugged. 'Her mother wants answers.'

'I see.' Colbert glanced across to where Rose stood with two friends. 'I hope you help the poor lady find some measure of peace.'

'I'll do my best.'

'Give me a ring later and we can talk.'

'I'll do that.'

Colbert said his goodbyes to Beth and Elliot, then walked quickly to the side gate and out on to the street.

John moved closer to the railings to watch him go. He climbed into the back seat of a black Mercedes Benz, which pulled away from the kerb and executed a smooth U-turn. Seconds later, it drove past where John was standing, allowing him to catch a glimpse of the driver as it passed the church. He was a young pug-nosed man, wearing a black suit with a crisp white shirt and tie. He looked oddly familiar to John, who copied the number plate into his notebook.

When he turned, Beth Gold was gone and Elliot was talking to another man. He decided not to follow the congregation to the graveyard and was walking towards his car when someone called him. 'Hey, Quigley. Hold on.'

John turned. Saul Elliot came up fast and grabbed his arm. 'I told you earlier you had no permission to search Dr Cooper's office. Now I learn you were in there snooping about. One of the nurses saw you leave with something. You've stolen hospital property. How dare you? I demand to know what you took. It may contain highly confidential medical information. I demand you return it or I'll have the gardaí regain it from you.'

'You need to calm down – and less of the demand talk.' John was aware that a number of people were glancing in their direction.

'I will do no such thing. I should have known the sort of person you are the moment I laid eyes on you. What did you take?'

'Calm down,' John stepped in closer and, lowering his voice, added, 'or I'll calm you.'

'You had no right,' Elliot said. He removed his hand from John's arm. 'I could have you arrested for theft and trespassing.'

'Whatever. Look, Bud, I took only personal items belonging to Dr Cooper. I didn't take anything medical. I'm not interested in it.'

'It doesn't matter. You had no right to take anything from the hospital. I insist you return it.'

'Okay, you can swing by the office – you have my card, don't you?'

'I'll be there after the funeral.' Elliot turned on his heel and walked away.

John watched him go. He wondered why Elliot had not already called in the cops if he was so incensed. Why had he been so upset?

He returned to his car and drove to Wexford Street. Back in the office he took off his damp jacket and hung it over Sarah's chair. He opened Alison's Filofax and sifted through it. On a whim, he decided to copy the entries from January. It was probably nothing but, as he'd told Karen Deloitte, sometimes nothing had an interesting way of becoming something.

He put the copied pages into his drawer and the original Filofax into an envelope with the notebook.

He made a cup of coffee and sat down to read through the last of Alison's monstrous leatherbound agenda, which he had removed from her home, with the receipts, cards, Post-its and illegible scribbled notes – God alone knew what they meant – that had been inside it.

He withdrew everything from the pouches and piled it on the desk before him. It was pretty generic stuff, work, school dates, nothing to write home about. Two birthday cards, which appeared handmade by her kids, work schedules, shopping receipts, scraps of paper and some more cards tucked into the cover.

John flicked through the cards. They were all thank-you notes, written in many different hands. The last was particularly interesting. It read:

Please don't blame yourself, I know you tried. I will always remember your kindness. Love Chris Day

John blinked. He had seen that name before. He opened the agenda again and found it written in the same black ink and encircled under Tuesday 12 February. He frowned and flicked back to December. Another name, Allen Foster, was encircled in black.

John wrote the two names down on a fresh pad and looked at them. Okay. It might be nothing, it might be something.

He was reading through her entries for the week she died when someone tapped on his office door.

'Come in – it's open.'

Rodney Mitchell poked his head through and smiled shyly. He's lost too much weight to be healthy, John thought immediately. And it wasn't as if he'd had much spare to begin with.

'I thought I heard you on the stairs.'

'Hey, Rod, what's shaking?' John closed his notebook and slid it under the agenda.

'Oh, nothing.' Rodney walked in, leaning heavily on his cane. His leg had been broken badly when he had interrupted a break-in to John's office. It had knitted, but never fully healed. John often wondered about that break-in. It had happened while he had been in England. It seemed a *lot* had happened during the few days he had been away.

John watched the tall man hobble across the floor. He wondered if Rodney was back on the hooch, but couldn't bring himself to ask. Rodney's weight was always on the low side but now he was gaunt, his pale pink scalp dry and flaky through his pale ginger hair.

'Can I get you a coffee, big man?'

'No, I'm … fine.' Rodney eased himself into the wicker chair and glanced at Sarah's desk. 'I take it you still haven't heard from her.'

'Not a sausage.'

'I thought she might have called, what with it being your birthday this week.'

'Guess birthdays don't mean much to Sarah.' John took out the phone book from a drawer in his desk and flipped through it to D.

'She might get in touch.'

'If she does she does, but I won't hold my breath.'

'Aren't you worried about her?'

'Why? Do you think my worrying will make a difference?'

'I don't know how you can be so calm about it.' Rodney frowned. 'She could be in trouble.'

John thought of the cop who had called. 'And why would she be in trouble?'

Rodney kept looking at his hands. 'No reason . . . I was just saying.'

'You ever going to come clean with me, Rodney?'

'What do you mean?'

'You honestly think I don't know you're hiding something? You're in here every other day dancing around the subject like you've ants in your Y-fronts. If you're so concerned about Sarah, why don't you tell me what you know?'

'John, I— There's nothing I can tell you.'

'Something happened when I was in England. I've worked that much out for myself. I was only away a few days, Rod. Everything's hunky-dory when I go. I come back and Sarah's acting like a cat on a hot tin roof. She's got bruises all over her face, and no good explanation for them, her sister's been run off the road and you're banged up in a hospital bed with concussion and a broken leg. Yet you both expected me to buy that these strange goings-on weren't connected.'

'She told you – she was mugged.'

'She was in her *hole*. Jesus.' John threw up his hands. 'She was walking Sumo the night she was attacked, right? Well, I didn't read any account of the cops finding a mugger half-eaten, because that's what I would expect if someone – *anyone* – had tried something that stupid. Jesus, even skagged off their heads no scobie's going to pick a girl walking a dog like Sumo as an easy target.'

'I don't know what to tell you.'

'See, and that's the real doozy right there, Rod. Because I think you know exactly what to tell me but you'd rather sit there pining like a dog than come clean.' John took out his notebook again and picked a pen out of the jar on his desk. 'But don't worry, it'll all come out in the wash. Some cop called here looking to talk to her. Maybe he'll be more forthcoming about why my so-called friend and partner is nowhere to be fucking seen. Maybe then I'll get to the bottom of that particular mystery.'

Rodney could not have looked more stricken if he'd tried. 'The gardaí were looking for her?'

'I don't know if he was the gardaí, Rod. He said he was a detective inspector but he had an English accent.' John wrote down the phone numbers of the four Chris Days in the book. 'Of course, I won't know more until Stevie gets back to me. *Assuming* Stevie learns anything and wants to share. But, hey, maybe he'll be another friend keeping secrets and I can sit here twiddling my thumbs like a gobshite until the cows come home.'

'There's no need to shout.' Rodney pressed his hand to his temple.

'If your head is hurting you,' John opened his other drawer and tossed Rodney a packet of painkillers, 'gobble a few of them. Should tide you over until Happy Hour.'

Rodney got up slowly. He put the tablets on John's desk and drew himself up to his full height. Two spots of colour sat high on his cheeks. 'There was no need for that,' he said softly, before turning and limping out of the office.

John replaced the tablets in his drawer and rested his head in his hands. After a few moments he ground out the untouched cigarette, picked up his phone and started to dial.

'Stevie? . . . Yeah, I know, I'm not taking the piss I swear. I need to add another number to the checklist . . . Nope, a car . . . Yeah, man, I really will owe you this time . . . What? . . . What the hell do I know about plumbing? . . . Yeah, yeah, all right.'

17

The aeroplane was a fixed-wing Cessna that had seen better days – hell, probably better years. Pavel – who had never flown in anything before – was initially dubious about its air-worthiness, but after forking out twice what they had agreed, he was stuck between a rock and a hard place.

He deeply regretted his choice when the pilot, a lanky German called Jans, overshot the runway on take-off and had to bank hard right to clear a group of unassuming trees.

Pavel spent the rest of the journey alternatively clinging to the armrest of his tiny seat and trying not to vomit as the small aircraft hit one pocket of turbulence after another. Rain lashed the windows and visibility was down to a bare minimum. He was unsure if that was a good or bad thing.

Somewhere across France Jans started to sing strange tunes. He shouted over the headset that these were songs to keep the spirits away. He was clearly a madman but that did nothing to dissuade Pavel of the notion that death had finally caught up to him. He was not sorry about that but he regretted he had not fulfilled his promise. He thought of Ana, lying cold and alone under the unforgiving earth above Zenica, and apologised to her that he had not avenged her.

No one was more surprised than he when, through his headset, he heard Jans cackle a laugh and declare they were flying over the Irish Sea. They would land, he yelled, weather permitting, within the hour. At that they hit another pocket of turbulence and the plane dropped out of the sky like a stone.

'Hold on!' Jans roared in broken Bosnian, as he throttled the small craft back up to a safe flying height. 'Ha ha! Up, you bastard, up!'

Pavel vowed there and then that, no matter what happened, he would never fly again. He didn't care how long it would take him to go places, he'd walk across the bottom of the ocean before he'd get into another plane.

They landed on a tiny gravel airstrip in a boggy windswept field in the middle of nowhere. Pavel climbed out of the small craft on shaky legs and stretched. It felt almost as good to be on solid ground as it had the first time he had been with a girl.

'Where is this place?'

'Welcome to Cork. Hey, my man, you're white in the face.' Jans slapped him on the back, laughing. 'Did you think we wouldn't make it? Did you? Hah!'

'How do I get to Dublin?' Pavel asked. He looked around him at the reeds and gorse bushes.

Jans jerked his chin toward a number of sheds and barns at the end of the dirt track that acted as runway. 'Follow that path. After about a kilometre you will reach a road. From there you need to turn left and it is about sixteen kilometres into Cork city. You can catch a train there to Dublin.'

Pavel pulled up his collar. The rain was getting steadily heavier.

'Better get going, my man.' The German pointed skyward

towards the clouds. 'Or I'll never make it.'

Pavel nodded to him, picked up his holdall and began to walk away.

'*Viel Glück*,' Jans called after him.

As he passed the sheds Pavel heard the roar of the engine and the small plane took off into the darkening sky.

Pavel made it to the road and, following the German's instructions, turned left. He had walked for nearly an hour when he came across an ancient open-bed jeep parked across a laneway. There was a small collie sitting in the back. It lowered its head and bared its teeth silently as Pavel approached.

Pavel stopped. The rain beat down on him relentlessly.

He walked around the jeep and peered in through the windows. It was in bad shape, strewn with rubbish and as filthy as it could possibly have been. He tried the door handle. The collie yelped at him, its bark high and frantic, but not vicious. He knew a vicious dog when he saw one. 'Go on.' He waved his hand at the dog. 'Get out.'

But the dog refused, hunkering low again.

Pavel walked to the gate and climbed up on it. He looked into the field but could see nothing, other than some bedraggled sheep huddled near the ditch.

He jumped down and looked along the road.

Sixteen kilometres was a hell of a walk.

He put his bag down and tried the handle again. He climbed up into the bed of the jeep and tried to open one of the three sliding window panels. The dog yipped and yelped at him until he aimed a kick at it. As lithe as a deer, it jumped over the side of the vehicle and disappeared.

Pavel looked around the truck bed. He found a crowbar under the spare tyre.

He hopped down, wiped the rain from his face and began to use it on the window, trying to get the lock to pop.

He had just managed to get the door open when he was struck on the small of his back with such force that he bounced off the jeep, closing the door again. 'You dirty stealing knacker, ya!'

Pavel fell hard into the muck. He reached for the door to haul himself to his feet when he was kicked again.

Then someone grabbed his hair and yanked his head up. 'Yer one of them fucks from up Knockananna, aren't ya? Well, I have ya, I'll have ya know, and you won't be stealing from a Redmond again in a hurry.'

Pavel groaned. He looked up. A red-faced man was standing over him screaming incomprehensible words in his face. The man hauled Pavel to his feet, probably to give him another few digs, but Pavel swung the crowbar and racked it across the man's shoulder so hard. He was big, dressed in a waxed jacket and wellington boots – but he never even saw it coming, although the damn collie did. As the man fell, clutching his surely broken arm, the dog was up and savaging Pavel.

Pavel stumbled to the side and shook it off. It ran at him again and he kicked out, but missed the dog, which latched onto the fingers of his free hand. Pavel yelled in agony and swung the dog around, finally sending it crashing into the side of the jeep. It bounced off, released him and rolled in the dirt. It made one more half-hearted attempt to attack him, but Pavel raised the crowbar and it ran back into the field.

'Ya dirty fuck, ya,' the man said, lying in the mud, his face contorted in pain.

Pavel wiped the rain from his face. He was sweating and his hand was bleeding badly. He leaned over the man and searched his pockets. He found the keys of the jeep and a wallet.

The man made a grab for him with his good hand, but Pavel kicked him in the gut. Then he picked up his holdall and climbed into the jeep. He managed to start the engine and pull out onto the road using only his left hand.

18

'Chris Day? Never heard of him.' Tom Cooper sounded tired and irritable. John could hear voices in the background and figured people had come back to his home after the funeral. 'Is that it?'

'You never heard Alison mention him?'

'I have a houseful of people – why are you asking?'

'I found his name in your wife's agenda. She has it written and circled. There were other names too. What about Coleen Clancy?'

'Never heard of her.'

'Allen Foster? Tobias Johnson? Somebody called Corrigan? That was on the day Alison died.'

'I've never heard of them. Is *that* it?'

John glanced at the page before him. 'I guess so. No, wait. I found a notebook at Alison's office, but I can't understand it. It's like she was writing in code or something. Do you know anything about that? Was that something Alison did?'

'Not that I know of.' Tom Cooper hung up.

The buzzer sounded. When John answered his reward was an even tetchier Saul Elliot.

'Come up, top floor.'

Elliot came in a few minutes later.

'Take a seat,' John said.

'I won't be stopping. Do you have Dr Cooper's property?' He glanced at the agenda. 'Is that hers?'

'This came from her home and has nothing to do with you. Her Filofax and a notebook are in here.' He reached into the drawer and handed him the originals. Elliot checked through them. 'Is this everything?'

'Yep.'

'Good. I don't want you harassing my staff again.'

'I didn't harass anybody and I'm only giving you this stuff as a courtesy so drop the attitude. But tell me something, do you know who Chris Day is?'

Elliot looked surprised, then angry. 'Where did you get that name?'

'It was in Alison's agenda. Who is he?'

'He's none of your business, that's who he is.'

'He sent her a thank-you card – she had a lot of them. So I'm guessing a patient?'

'Goodbye.'

After Elliot had left, John leafed through the rest of the agenda. There was no doubt in his mind that Elliot had recognised the name. He'd need to check with Beth Gold. He flicked the agenda open to the month before Alison's death. There were a lot of nonsensical notes scribbled across the pages here too. What did they mean? He scowled at Sarah's desk. She was the one who normally dealt with this kind of thing. That was their unspoken agreement. John would drive too fast and risk flouting the occasional law or two, and Sarah would use her great bonce to work shit out.

'Thanks a bloody bunch,' he said, to the empty space. He scowled some more, but eventually realised that that wasn't going to solve the puzzle. He picked up the agenda, fetched the copied pages of her notebook and made his way downstairs to the pirate radio station. Hopefully Clique was available and, if not, surely one of the other little short arses in big pants would help him out.

He knocked on the reinforced door and sat on the steps to wait. He heard some indecipherable mumbling and the door was opened one full inch. Plumes of rich, heavy smoke drifted out through the gap, rendering the air in the stairwell sweet and cloying in an instant. Something – he wasn't sure what – wearing skinny jeans and winkle-pickers glanced out through the haze. 'Yeah?'

'It's John from upstairs.'

'Oh, yeah.'

'Click there?'

'Hold on.'

The door closed. After a minute or two it opened again and another scrawny young man emerged, blinking, into the light. This one had half a head of electric blue hair and various piercings. 'Hey, John.'

'Click.'

The young man sighed. 'Clique. You'd think by now that would get old, John.'

'Only thing old around here is me. How you doing?'

'Um, pretty okay, you?'

'Good. How the hell do you lot manage to keep your eyes open in that room with all the smoke?'

Clique gave John his best attempt at an enigmatic smile.

'Nice hair job.'

Clique patted the side of his head that was completely shorn. 'Glad you like it.'

'You need to eat something every now and again,' John said, eyeing him. 'You look like a walking skeleton. And how can it be comfortable wearing your pants that low? Aren't you afraid they'll fall down about your ankles when you're walking up the street?'

Clique raised one perfectly shaped eyebrow. 'Gosh, John, if you could swing by my house later and tuck me in I'd really appreciate it. I like *Where the Wild Things Are* and Dr Seuss.'

'Smartarse,' John said, but with no malice. He had a genuine affection for the gawky, bouncy kid with his skinny arms and unnatural fondness for make-up. Underneath the street garb Clique was a smart, soft-hearted gentleman, and kids like him were rare jewels in post-Celtic Tiger oh-so-entitled Dublin.

Clique leaned against the wall and folded his arms across his chest. 'So, like, I was wondering if you'd heard from Mike.'

'Nope. He's still got a way to go before he's out.'

'Right . . . right.'

'Something the matter?'

Clique shrugged. 'Just some of the guys need paying and I haven't been able to get hold of Suzy.'

John wasn't surprised. Suzy was Mike's younger sister. She was a wild card who liked to party hard and date men who took her money. 'I can lend you a few quid if you're stuck.'

'Nah, I'm okay. I live with the 'rent now, so I won't starve, but I feel bad for the lads.'

'Want me to talk to Suzy, see if I can get her to focus on the payroll?'

'Would you mind? I don't want to cause any trouble.'

'It's no big deal. Me and Suzy know each other a long while.'

'That would be cool, John, thanks.'

'No problem. So, can you do me a favour?'

'Sure?' Clique laughed. 'What do you need?'

'You're smart, right?'

'If you say so.'

'Take a look at these entries and see if you can figure out what they mean.'

Clique took the agenda and photocopied pages from him and read the entries John had highlighted. The hair that had not been shaved off hung almost to his nose as he bent his head in concentration. 'Well, it's obviously written in code.'

'That part I managed to work out for myself. I need you or some other brainiac to break it into lay person's language.'

'Can you give me half an hour? I've got to set some tracks up and do a few shout-outs.'

'Half an hour?'

'I'm guessing it's not that complicated.'

John scowled.

'Or maybe it is,' Clique said, with an angelic smile that was hard to fault. 'And I'll get lucky.'

'I'll be upstairs.'

John returned to his office and sat down. While he waited for Clique to do what he knew the young man could do, he read through the receipts he had removed from the Filofax, hoping to piece together Alison Cooper's daily activities.

He called Beth Gold and left a message asking her to contact him. As he was hanging up, the fax beeped. It was the mortuary, sending through a copy of the coroner's report. Rose Butler had requested a copy be sent to him.

John read it. Alison had been a healthy woman, with no obvious sign of illness or trauma. There were no signs of a struggle or injury, although there were traces of alprazolam in her system and also of citalopram, the antidepressants Xanax and Cipramil, and, more alarmingly, propofol, an anaesthetic.

'So much for not pill-popping,' John muttered. She had to

114

have been three feet high and rising. Probably needed to be to do the deed.

The coroner had ruled 'death by misadventure'. She had slit her wrists vertically and bled out. Cause of death had been heart failure.

John leaned back in his chair and tapped his fingers on the desk. Xanax and secret antidepressants, a cheating husband, tough job. Maybe the poor woman had simply had enough.

He was still there when Clique appeared at his door with the cheery expression of one who knows he's smarter than the average bear.

'You've cracked it, I gather?'

'Dib dib dib.'

'What are you on about? Did you do it or not?'

'Sure.' Clique flicked his fringe out of the way and bobbed into the room. 'Well, I'd like to brag but, as I said, it wasn't exactly difficult.'

'It wasn't?' John took the agenda and the pages from him. 'It had me bloody stumped.'

'Well, you were probably never a Scout.'

'Fuck, no, that shower wouldn't have me.'

Clique grinned and folded himself into the wicker chair. John jammed a cigarette into his mouth and lit it.

'I thought you weren't supposed to smoke in here?'

'Now who's acting like a daddy? So, come on, hot shot, stop smirking and educate the idiot.'

Clique pulled out a sheet of paper and slid it across the desk. On it was the gobbledegook from the agenda, but below each line was a perfect and easily understandable English translation.

Sofia Johnson: kidney – rejected

Allen Foster: kidney – rejected

Coleen Clancy: liver – rejected

Chris Day: liver – rejected
Ann-Marie Corrigan: kidney – rejected

John frowned. There was the name that had been in Alison's agenda for the day she died. Were these people patients? Alison Cooper had been a hospital doctor: she probably ran across patients who had organ failure every day of the week. What was so special about these five? 'So spill it. What's this Scout stuff?'

'She was using reverse alphabet. I imagine she was in the Brownies at some point. Her Z is an A, her Y a B and so on.'

'Clever!'

'Not really. There are much tougher codes she could have used. I guess she wasn't expecting anyone to study this too hard.' Clique waved away some smoke. 'I suppose the question is, why write in code at all?'

'Is it?'

'Well, that's what I'd be wondering if I was a detective.'

'Yeah, yeah,' John said, scratching the stubble on his chin. 'Thanks for this, kid. I'll be sure to shake some coins out of Suzy for your help.'

'Happy to help either way.' Clique shrugged his bony shoulders. 'Can I ask you something?'

'Shoot.'

'Have you spoken to Rodney recently?'

'A bit. I haven't seen much of him.'

'He's not looking so great, like, he's . . . um . . .'

'I know,' John said. 'Like he's back on the sauce.'

'Well, okay, I just thought I should say something.' He glanced over his shoulder to the invisible elephant in the room. 'I think he misses Sarah.'

'Yeah, well.' John glowered at the page before him. 'Reverse alphabet, how about that? I thought the Scouts taught kids to build fires from sticks or whatever. I never knew they taught useful shit.'

Clique stood languidly. 'I'd better get off.'

'How's the moped?'

'It's going, that's the main thing.'

'Thanks again for this, Click.'

'Getting old, man, getting old.' Clique sighed and sloped out of the door.

John read the list again. So, what had he got? Five names, probably patients, one of whom, Chris Day, had sent Alison a card telling her not to beat herself up over something, the name Corrigan in her agenda for the day she died, and a depressed doctor with a cheating husband.

Time to get chatty.

He took out his notebook and started to work his way through the four Chris Days he had found in the phone book.

After twenty minutes and some minor confusion with one Christina Day, John had struck a further two of the Days from his list. The last was not at home and his answering machine was the electronic voice that John hated so much. Nevertheless, he left a message asking Chris Day to get in touch with him as soon as possible.

Then, with bugger-all else to entertain him, he called Ivan Colbert to set up a meeting. After that he decided he'd better find Suzy Brannigan and discover what the crazy doper was doing with Mike's money.

19

Pavel parked the jeep behind a block of flats. He climbed out and removed the holdall, which he put a short distance away. He returned to the jeep, popped open the petrol tank and stuffed part of his torn T-shirt into the mouth. He lit the rag, made sure the flame had taken hold and left it.

He was half a block away when he heard the explosion. He noticed a few people on the street frown and look around at the dull *whap*. They didn't seem to realise what it was. He wasn't surprised: Hollywood never got that sound right.

He asked for directions from an elderly couple, and although it took two or three attempts before he fully understood them, he was pleased to find he was not a million miles from the railway station. He went into a supermarket where he stole a packet of plasters and a bottle of Dettol.

He walked down the hill to the station and checked train times for Dublin. He had two hours to wait.

He emptied the wallet he'd stolen and dumped it in a bin.

There was more than eighty euros in it. He bought a ticket, then a sandwich, coffee and a newspaper, and went into the toilets to attend to his injuries. He ran the tap over his fingers of his right hand and then applied Dettol liberally. He winced as it dribbled into the wounds. One of the bites was bad – the dog's incisor had caught him on the knuckle and torn the flesh. He washed it twice and disinfected it. He used blue paper towels to dry his hand and plastered it up as best he could.

He returned to the platform where he pretended to read a newspaper. His mind would not settle and wandered freely through the halls of his memory, conjuring up emotions and feelings he'd thought long discarded, and the path that had led him to this point. He was not sorry to be here. He was nothing now, only a husk.

He watched an old man pass on the way to the ticket kiosk, gnarled hands by his sides. He was reminded of his father, how bent and twisted the old man had become in his final years, ground down by grief and fear and hopelessness. That was how Pavel remembered him – ground down by war and death. All those years he had spent trying to do the right thing, trying to eke out a living, while the world was ripped asunder by hatred and violence. Pavel remembered the fights they had had, his father's pleas that he should stay and work with him. Even then, in the face of ridiculous odds, he had worked to keep his family together.

Ana had been a child when the war had begun, a small, dark-eyed nymph. He had been older, wilder, a nervy teenager, on the bottom rung of a street gang. They had run around the neighbourhoods, keeping a close eye on the new factions opening before them. Pavel had not understood then what people could do to each other, the justifications good people uttered to do evil. It had not taken him long to discover that hatred lurked beneath even the slickest veneer. Why not cast off the veneer – what was the point of pretending? Where did it get you?

He had seen things in the past that no youth should have to see, friend turning against friend, neighbour against neighbour, brother against brother. Something had turned in Pavel, soured. If he had been a fanciful man he would had said his soul had died.

He and his little ragbag gang of friends had never really stood a chance. To be successful you had to be invisible, the lone wolf, not the dog pack.

Pavel had abandoned the group in the days after his father's death. He had rejected his uncle's offer to become head of the family. He wanted no ties other than to his immediate family. When his mother had died shortly afterwards, he had transferred his loyalty to Ana, until she married. When her husband was killed, he watched out for her.

And now she was dead too.

People talked of the future while blood still stained the walls. But there would always be evil. There would always be those like him on the fringes.

But more and more he understood that it was not only on the fringes that evil flourished. Men like Travnic and Flintov were regarded as respectable. They wore suits and drove nice cars, they listened to music and wept over the tragedy of the masses, no doubt. Predators. Jackals. They slipped through society, veneer polished to a high sheen, implacable enemies. What chance did ordinary people have against them? What chance had Ana against such men?

He curled his hands so hard into fists that blood seeped through the plasters. Though he told himself nothing mattered any longer, Ana was a blade to his heart. She had died to save him. He would carry his guilt to the grave. That was his burden and he accepted it willingly. They had killed her with their promises, their charm and their lies. They had taken, as predators always did. They had fed on her flesh as surely as the packs of wild dogs had fed on the dead and dying during the war. Remorseless creatures, eating their fill and moving on to their next victim.

'Hey, are you okay?'

Pavel glanced up. A girl stood on the platform before him. She was chubby-faced and wore a long dress, a man's coat and what looked like hob-nailed boots. Strands of curly strawberry-blonde hair stuck out from under a black beanie cap and she carried a battered guitar case slung over her shoulder.

'What?'

'You were crying – are you okay, like? Are your hands killing you? They're cut to bits, aren't they?'

'Yes. I am … okay.'

She sat down on the bench beside him. 'It's fierce cold, huh?'

'It is not so cold.'

'Train should be along soon enough. Least we can get out of this bleeding hole.' She looked down the platform. Her ear, the one closest to him, was pierced many times. 'So, where you heading?' she said, turning back to him.

She had the palest blue eyes he had ever seen and a smattering of freckles across her snub nose. Pavel put her age at sixteen. 'Dublin,' he said.

'Cool. Me too. I'm Grace by the way.' She stuck out a gloved hand.

Pavel stared at it. It was tiny, like a child's. He thought of Ana, lying in the cold dark earth. 'Pavel,' he said finally, taking her hand in his. 'I am Pavel.'

'Where you from, Pavel? Poland?'

'Yes,' Pavel lied.

'Yeah? You live here?'

He looked at her for a moment, saying nothing.

121

She flushed under his gaze. 'I know – a priest wouldn't ask you that, right? My old lad's always telling me I shouldn't be talking as much. Sorry, if you want I can leave you alone.'

Pavel took out his cigarettes. He shook one loose and put it into his mouth. After a moment he offered one to Grace. She took it. 'Thanks. What are these?'

'Cigarettes.'

'Yeah, I *know* that. What kind?'

'Polish.'

Grace took a drag and started to cough. 'Strong, aren't they?'

Pavel shrugged and continued to smoke. Like everyone he knew he bought his cigarettes from a trader and never from a shop. He did not recall when he had last smoked a legal one. He had twelve packets left in the holdall. After that he would need to roll his own.

'You don't talk much, do you?'

'No.'

'That's okay.' She took another drag of the cigarette, but he could see she didn't like it. After a few moments she ground it out under the bench.

'So, how come you're going to Dublin? Do you live there?'

'No.'

'Looking for work? Gone shite, isn't it? Mad how it changed so quick.'

'I am looking for job.'

'Were you working long here, like?'

'I work on building. Now job is done.'

'Fuck. Sorry. It's hard right now. I know tons of lads that were laid off, like. Unreal how bad it's gone.'

'Yes.'

'Don't know if Dublin's much better, to be honest. There's signs up now in some places saying don't even bother asking. I reckon you need to have someone in the know to get in anywhere.'

Pavel said nothing. He ground out his butt with the heel of his shoe. He wished he had thought to get painkillers. His left hand was throbbing.

Beside him Grace prattled on. He had no idea what she was talking about or why she had chosen him to talk to, but by the time the train pulled in he was pretty sure he was getting a headache.

20

From the outside looking in, Suzy Brannigan lived in the most expensive flophouse in Dublin. Mike, albeit hardly from the goodness of his heart, had sunk a fair chunk of money into property using various siblings and relations as cover for his property portfolio, and Suzy had landed a two-bedroom apartment situated on the third floor of a redeveloped convent in Kilmainham.

Suzy was Mike's youngest sister, a twenty-eight-year-old beautician who rarely worked a full day and made the bulk of her money selling X tabs and wraps of cocaine so cut down that only the greenhorns or the already strung out of it got high. She'd been pulled over more times than John could remember, but that didn't stop Suzy partying and it sure as hell didn't convince her to go straight.

'Fuck it,' she would say to the cops, whenever she was hauled in. 'This is against my human rights! I'm a bleedin' libertarian. People should be allowed do what they fucking want. That's what's wrong with this country, that and the fucking Catholic Church. Not arresting them, are ya?'

'Shut the fuck up and mind your head,' the cops would say, sticking a black-eyed Suzy into the back seat, where she would proceed to sing rebel songs and cadge smokes until she passed out or was released into the loving arms of her solicitor, whom she had on speed dial.

Suzy might have been wild but she wasn't dumb and knew to keep her yap shut in court. She would turn up dressed like a Stepford wife and weep gently as her solicitor reeled off her 'tragic' background, the trauma of her dead daddy and her 'many attempts to regain sobriety'. Usually the court fell for it, and because large amounts were not involved Suzy would get a slap on the wrist or, at very worst, a quick spin round the revolving door of Mountjoy and be back in the clubs, shaking her bony arse and necking pills, in no time. Apart from her long-suffering mother nobody really had a problem with this. Suzy was Suzy, the same as she had always been, and frankly all of the Brannigan children were a sandwich short of the full picnic. But of late Suzy had taken to hanging around with a less than salubrious group, and currently the wild party girl was shacked up with a bloke from the Midlands. John had met him once and taken an instant dislike to him. Mike didn't think much of him either and reckoned this guy had more bite than Suzy could safely handle. But Mike knew if he said that to Suzy she would accuse him of trying to run her life. He had been planning to run the guy off when he'd been nabbed with the black cigarettes.

John tried to think of the bloke's name. Jiffy? Jaffa? Something stupid like that.

Though it was almost twenty past five, Suzy was still in her dressing-gown when she let John in. 'Johnny boy, the pipes, the pipes are calling . . .' she sang, as she opened the door.

'Hey, Suzy,' he said, smiling – despite himself he had always had a soft spot for this hare-brained girl and her crazy ways. He leaned in and gave her a hug. She smelt of stale perfume and something acidic.

'Come on in. What can I get you? Beer?'

'Beer would be great.' He didn't want one as he was driving but she was a Brannigan: there was no point in arguing with her. He followed her up the hall into the living room. Otis Redding played in the background and the air reeked of grass and air-freshener. Suzy stepped through a set of swing doors into a galley kitchen and pulled open the fridge. She rummaged around inside, then threw some ice into a glass. She handed John a beer, then poured a vodka over the ice that would have felled a horse and added the tiniest splash of lime. She peered at John as she stirred her drink with an index finger. 'So, long time no see, yeah? How's tricks?'

'So so, Suzy, so so.'

'What the fuck kind of answer is that?' She slid into a white bucket chair that was suspended on chains from a beam. Some of her drink spilled down the front of her dressing-gown. 'Oops.'

'Everything's going okay.'

'Yah? She back, then, is she?'

'Sarah? No.'

'Figures – you've a face on you like a mutt we used to own back in the day, stupid thing, always miserable. Used to sit out in the back garden and howl until me old lad got rid of it.' Suzy sipped her drink. 'Why don't you go after her?'

'Why would I? She can make her own mind up if she wants to come back – she knows where I am.'

'There is that.' Suzy nodded. 'So, whatcha doing here? Mike call you, tell you to check up on me?'

'He didn't.'

'Surprised. He's been like a bear with a sore head lately.'

'He worries about you, you know that.'

'Yah, he does. Like an old lady, that one.'

'He's just looking out for you.'

'Hah. I don't fucking need Mike no more. I got my own man to keep me from harm.'

'Oh, yeah . . . How is . . . Jaffa?'

'He's grand.'

John looked at her more closely. She was rail thin, her skin was pasty and there were cold sores around the corners of her upper lip. She had once been a cute young one. Now she looked ten years older than she was. 'Look, Suze, I don't want to come across as nosy or anything, but is everything okay money wise?'

'Yeah, why wouldn't it be?'

'Some of the guys from the station were wondering when they might be getting paid.'

She took a slug of her drink and shot him a side-eye. 'Who's been complaining?'

John spread his hands.

'They'll get their money. There was a mix-up this week, that's all. And, John, there's no need to go worrying Mike with this shit.'

'Okay.'

'A mix-up, okay? You tell them that. Mike left me in charge. You tell them, they got a problem they come speak to me.'

'Okay.'

'Fuckers.' She shook her head. John didn't know to whom she was referring. Maybe everyone.

'You're all right, John.' She looked at him over her glass. 'Don't know what you ever saw in that stuck-up bitch. You're too good for the likes of her, no matter how high and mighty she tries to pretend she is.'

'Suzy, listen to me. You ever need anything, I'm only a call away – okay? Don't be a stranger.'

'I got a man, John, but sweet of you to offer.'

John actually felt himself blush. 'You know what I mean.'

'Yeah, I do, you eejit. Man, you should see your face – scarlet!' She laughed, spilling more of her drink. Then, abruptly, she stopped. 'You tell them kids I'll see them right. You tell them not to bother Mike with this shit. Okay, John? I'll take care if it.'

'Okay, Suzy.'

'Good man.' She laughed again, but there was no humour in it, and John was glad when he said goodbye and left.

He drove across town to Raglan Lane, where Ivan Colbert invited him into his stone-fronted townhouse.

'Nice digs,' John said, when Colbert led him into a sunken living room. It was gorgeous, with large soft furnishings and a fire burning brightly in a red-brick fireplace.

'Thank you,' Colbert said. 'Drink?' He lifted the glass he was carrying and tinkled it.

'No thanks. I'm good – I have the car.'

'Please, take a seat.'

John sank into one of the cream sofas and Colbert took a large carved chair by the fire. He had changed from his funeral clothing and was in chinos and a soft blue cashmere jumper over a white shirt open at the throat.

'I didn't see you at the burial,' Colbert observed.

'I'd had enough for one day.'

'I understand. Distressing events, funerals.'

'You and Alison knew each other a good few years, I hear.'

'We met when I worked in Toronto.'

'You were in the same hospital?'

'Yes. Alison returned home when her father was ill and I came back a number of years after.'

'You work at the Alton, right?'

'Yes.'

'You're a surgeon there?'

'Ah, no, more a consultant.' He smiled sadly. 'I have arthritis, I'm afraid. These hands are no longer dexterous enough for surgery. I have, however, retained my keen eye for beauty and, as you can imagine, the surgeons at the Alton are top-notch.'

'You and Alison stayed in touch all these years?'

'On and off. More off than on.'

'You know her husband, Tom?'

'We've met.' Colbert glanced towards the fire. He leaned out of his chair, grabbed the poker and jabbed at a log that had been burning perfectly happily. Avoidance – even John knew that when he saw it.

'Did you speak to Alison recently at all?'

'We had lunch a while back.'

'Talk about anything interesting?'

'Well, it depends on what you consider interesting. We usually engaged in shop talk, and we know a number of the same people, of course – not that Alison was a gossip or anything remotely like that.'

'When was it you had lunch?'

'I'm not sure . . . first week in February? I'd need to check my diary.'

'How did she seem when you spoke to her?'

'Seem? Well, like she always seemed, perhaps a bit under the weather. I thought she looked pale. I may have said so. She did mention that she hadn't been sleeping well.'

'Did you get the impression she might have had something on her mind?'

Colbert looked down into his glass. 'She was unhappy, Mr Quigley. I could see that.'

'Did you know she was on Cipramil?'

He looked up. 'Yes.'

'The coroner's report lists it as an antidepressant. I looked it up online – it's heavy stuff.'

'Mm, it is.'

'How do you know she was taking it? Her husband didn't.'

'I prescribed it.'

'You did? You were Alison's doctor?'

'No, I was her friend. It's not unusual for a doctor to prescribe medication to a colleague. I knew she was depressed. I knew she was struggling.'

'I found Xanax in her desk at the hospital too. Would Cipramil and Xanax mixed be a potent cocktail?'

'Certainly, if taken with alcohol.'

'How about if you topped it off with propofol?'

'Propofol?'

'Yep. She had some of that sloshing around her system too. Did you prescribe it?'

'Oh, of course not.' He looked genuinely shocked and upset. 'My God. Poor Alison. Why would she do that?'

John was beginning to think Alison's death had been far better signposted than Rose Butler cared to admit.

'She was a very fine woman, Mr Quigley,' Colbert said softly, 'a very fine woman. The world is less for her passing.'

'Did you ever get any sense from her that she would kill herself?'

Colbert looked up. His face was composed, but there was something bleak about his expression. 'No, but then none of us ever knows when the demons will surface, do we?'

John closed his notebook. 'No, I guess we don't.'

21

'Are you serious? You don't even have a place to stay or anything? You mad fuck, you. That's mental.'

They were pulling into a station in Dublin. Grace tried to lift her guitar from the overhead shelf but it had slid to the back and she was too short to grab it. Pavel watched her struggle for a moment then stood up, grasped it and passed it to her.

'Cheers.' She took it from him. As she did so, her fingers brushed against his. Pavel jerked his hand away. She laughed, but looked embarrassed. 'Relax the cacks – I'm not infectious or anything. Are you always this jumpy?'

Pavel forced a smile. She had been beside him for the entire three-hour journey, talking about so many subjects so fast that his head was spinning. He had barely understood a word.

'Well, what are you going to do? Stay in a hostel or some shit? There's loads down around my way but, to be honest with you, they're rough as fuck.'

'I do not know,' Pavel said truthfully. He needed to change

some of the money he had taken from Flintov's safe, but he guessed the banks would be long closed.

'Look, it's cool you're looking for work and shit, but listen, man, Dublin's not safe, you know? Lot's of fucked-up people out there.' She indicated 'out there' with a jerk of her chin.

Pavel glanced out of the window. They were pulling in at platform five, slowing to a near crawl.

'Look, if you want you can kip at mine for a day or two, least until you get your bearings and shit. Can't believe you don't even have a map nor nuthin'.' She shook her head in wonderment. 'I mean, I went busking all over the country during the summer, you know, but least I had a place to sleep and shit lined up first. You're mad you are. There's killings out there.'

'I will find place.'

'You will in your bollix. Look, it's no hassle. You can kip down on the sofa for a day or two – my flatmate Rick won't mind. For a start he's a complete dope-head so I doubt he'll even know you're there since you don't talk much.'

Pavel thought fast. Although he did not want to be tied to anyone, he could see the sense in what she was proposing. He needed to get his bearings, find a base and a map and think things through carefully. He was tired, his hand hurt and he was in a foreign land. He needed time to formulate his plan.

'So, are you coming or what?'

She was waiting for him at the now-open door. Her red-blonde hair glinted under the platform lights.

He shouldered his bag. 'Okay.'

'Good man, Pavel. Don't worry, it'll be fun – a bit of *craic*.' She linked arms with him on the platform, chattering away about the state of her flat, telling him not to get his hopes up, that it was a dump. Pavel let her talk. It was at last becoming white noise to him.

'Gardiner Street,' she said, after they had walked along by a river and crossed a large gaudy road she told him was O'Connell Street, the main street of Dublin. 'Used to be posher – for a while anyway, loads of apartments and shit, then all the darkies started to move in, then the Chinks, or maybe they were first. Anyway, doesn't matter. Fuck, you'd be hard pressed to see a white face round here these days. Go along Parnell Street and it's weird food shops a-go-go.' She looked at him. 'But you'd be all right – you're kind of foreign-looking anyway. Not that you're dark nor nothing like, but you're – no offence nor nothing – foreign-looking.'

Pavel glanced about him.

'Yeah. Well, fuck, least you're European, right? Some of them darkies are fucking headcases. Into all sorts of weird shit, voodoo and all that, they're mental, I swear. Just before Christmas one of them cut another one to pieces with a machete, right outside the steps of the flat. I was on me own and scared shitless. I could hear your man shouting and screaming and then nothing. And you know the weird thing? I never seen nothing about it in the paper neither. That lot keep their mouths shut and look after their own. Only thing left of that poor fucker was a tooth and a blood splatter. Turned me green, I tell you, when I saw it there next day. But everyone acted like they didn't even notice.'

Pavel thought that sounded ideal. People minding their own business was good, as far as he was concerned.

'Now, listen, don't say nothing to Rick about us meeting on the train or any shit like that. If he asks you shit, just say you know me from Cork.' She furrowed her brow. 'Can you sing?'

'Sing?'

'Yeah, carry a tune, like.'

Pavel nodded.

'Fucking brill. He asks, you can say we did some busking

together. Tell him this is the second time we've met. He won't have a clue – he gets a nosebleed going to Bray, for fuck's sake, so he won't know where we met. Galway – tell him we met in Galway during the summer.'

'Galliwhey?'

'Yeah, Galway – don't worry, I'll do most of the talking.'

Pavel wasn't worried about what some teenage dope-head thought. 'I need map.'

'A map? Okay, there's a shop I know sells them.'

She squeezed his biceps. 'Don't you worry, Pavel, you and me will have a right bit of *craic* over the next few days. Wait till the weekend – if you don't get work before that we can hit Temple Bar and get a few quid.'

'Crack?'

'Yeah, *craic*, a laugh. You know, doing fun stuff.' She grinned again. 'You know how to have fun, don't you?'

'Crack,' Pavel said, rolling the word over his tongue. Yes, he would have crack. He would do fun stuff, but first he had to find his quarry. Then the crack could begin.

22

It was a basement flat, and once Grace had managed to shove open the peeling door it was pretty much as she had described it. It was a small, poorly furnished flat, no better than a squat, really. It was dimly lit, reeking of damp and cigarette smoke.

'Here we are! Home, sweet home.'

A skinny kid of about eighteen was sitting cross-legged on a faded blue sofa, watching television and smoking a bong. He glanced at them, his eyes vacant and sullen. His expression told Pavel he was not wanted.

'Hey, Rick,' Grace said. 'This is Pavel. He's a friend of mine from Galway. He's going to kip here for a day or two. Say hello!'

'Hello,' Pavel said.

''S up, man.' Rick gazed at them through the smoke with bloodshot narrowed eyes. 'Wasn't expecting no house guests, Grace.'

'It's only for a little while. He's looking for a job.'

'Yeah? Good luck with *that*.'

She put her guitar case down and began to remove some of
the layers of clothing she wore. 'Sit down, Pavel. Do you want
some tea?'

'I am fine.'

'Rick?'

'Sure, if you're making it. But, like, I think we're out of milk
'n' stuff.'

'How the hell can we be out? I bought two litres the day I left.'

'Yeah, I had, like, cereal, though. Stella stayed over the other
night and she might have had some too.'

Pavel noticed Grace's mouth tightened at the mention of
Stella. He looked around him for somewhere to sit. Rick didn't
offer to move any of the newspapers and assorted crap beside
him on the sofa and there wasn't another chair. In the end Pavel
had no choice but to flump down on a grubby bean-bag.
Something stuck to his palm. Jam?

While Grace bashed about in the tiny kitchen just off the
sitting room, Rick took a last hit off the bong and offered it to
Pavel, who shook his head. Rick put it to one side. He skinned
a cigarette with practised ease and lit it. He looked at Pavel and
blew twin streams of smoke out of his nose. 'So, like, Pavel,
where do you know Grace from?'

'Around.'

'Yeah? I never heard her mention you before.'

Pavel shrugged.

'Where you from?'

'Around.'

Rick took another drag. 'You're Polish or some shit, right?'

Pavel did not answer.

'Yeah, well, don't get too comfortable here, man.' Rick
jabbed his thumb towards the kitchen. 'Grace is pretty cool, but
way too soft, always taking in the fucking strays. People take
advantage, you know?'

They sat in silence until Grace came back into the room carrying two steaming cups, one of which she handed to Rick. 'Are you working tonight, Rick?'

'Yeah, going in shortly.'

'Rick works in Fibbers bar. It's just down the road,' she explained to Pavel.

Rick coughed and wiped his eyes with his hands. 'Going to an after-party later. Marty and the boys are launching their album this week. Should be a blast.'

'No way? That's this week?'

Rick and Grace waffled on. Despite the territorial piss from Rick, Pavel felt himself relax a little. He was tired and needed to sleep for a while. But he would not be able to sleep with the boy in the house.

Luckily there was no real need to speak. Grace did most of the talking for all of them and, before he knew it, it was time for Rick to drag his skinny arse off the sofa and disappear into a bedroom to change into a marginally cleaner shirt. When he returned he put on a military-style jacket with a lot of buckles and – oddly – a top hat. At just after six he grabbed his keys and skipped out.

After he'd left, Grace let out a long, deep breath. 'Sorry about that. He can be a moody git sometimes but he's all right, really.'

'He is your boyfriend?'

'Rick? Hah, no way, man. Me and Rick, no way.'

Pavel lit a cigarette and smoked. He let his eyes travel around the dingy room. There were three doors leading off the sitting room. He knew that the one to the right of the kitchen was Rick's room and the one behind him was the bathroom. He guessed the other room belonged to Grace. The apartment was tiny. He had been in bigger cells.

'What age you are?'

'Why? How old d'ya think I look?'

'Sixteen.'

'Yeah, well, I'm not. I'm older than that.'

'You have family here in city?'

Grace grimaced. 'Not really. Me mam's dead and me old fella . . . We don't get on that well. He actually lives in Cork.'

'You have brothers, sisters?'

'Only a sister, but she got married to a Greek guy and they live in England. I usually only see her at Christmas, if she's over. She's a good bit older than me, though, so we're not on the same, like, level.'

'You are alone.'

'I *have* people, friends, like, Rick and them others.'

'Friends are not family.'

'They're as good as – least you get to pick *them*. How about you? You got family here or back in Poland?'

'No, I have no family.'

'So you could say we're in the same boat.' She cocked her head, happy now that they had something in common.

'You live by your music?'

'Sort of. I get some dole and the busking gives me a bit extra. The rent on this place's not bad and I've sent in an application for RA.'

Pavel stared at her blankly.

'Rent allowance. Rick's usually too broke to pay much and there's another guy crashes here regular, Mark. Really sound, he is. There used to be a girl, Paula – she was my original flatmate, but she's gone now, moved to fucking Scotland of all places with this shit-hole band – you should have heard them. They call themselves the Virgin Eaters. She's supposed to be their bassist but she's shit. And they're shit too. The lead singer, Seb? He's not half as hot as he thinks he is. Total loser. His breath stinks for one thing and he can't hold a note. They played in Eamon

Doran's time and I heard not one person bothered to turn up and that'll tell you.'

Pavel closed his eyes. He had not the faintest idea what she was talking about.

'Hey, are you hungry? We can go grab a bite to eat if you want. I'm starving.'

'No. Please, I am very tired.'

Grace looked disappointed but after a moment she got up from the couch. 'C'mere to me. You can sleep here for a while. I'm going to nip down the road to Silvio's, get a bag of chips and see about getting some milk. You want anything back?'

'No, thank you.'

'I can pick you up a bag, if you like. It's not a problem.'

'No, please, I want only to rest for time.'

'Oh, okay. I won't be long.' She picked up her scarf and coat from the back of the sofa.

Pavel worked his way up from the bean-bag. 'You should take careful of people you trust. I think you should not let strange men into your home.'

'Like sad Polish men, you mean?' Grace grinned. She offered him her hand and helped him to his feet. 'I can tell a lot about people from their faces. I knew you were harmless the minute I saw you at the station. You looked so freakin' sad sitting there with your hands all in bits. I just had to talk to you.'

'People who are sad can be also dangerous.'

'Yeah, right. You're not dangerous.' She pulled her cap down over her curls. 'Back in a few minutes. I'd say don't rob the place, but apart from the telly there's fuck-all to take.'

She went out and closed the door behind her. Pavel lay down on the sofa. He put one arm behind his head and closed his eyes. By the time Grace returned with the chips and a battered sausage he was fast asleep.

23

The Alton Clinic was a large, modern structure of smoked glass and smooth pale concrete set on an acre of neatly maintained grounds just outside Lucan village. Frieda Mayweather parked in her reserved bay and strolled along a footpath of palest gravel. A large water feature tinkled gently, sending a constant stream into perpetual motion over a series of levels and ornamental stones. Money, she thought, could make even the bleakest landscape into something worth having.

She walked through a set of sliding doors and into a cool triple-height foyer. The reception desk was marble and behind it sat two of the most beautiful women she'd ever clapped eyes on. One was on the phone. The blonde with the headset smiled when she recognised Frieda. 'Hello, Miss Mayweather. I wasn't expecting to see you this morning. Your secretary hasn't arrived.'

'Good morning, Lucy. That's okay, I have a little paperwork that needs to be attended to. Is Ivan in yet?'

'He is. Shall I contact him for you?'

'Please do. Ask him to come up to my office when he's free.' Frieda tilted her head. 'What did you choose for the funeral?'

'White roses on scented eucalyptus.'

'Excellent.'

'I knew you wouldn't want anything ostentatious.'

Frieda walked away from the desk. Normally she enjoyed interactions with her staff, but today she was in a foul mood. She had handpicked Lucy, just as she had handpicked the girl, Eleanor, sitting next to her, and every other member of the front-of-house staff. They might all work in a medical centre, but that didn't mean the shop floor had to be neglected. Frieda's father had been a shop steward and had known the value of being hands-on, of presenting a polished and competent front. He had taught Frieda everything she knew about people, namely that they were stupid, easily manipulated and not to be trusted.

She walked across the marble floor to the lifts. She knew the receptionists watched her leave. She was not overly vain, but she knew she carried herself well. She was tiny, barely over five feet one, but she looked after her body almost to the point of obsession. She ate well, performed yoga daily and played squash at a highly competitive level three times a week. She did not eat junk food. Frieda knew her looks were important: she was a figurehead for the business, and it did not do for a figurehead to be slovenly.

On the fourth floor she alighted and made her way to her suite. It was from here she ran the Alton. She had opened the clinic in 1996, when the Celtic Tiger was finding its feet. With money becoming more plentiful the Irish lady had begun to look to the fashion magazines. Beauty was no longer unattainable. With a small investment, a waist made thick by childbearing could be whittled away, sagging breasts could be lifted, noses straightened, prominent veins blasted away, lips plumped and chins carved to perfection. Frieda, a plastic surgeon, revelled in the business. She was a sociable woman and on the board of anything she believed would send business her way. She was a regular face at the races, at art openings and at auction houses. She played the game with the same vigour she played squash, and the business had taken off.

Now, though, the Tiger had been pussy-whipped and business had slowed to a trickle. The women who had willingly allowed the fat to be sucked from their bodies twice a year – before summer, after Christmas – were now quibbling about price and talking about food-replacement diets, like SlenderTrim and OptiFit. In the last three months Frieda had lost four long-term clients.

It was nothing to do with her and she knew it. It was the goddamned economy. Her reputation was unimpeachable. She had charm and a confidence that attracted only the big money, the society ladies who could not afford speculation on their advancing years. Her work, and the work of her staff, was exquisite and delicate. Not for her clients the perma-surprised expression or frozen wax mask. She was an artist, a sculptor, and a woman of finesse. She was, she thought, without pretension, gifted.

She sat behind her hand-tooled desk and unbuttoned her jacket at the waist. She was glad her secretary had not arrived. She was tired and did not want anyone to question her about anything.

She had been there only ten minutes when Ivan Colbert came in. Without knocking, she noticed with annoyance. When had he started that practice?

'Ivan.'

'Frieda.'

She gave him the once-over. He was still a tall, good-looking man, but losing something every time she saw him. He had once been a great surgeon. He still was a surgeon – in name at least – but not even close to the league he had once presided over. Alcohol had claimed him a long time ago.

'There you are. I've been calling. Why the hell is your phone off?'

'It's not even nine, Frieda.'

'You look terrible. Was the funeral awful?'

'Yes, it was.'

'I sent flowers, of course.'

'I appreciate that.'

'Well, Alison and I had our differences but she was a very dear friend to you and you're a dear friend to me.'

'Yes, she was, and thank you.' Colbert slipped into the chair opposite her desk, pulled the crease out of his trousers and crossed his legs. 'What was it you needed to speak to me about so urgently?'

'I have some bad news, I'm afraid.'

'Oh?'

'I'll need you for surgery at the end of the week.'

His face remained unnaturally still. 'Frieda, we had a deal. I helped you that one time and you promised me it would be the last.'

'I have no choice. Flintov is dead.'

'Andrei? Dead? I don't believe it.'

'Yes – and his wife, Mariana.'

'What happened?'

'I don't have all the details just yet but they were murdered, as far as I can tell.'

'*Jesus.*'

'From what I can gather, the police think it was a break-in that went wrong.'

'Jesus,' Colbert repeated. 'That is awful. I'm so sorry, Frieda

143

– what a shock when you've known Andrei for almost fifteen years. My God, what is the world coming to at all?'

Frieda clasped her hands before her. 'Yes, he was a brilliant man. It's such a terrible waste. I warned him to be careful after that carjacking. Why the hell he wanted to live in that accursed country I will never understand.'

Colbert shook his head. 'I can't believe it. They say it comes in threes, you know.'

'What does?'

'Death.'

'For God's sake, Ivan, since when did you get so superstitious?'

'I'm not.'

'Alison's suicide had absolutely nothing to do with Andrei Flintov's murder.'

'I know, but …' He trailed off. 'When did you say this surgery was for?'

'Sunday.'

'Sunday – Jesus, that's so … I have no time to prepare.'

'What the hell preparation do you need? It's a kidney, Ivan, the type of surgery you used to do in your sleep.'

'Who's the patient?'

'A woman, early twenties.'

'What's her name?'

'Why do you need to know?'

'Jesus, Frieda. To add some humanity to the procedure, as I do with all my patients.'

'So you'll take her as a patient?'

'I didn't say that. But you're hardly giving me much choice, are you?'

'There *is* no a choice. Not with Andrei dead. It takes time to find someone of his … calibre and enlightened thinking. '

'Who is the donor?'

'We were remarkably lucky. The family found a superb match.'

'Who?'

'A relative – a cousin, I believe.'

'A cousin?'

'Yes.'

Colbert ran his hands over his face. He didn't believe the family had found a cousin or any relative. If such a person existed, the surgery would not be so convert and hurried. 'I don't know.'

'Ivan, you owe me.'

'I never signed up for this, Frieda.'

'Without me, the only thing you could be signing up for is unemployment.'

He looked at her. 'Uncalled-for.'

'I'm sorry.' Frieda sat forward and gave him a tight, apologetic smile – or, at least, the pretence of one. 'But do you think you're above everything, Ivan? Do you think I bend the rules for the sake of it?'

'Of course not.'

'What we do is important. We save lives. Every day, Ivan, I weigh up the odds. I understand the risks and the cost and I sleep soundly at night. Can you say the same?'

He looked away.

'You have the skill. You have the ability. I need you to do this for me. For her, for her family.'

He looked down at his hands. They were still. They were not always so. 'Okay. But then we're even, Frieda. I can't do this any more.' He stood and left, sickened to his core. If a cat could smile when it cornered a mouse it would smile like Frieda Mayweather.

24

The day had started badly for John Quigley. By ten o'clock he had managed to spill coffee on his jeans and get ketchup on his shirt. He called and left messages for Chris Day, then tried to ring Stevie, but he wasn't answering. He rang Rose Butler to give her a progress report, such as it was, and discovered her in bullish form.

'So what if she was taking tablets? If she was, she must have been trying to get better. That wouldn't make her kill herself.'

'I've looked up Cipramil.' John turned to his computer and brought up a web page he had marked. 'I know there can be serious side effects with it. In some cases it can cause anxiety, even suicidal thoughts. According to Ivan Colbert, she's been on it since last July.'

'When she found out that yoke was messing around behind her back.'

'You know about that?'

'I do. Did you see him at the funeral?'

'I saw him.'

'Did you see the way he was acting?'

'Mrs Butler, I don't know your son-in-law from Adam. And, to be fair, grief affects people in different ways.'

'I asked him to bring the children over for a while today. He said no, he didn't think it was advisable under the circumstances.' She took a ragged breath. 'Is this it now? Is this what it's going to be like? Am I going to lose them too?'

'Of course you won't. It's just early days. Maybe he feels they might like to be with him in case they're afraid they'll lose him too. Maybe he doesn't want them to see you upset, or for you to see them upset.'

'I wish I had your belief in human kindness, Mr Quigley.'

John rested his forehead on his fingers. 'Everything will be okay, Mrs Butler. Give him time.'

After he'd hung up, he studied the flyers and business cards he had taken out of Alison's agenda. He fingered the lush card from the Le Vin dans les Voiles. He flipped it over and looked at her scrawled handwriting. Corrigan. There it was again. Maybe she had met this Ann-Marie Corrigan there on Friday.

When he got to the restaurant it was busy. He nursed a soda water and lime at the bar and observed the diners. The lunchtime crowd were mostly businessmen and -women, interspersed with the occasional table of pastel-clad ladies who clearly lunched on water, air and black coffee. It did not strike him as the sort of place Alison Cooper would have frequented on a regular basis.

Finally the maître d', floated his way. 'Now, Meester Quigley,' he said, 'how is it I can be of assistance?'

'Like I told you already, I need you to look at this photo and tell me if you recognise her.'

The man reluctantly took Alison's photograph from John, tilted it to the light and wrinkled his nose. He handed it back. 'I cannot say.'

'No?'

'*Non.*'

'That's a hell of an accent you have. French?'

'*Mais bien sûr.*'

'Whereabouts in France you from?'

'Why does this concern you?'

'I'm just curious.'

'Paris.'

'Nice. I was there once on a stag.'

'How pleasant for you.'

'This woman,' John tapped his hand, 'maybe some of your staff would recognise her.'

'As you can see, we are very busy.'

'Yeah, I get that, but it doesn't take much to look at a photo. Maybe I'll try the patrons – you wouldn't mind if I asked them, would you?'

'*Mind?*' He looked horrified. 'Of course I mind! You cannot disturb them during lunch.'

'I'll wait outside then, snag them when they come out.'

The maître d' snatched the photo from his hand. 'That will not be necessary. I will ask the staff. Please wait here.'

He floated off – how did he do that, John wondered, checking his feet – and discreetly spoke to a number of the waiting staff. After a few moments he was back with a pretty girl, whose dark hair, in a plait, reached her waist.

'Vicky, this is Meester Quigley. Please, if you would.'

He handed John the photo and turned to scan the room.

'Hello,' John said. 'I'm sorry to be a pain in the arse, but do you recognise this woman, Vicky?'

Vicky glanced at the maître d', but he moved away, snapping

his fingers towards an empty water glass. 'Yes. She was here.' Her voice was high and heavily accented. 'On Friday.'

'Alone?'

'No, with another woman.'

'Good girl. What kind of woman? Young, old, fat, thin?'

'I do not remember. We were very busy. I remember this woman,' she tapped the photo, 'because she was upset.'

'Upset?'

'Yes, she was with tears.' She pointed to her eyes.

John sat forward. 'Did you manage to hear anything of what they spoke about?'

'No, but I do not listen to conversations.'

'Right.'

'This woman, she is okay?'

'She's dead.'

'Oh.' Vicky's dark eyes dropped to the photo again.

'Can you remember who paid the tab?'

'I do not know. I leave the bill on the table and it is paid.'

'Were these women friends, do you think?' John asked. Maybe the other had been Beth Gold.

'I do not know.'

'What table were they at?'

'It was fifteen, the corner one.'

John stood and slipped the photo into his jacket pocket. 'I'll leave you my card. Can you think over the lunch again? If something comes to you – anything at all, maybe a gesture, a comment – please call me. Anything you can remember might be of some use.'

'Okay.'

He handed her the card and she slipped it into the folds of her apron.

'Ah, you are satisfied?' the maître d' said, hustling John towards the door.

'Nope. I need you to flick through your reservations book and tell me who might have been here for lunch on Friday of last week.'

His face fell. 'What?'

'I'm kidding. Table fifteen will do the job.'

He looked so relieved that John almost laughed.

After a few flips through the book, the maître d' said, 'Ah.'

'"Ah" what?'

'On Friday there were two parties at table fifteen for lunch.'

'Shoot.'

'What?'

'Tell me.'

'There was for a booking for Sharkey, a good client, accountants.'

'The other?'

'Cooper, Alison Cooper.'

'She booked the table?'

'Yes.'

'Did she pay the bill?'

'I do not know.'

'Can you find out?'

'I have not the time to look through receipts!'

'Not right this second, but later. Huh? It's important. I need to know who Alison Cooper was dining with on Friday lunchtime.'

'Yes, yes, I will look. Now, please, the floor must be covered. Ah, Mrs Rosenburg, a beautiful day, please allow me . . .'

He hissed at John to move aside and John was happy to oblige as a hundred pounds of stringed beef with a blue rinse handed over her coat.

Really, John thought, trotting past the baby grand on his way to the stairs, how the other half lives.

25

Pavel woke to the sound of metal music blaring. He sat up, groggy and disoriented. He looked about the room, then remembered where he was and why. He checked his watch and was amazed to find it was nearly midday.

'So you're awake?' Rick was standing in the doorway to the kitchen, barefoot and bare-chested, his jeans slung so low on his hips that Pavel could see traces of his pubic hair. He was eating a bowl of cereal. Both his nipples were pierced and he had a Celtic band tattooed around his left bicep.

Pavel rubbed his eyes. 'Where is Grace?'

'Bathroom. Yo, man, you're going to be looking for work today, right? It's cool Grace helping you out and shit, but you can see we don't have a lot of room here.'

Pavel lit a cigarette and blew out a stream of smoke.

'That's all I'm saying, man. This is no doss-house, don't think any different.' He turned and walked back into the kitchen.

Pavel stood and stretched. He had much to do. He yawned and scratched his belly. He grabbed his holdall and rummaged through it for fresh clothes.

'Hey, you're awake.'

He turned his head. Grace walked through the room with a towel wound tightly around her body and another around her hair. She had a tattoo of a dolphin on her pale shoulder. Her eyes were rimmed with smeared mascara. She was, Pavel thought, a singularly unattractive young woman. 'Yes.'

'You were out cold last night when I got back so I thought it would be better to leave you sleep. But you must be starving, right?'

Pavel had not been thinking of food, but the moment she mentioned it, he realised he was famished. 'Yes.'

'Cool. Tell you what, I'll get dressed and we can go out for a bite. Give me a few minutes, okay? I left a fresh towel for you in the bathroom in case you wanted a quick shower. Okay? I'll only be two shakes of a lamb's tail.'

Pavel watched her go. He hadn't wanted any company on his excursion and had thought to leave as soon as he woke up. He glanced at the holdall. Maybe he should just slip out of the flat while she was getting dressed.

Half an hour later he was smoking a cigarette at the outdoor table of a café. A street map he had bought was open before him.

'You've got the maddest tattoos,' Grace said, pouring three sachets of sugar into her coffee. She stirred it with the wooden stick the coffee shop had provided. 'I saw them when you were taking a wash. And what's with the scars, man? Were you in an accident or something?'

Pavel took a sip his own coffee, black no sugar. He grimaced. It was as weak and as tasteless as dishwater. 'Car crash.'

'Do they mean anything?'

152

He looked at her, puzzled.

'The tattoos?'

'Different things.'

'Did you see mine?'

'Yes.'

'Know why I got a dolphin?'

He shook his head.

'Because I'm afraid of water.'

'Water?'

'Well, maybe not water. I'm afraid of drowning.'

'Tattoo will not save you.'

She grinned. 'Ha, ha.'

Pavel refolded the map into a smaller and more manageable size. He studied the various streets.

'You should do a tour,' Grace said. 'You can get this yellow bus, it sort of looks like a Viking boat – you get to wear a helmet and everything.' She glanced at his face. 'Yeah, I know, sounds kind of stupid. I've never been on it, but if you felt like—'

Pavel tapped the map.' Where is Loo-kan?'

'Lucan? What the fuck do you want to go to Lucan for?'

'I know person there. Maybe can give job.'

'I could show you where it is.'

'No, I go alone.'

'You don't need to say it like that. I was only trying to help.' She turned sideways in her seat and looked out across the street.

'Where is place?'

'You need to go out the M50.'

'M50?'

'It's a road. Here, look.' She explained how to get there.

Pavel listened intently. He would have to lose her somehow. It was ridiculous that he was drinking coffee with a sullen teenager in bad shoes. 'I need go bank.'

'Yeah? Which you with?'

'What?'

'Which bank, like?'

'No, to make over money.'

'Make it over?'

Pavel reached into his holdall and took out some of the money he had removed from Flintov's safe. He handed a note to Grace.

'Weird. You mean you need a *bureau de change*. Is this Polish money?'

'Yes.'

'I'll take you to the Central Bank. Then do you want to see where I do most of my busking?' she asked.

Pavel did not but he nodded, and when they had finished their coffee he let her lead him through the crowds.

She brought him to the bank. He changed only a small amount of money because she was watching and he did not want her to know how much he was carrying. He figured he could always come back later and change more as he needed it. Then they were off to the busking zone.

'I like this place a lot,' she said. They were on Castle Market Street, standing outside a second-hand clothes shop, which Grace assured him sold something called 'amazing vintage'. It looked like junk to him.

'People here are usually nice and you can get great coffee in the kiosk across in the arcade. I've been on Grafton Street loads too. Used to be good, but there's so many of us now that unless you have an amp or a gimmick nobody takes any notice. Well, unless you're in a band, that is. Bands do okay, but I'm not in a band … Well, obviously – I don't know why I said that.'

As she spoke she tuned her guitar. Pavel watched, wondering how she could hear the subtle differences between the notes and talk at the same time.

She glanced up at him again. 'Okay, I'm ready.'

'I go. You work.'

'Don't you want to hear a song before you go?'

Pavel shoved his hands deep into his pocket. He wanted to get going. 'Okay.'

She slung her guitar strap over her shoulder. 'Got any requests?'

He shook his head.

She strummed once and closed her eyes. She began to sing. '"I waited for you. The night was so cold, like your voice, like your heart ..."'

Her voice was stunning. It was deep and unwavering, yet it soared on the high notes, swinging up through the ranges in an effortless arc. Pavel stared at her. How did this podgy little mess of rat ends, chewed fingers and ugly dolphins possess such an instrument? Around him people slowed, stopping to listen without realising. She reeled them in with her hypnotic voice.

When she finished, she opened her eyes. 'Did you like it?' she asked Pavel, taking little notice of the people who dropped coins into the cap she had laid on the ground before her. She looked only at him.

'Very good.'

'I wrote it myself.'

He raised an eyebrow.

'No, seriously, I did.'

'Good.'

'Do you want to hear another?'

'I go now.'

'Oh. Are you coming back?'

'I do not know.'

'I'll be here for a few hours, if I don't get moved on.'

Pavel nodded, unsure of what he was supposed to say.

'It's okay, you've got to go – I know, I get it. People always have to go.'

'You are good singer. Very good.'

'Yep.' She looked at her feet. For some reason Pavel patted her awkwardly on the arm. Then he shouldered his holdall and walked away.

He walked through the George's Street Arcade and out onto George's Street, turned and went down to the Central Bank, which Grace had shown him earlier. He went to the *bureau de change* and changed a larger sum of Flintov's money into euros. When he was finished he came back out onto the street, bought a large bouquet of flowers from a shop across the street and hailed a cab.

'Where to, mate?'

'Loo-kan.'

'Whereabouts?'

'The Alton Clinic.'

'Put your belt on. Nice flowers.'

'Thank you.'

26

John was taking the fake blue disabled notice off his car dashboard when Stevie finally returned his call. 'Well?'

'How you doing, John?'

John knew immediately from his friend's tone that something was up. This was confirmed by Stevie's next line.

'You sitting down?'

'Pretend I am.' John said, putting the sign in the glove compartment.

'That cop who called you yesterday. He's here from London, investigating the death of a man called Victor Wright.'

'Never heard of him.'

'Yeah, I sort of figured that might be the case.'

'Okay, so why does he need to speak to Sarah?'

'John, listen to me now. According to what I've been told, this guy Victor, well, he was Sarah's husband.'

John watched the traffic go by. The day was dry, but the sky was heavy with clouds. It was surely going to lash out of the heavens soon, he thought. 'Sarah was married?'

'I did some checking. She got married ten years ago in a register office in Slough.'

'In Slough?'

'You okay?'

'Yeah. So, Sarah was married and now this guy's dead. '

'His body was found on a beach in Wales.'

'Wales?'

'Yeah, washed ashore there. He had been stabbed.'

'Stabbed?'

'Are you going to keep doing that?'

'No, sorry, go on.'

'Right. It took a while but apparently the police have managed to trace his last movements and it seems he was here, in Dublin. He came over on the ferry back in October.'

'I see,' John said, thinking.

'His body was found on the eighteenth of November.'

November. That was the month John had travelled to England on the missing-person case. It was the month Sarah had been mugged and his office had been trashed. November was the month in which Rodney Mitchell had been beaten to a pulp and when Jackie, Sarah's sister, had been driven off the road. November was the month when Sarah had gone from red hot to ice cold.

'They're tracking his movements at the moment, trying to find out where he stayed.'

'Right.'

'That's probably why they want to talk to Sarah – to see if maybe he tried to contact her while he was here.'

'Yeah. That's probably it.'

'Did she ever mention this guy to you, John?'

'Nope, can't say she did.'

'You think she saw him while he was here?'

John thought of his Sarah, her haunted eyes, the bruising around her face. 'I doubt it, Stevie – ten years? They'd probably be well moved on by then.'

'Wonder what he was doing over here.'

'Fucked if I know.'

'Well, if I hear anything else I'll be sure to let you know.'

'Thanks, Stevie, I really appreciate this.'

'Sure, and I'll be talking to you about that other matter.'

'What other matter?'

'The car reg you asked me to trace. I haven't had a chance to run it yet. I thought you'd need to hear this first.'

'Okay, Stevie, thanks.' John hung up.

Married. Wales. Dead. Stabbed. Bruising.

Sarah.

'You stupid fool.'

He took the stairs in Wexford Street two at a time until he reached the second floor. He barged into Rodney Mitchell's office, nearly taking the door off its hinges.

Rodney was seated behind his desk, a glass of Jack before him. When he looked up his eyes were dull and bloodshot. 'Can I offer you a drink? I think you can classify it as medicinal.' His words were slurred.

John glanced at the half-empty bottle by his elbow. 'Medicinal, eh?'

Rodney shrugged. He knew he was caught and he really didn't care.

'Rod, look at me. I need you to tell me the truth.'

'About what?'

'About Sarah's injuries, about your injuries. What the hell happened?'

'I don't want to talk about it.' Rodney lowered his gaze to the glass.

'Damnit, Rodney, I'm fucking serious here. You'd better start talking.'

'You need to calm down.'

'Don't give me that. Did you know Sarah was married?'

Rodney's face went through a series of expressions before finally settling on flabbergasted. 'Married? To whom?'

'To some corpse the cops found washed up on a beach in Wales back in November. You remember November, don't you?'

'Oh.'

'Yeah, oh.' John dropped into a chair and ran his hands through his hair. 'I need to know what happened when I was away.'

'I'll pour you a small one,' Rodney said, taking a dusty glass off the shelf behind him and blowing ineffectually into it. When he was satisfied he filled it with three fingers of Jack and slid the glass across his desk to John. His hands were steady as a rock.

John accepted it. 'I want to know what happened.'

Rodney took a sip of his drink. 'You know most of it. I was here late when I heard noise upstairs. I knew you were away, so I thought … well, I just thought I'd make sure everything was all right.' He gave John a miserable half-smile. 'The man I discovered wrecking your office roughed me up. Then he told me to deliver a message.'

'What was the message?'

Rodney took another drink. 'I promised her I wouldn't speak about it. I promised her.'

'Sarah's not here, Rod. I am.'

'I know that.'

'What was the message?'

'He wanted Sarah to meet him that night. He shoved a note into my pocket, then slapped my face a few times. I thought I was a goner, John, but he left. I think I passed out. Next thing I knew Sarah was pulling furniture off me, and she was crying.'

'Jesus Christ, Rod, why the hell didn't you tell me?'

Rodney looked forlorn. 'She came to see me in the hospital. She was all banged up and I knew something terrible had happened, but she made me swear, John – she made me swear to keep what happened in the office to myself.' He shrugged. 'I should have told you but I couldn't.'

'What did she say?'

'She told me she'd taken care of him. That he wouldn't be bothering us again.'

'Fucking hell, Rod.' John leaned forward and pressed his fingers to his forehead. He felt as if someone had just punched him straight in the gut. 'You must have known what she'd done. Don't sit there and tell me you didn't know what she meant.'

'I'm sorry.'

John pushed his glass away and stood up. 'I've got to go.'

'John, wait. What are you going to do?'

'I don't know. I need time to think.'

'John!' Rodney said, alarmed. 'What are you going to do? John!'

'I've got to go.'

John left the office, got into his car and pulled into the traffic. He couldn't think. He felt ill, trapped, weighed down by anger and fear and a sinking sensation that Sarah was so deep in the shit he'd never pull her out.

After half an hour he pulled up outside a smart house in Rathgar. He rang the doorbell and waited, stepping from one foot to the other as he did.

The door opened. Jackie Kenny, Sarah's sister, appeared. At John's expression the welcoming smile slid from her face. 'What is it?'

'Jackie, we need to talk.'

'You'd better come in, then.'

27

Jackie showed John into the kitchen and made a pot of tea. John had been to her house a few times with Sarah but, as always, he was struck by how calm and welcoming Jackie's home was compared to how Helen and Sarah, kept theirs. The kitchen was an addition to the original house. It had a pitched roof and was dominated by a long refectory table and a deep red Aga. A number of Jackie's brilliantly coloured paintings hung on the white walls and vases stuffed with flowers sat in odd nooks and crannies.

'You're looking well, John. Life must be treating you kindly,' Jackie said. She placed two cups on the table and put the teapot on a wire stand. She got out the milk and the sugar and put an open packet of biscuits on a plate between them.

'Looking pretty good yourself, Jackie. How's the arm doing?'

'It's a lot better, thank you. Once that wretched cast was off the relief was indescribable.'

'You back painting again?'

'I am.'

'Good.'

John poured his tea and added milk and sugar. He liked Jackie, he always had. She was an artist and art teacher in a local secondary school. She was the middle Kenny girl and the long-standing peace-maker of the family. She was shorter than either Sarah or Helen and heavier set. Her long dark Kenny hair was untidily pinned high on her head and numerous strands had worked their way loose. Her eyes, lighter in colour than Sarah's, were kind and sad in equal measure.

John stirred his tea. He was stalling, searching for a way to start the conversation.

Jackie reached out and placed her hand on his. 'So, I take it he called you.'

'Who?'

'The detective from the UK.'

John looked at her, surprised. 'Floyd. Yes, he did. Did you know she was married?'

Jackie shook her head. 'No, I did not. None of us had any idea. Helen is fit to be tied. Absolutely furious. It was such a shock when he called and told us.'

'I can't believe it myself. She never let on.'

'She's a secretive girl, our Sarah.'

'She's a widow, that's what she is. A widow with a cop on her tail.'

Jackie retracted her hand. 'Well, like I told that detective, the poor man is dead and that's awful, but I don't really see what any of that has to do with Sarah.'

'You don't?"

'No.'

John barked a laugh. 'Really, Jackie, this is going to be your line?'

'It's hardly a crime not to tell people you were married once and that it failed.'

'No, it isn't, and that's fine. All of us have made our mistakes. It is a crime, however, to gut your ex-husband and toss him in the sea.'

'What the hell are you talking about?'

'The night of your car crash, what happened exactly? You told Sarah you thought someone had clipped your car. She found paint, didn't she? On your bumper?'

Jackie grew pale. She looked at her hands for a moment. 'I was coming home from Mum's house. I was tired, I'd had some wine … I thought there was a van right behind me, but I don't know what happened.'

'You don't know?'

'I don't remember, John. I've thought about it so many times, but it's all a bit of a fog. There was a van in my rear-view mirror, I know that, then something hit me and the car spun – I remember it spinning – and then it hit a bollard and went into the side of a building.'

'Is that all you remember?'

She lifted her hand to her face and traced a finger down it. 'There was a man, I think, at the scene. He had a scar – here – and a pale eye. I don't know, maybe he called the ambulance.' She shook her head. 'I can't really remember.'

'Did you tell Sarah about the man?'

'Again, I don't remember. I was pretty out of it and had bad concussion.'

'I think Victor Wright might have been the one to hit your car.'

'But why would he do that? I'd never met the man.'

'I don't know why but I think he did, and I think Sarah knew he was here.'

'What are you saying, John? That Sarah killed him? That's

164

ridiculous. Sarah? Come on. How can you sit there and even think such a thing? You know her.'

'Yeah, well, I thought I did.'

'Don't say that.'

'Then why did she run, Jackie? Where is she?'

'I don't know.' Jackie tucked a loose strand of hair behind her ear. 'I really don't. She hasn't been in touch.'

'She hasn't called about your mother?'

'She hasn't called *us* about her. She might very well be checking with the home.'

'Well, I'm sorry, that doesn't sound like the Sarah I'm supposed to know.'

'She's not a killer, John. She wouldn't kill a man.'

'She has before.'

'You're talking about Patrick York?' Jackie's features shifted and she stiffened visibly. 'He *was* going to kill you. She did that to save you.'

'Maybe this time she killed to save you.'

'I think you should go, John.'

'I need to find her, Jackie – I need to find her before this guy Floyd does.'

'Are you going to tell him your notions?'

'No – because right now that's all they are.' John pushed his cup aside and stood. 'But you can be sure Floyd is going to come to the same conclusion, even if it's by a different pathway.'

Jackie raised her head and folded her arms. She looked at John with fear in her dark eyes. 'For fuck's sake, Jackie, do you really think I'm out to burn her? Do you? If you know something you've got to tell me!'

'I don't want anything to happen to her.'

'Jesus, Jackie, I wouldn't hurt her. I love her, goddamnit.'

'I know you do.'

'Then you've got to help me find her.'

Jackie stood up and left the room. She returned with her handbag, a monstrous blue thing with tassels. She opened it and took out a purse so stuffed with God knew what that she'd put an elastic hairband around it to keep it closed.

She opened it and riffled through it until she found a well-folded piece of paper. She found a pen next, copied a number onto another scrap of paper and passed it to John.

John read it. An English phone number. 'She's in England?'

'I don't know where she is,' Jackie said. 'I took that number from Mum's telephone bill. I sorted out her bills after she went into the home. Sarah called this man. Sid is his name – I know because I called him .He wouldn't tell me anything initially, but a few days later he rang back and said I wasn't to worry, that Sarah was okay and she'd get in touch when she could.'

'You should have told me.'

'There was nothing to tell, John. She never called.'

'When was this?'

'Just after Christmas.'

'Have you spoken to him since?'

'Once. When I didn't hear from her I rang him again. He said he was sorry but he couldn't force her and assured me she was well.'

John folded the piece of paper and put it into his wallet.

'John, listen to me, Helen doesn't know about this.'

Well, if you won't tell her, Jackie, I sure as shit won't.'

Jackie's face twisted in on itself. 'Secrets and lies.'

'What?'

'Something Sarah said to me just before she left. Our family is full of secrets and lies.'

John bent down and gave her a kiss on the cheek. 'I'll find her, Jackie, and I'll make sure no one harms her.'

'Promise?'

'Scout's honour.'

28

'Can I help you?' The receptionist offered Pavel a non-smile.

Pavel glanced at the blank card tied to the flowers. 'I look for Mayweather.'

'Oh.' The non-smile became a real smile. 'Of course. Fourth floor, suite nine. You can take the lift over there.'

As Pavel rode up he felt calm and relaxed. On the fourth floor he studied the various plates bolted into the walls. He turned left and walked until he came to smoked-glass double doors. He pushed open the outer door and walked into a reception area where a woman sat behind a desk.

'Can I help you?'

'Mayweather?'

'I can sign for those.'

Pavel shook his head. 'No, only she.'

The receptionist frowned, but she lifted the phone and pressed a button. 'Ms Mayweather, I am sorry to disturb you, but there is a gentleman here with flowers for you and he is insisting you sign for them . . . Of course.' She hung up. 'She will be with you in one moment.'

Pavel waited. After a minute the inner doors snicked open and a short woman in a tight pencil skirt approached him. 'These are for me?'

'Frieda Mayweather?'

'Yes.'

'Then for you.'

She took the flowers and looked at the card. She frowned. 'There's no note with these.'

Pavel shrugged.

She put the blank card back and looked at him. Pavel felt a slight start of recognition. Her eyes were grey, but alert, clever and cold. He had seen eyes like these before, but never in a woman.

'Do you need me to sign for my mystery flowers?'

'No.'

She passed them to her receptionist. 'Put these in water.'

'Of course.' The woman took them and walked off.

Frieda Mayweather turned back to Pavel. 'In future my secretary has my consent to sign for my deliveries.'

'Yes.'

She turned and went back to her office. Pavel pretended to walk to the smoked-glass doors. When he heard the click of the inner doors he doubled back and vaulted over the secretary's desk. He grabbed the Rolodex and spun it, his finger almost a blur as he chased down the two names he needed. There . . . and there.

He ripped the cards out, pocketed them and vaulted back over the desk. His feet had barely touched the carpet when the secretary returned with the flowers in a crystal vase. She looked at him suspiciously. 'Did you need something else?'

'No.'

He walked through the doors and along the corridor. He was almost at the lift when he heard, 'Excuse me?'

He turned.

Frieda Mayweather was walking towards him.

He waited. She stopped a foot away.

'I forgot to ask which shop you're delivering for?'

Pavel blinked. He tried to think of its name but it wouldn't come.

The woman was watching him. 'Cat got your tongue?'

'English, bad,' he said. 'Shop is Mad Flowers.'

She smiled. 'Ah, I know it. I will ring them and see if they can't let me know who was kind enough to send the flowers.'

Pavel nodded.

'Well, take care, Mr—'

'Ademi,' Pavel said.

'Take care, Mr Ademi.'

She walked away and Pavel stepped into the lift. He was sweating and light-headed with the effort of remaining outwardly calm. When he reached the ground floor he walked out of the lift and glanced up.

Frieda Mayweather was staring at him from the landing. He walked across the marble foyer and out into the cold air, relieved to be away from her.

He hurried back onto the main road and, after a few attempts, managed to flag down a taxi. He slid into the back seat and pulled out the card he had stolen. 'Here.'

'Sandymount? Okay.'

Pavel got out on the Strand Road and waited until the car had driven away. He lit a cigarette and stepped back as two thin women with blonde hair and skin the colour of copper stomped past him being led by a short breathless pug.

He took a deep breath, drawing the sea air deep into his lungs. It was cold and wet but he didn't care. The weather was hardly a concern. He had seen her. He knew where she lived. He knew where the man lived. He was closer to his goal.

He thought of Frieda Mayweather watching him and shuddered. She had not been what he had expected. She was something else entirely. She was a demon in human form.

He shouldered his bag and walked along the road. He took out the map he had refolded in the taxi and checked which direction he should go.

He turned off the main stretch of road onto Sydney Parade and strolled along the leafy avenue, counting corners and peering through ornate gates into gravelled drives. It was such a dull day that many of the magnificent homes were lit from within. Large airy rooms filled with beautiful people.

Pavel turned off Sydney Parade and entered a sort cul-de-sac. He counted the houses. Her home was the second from the end. He paused at the gate and bent as if to tie his shoelaces. A Land Cruiser by a bay window. A bike lay on its side half under the bushes and a football just inside the gate.

Children.

He straightened and walked on, performing a full sweep of the cul-de-sac and going into the street behind to survey the way the houses overlooked each other, searching for a security weakness.

He found one. The house whose garden backed onto the woman's was less well maintained than the others. The windows were single-glazed, it needed a coat of paint and there were no security gates, just normal ones he could have stepped over if he had so wished. There were no cars parked out front and no light from within, although this did not mean it was unoccupied.

He made a mental note of it and left.

He caught a DART train to Dun Laoghaire and found the second house he was searching for. This would be easier, he thought, sitting on a low wall directly opposite his quarry's home. Brendan O'Brien would be an easier target. It was modern, semi-detached, with a side gate and a lawn set a few feet off the main road. People were less watchful in more urban areas, less suspicious of people like him. If he needed to put the squeeze on he would start here. Let them decide how they wanted to play the ball in their court.

He did not like to admit to himself that meeting Frieda Mayweather had unnerved him.

Satisfied with his afternoon's work, Pavel made his way back to the station and waited for the train to return him to the city.

Once he alighted at Tara Street he consulted his map again. He could find a hotel – he had enough money for one now. Yet for one reason or another – none that he could explain – he found himself crossing at the traffic-lights and making his way back towards where he had last seen Grace.

It was just coming up to rush-hour and the streets were filling. He hurried up College Green, passing the café where they had had coffee that morning. If she was gone that sealed it: he would get a hotel. Let the fates decide.

But she was there. And she was not alone.

Two youths were crowding her. She was backed against the wall to the left of a rack of men's jackets that belonged to the second-hand clothes shop. The one on the left, shaven-headed in a white Adidas tracksuit, was holding her guitar by the neck.

Pavel stepped into the door of a burger bar and watched through the corner window. If this was a friendly chat why did Grace look so frightened?

The other youth made a grab for the cap Grace was holding. She flinched and hugged it closer to her body. The boy dug into her arm with his closed fist, not hard, but enough to make Grace yelp. Pavel rounded the corner and moved towards them, not running but moving fast. The one who had struck Grace noticed him coming, but by the time he swivelled around Pavel had grabbed the boy with the guitar by the back of the neck and slammed his head into the wall. He caught the guitar before the kid dropped it, and spun.

The one who had struck Grace stepped forward. 'Here, what the fuck—'

Pavel swung the guitar up with both hands and caught him flush beneath the jaw. The sound of wood on bone was musical in a crunching way. The kid's knees buckled and he went down hard and heavy.

Pavel turned to Grace. The boy whose head he had bounced off the wall was groaning. The other was spitting blood, but wisely stayed down. 'You are hurt?'

She shook her head. She was staring at him, her tearstained face upturned to his, her mouth hanging open. 'You came back.' Her voice was high and strained, as though she couldn't believe what had just happened.

'Yes.'

She looked at her antagonists, then back to Pavel.

'Come,' Pavel said, handing her the guitar.

She took it, skirted around the fallen youths and stepped into stride beside Pavel. She said nothing, but every now and then she would gaze at his profile.

Pavel paid her no attention. His thoughts were of buildings and meetings and Frieda Mayweather. Now that he had seen her he knew he was on the right track. He would keep to his work. He would make his demand the next day and if they did not comply – and he understood that it was likely they could not – he would avenge his sister. He would do whatever it took to see it that no other sister, no other desperate person, would be carved up by these monsters in the name of science.

'Pavel?'

He glanced at her.

'Thank you so much for helping me. No one else would.'
'The street is dangerous for woman.'
'I thought I would be safe there – it's so busy normally.'
'There are always bad people. Always, everywhere.'

Grace did not say what she wanted to say: that as long as he was by her side she felt safe. He had come back for her. He had rescued her from certain harm.

Grace Whelan was beginning to fall in love.

29

Back at his office John tried the number Jackie had given him but it rang out. He tried it again half an hour later, still with no success. He smoked incessantly and paced his office. Finally he gathered up his belongings and made his way to his car. In between calls to 'Sid' he had eliminated the third Chris Day from his enquiries and left a message for the last one. Rather than wear a groove in his office carpet, he had decided to pay a personal visit.

According to the phone book, Chris Day lived in Clonee. John drove out along the M50 and found the address after driving around in circles for a ridiculous length of time. It was a townhouse set in a huge complex made up of other townhouses and apartments, all nearly identical. There were a lot of for-sale signs.

John parked the Manta on the street and knocked. No one was at home. He tried to see in through the window to the left of the door, but bamboo blinds were rolled all the way down.

After a few minutes he took out a business card, wrote 'call me' on it and slipped it through the letterbox.

He was still debating what to do when a people-carrier packed with kids pulled into the drive of the house two doors up. A woman climbed out and began to unload a ton of shopping from the boot. The side door pulled back and kids of all ages poured out.

'Excuse me?' John stepped over the box hedges to reach her.

The woman glanced at him. She looked tired and a little startled. 'Yes?'

'Hi, I was wondering if you knew Chris – Chris Day? He lives in number eight there.'

'No. I mean I knew the man by sight, but we didn't know each other. DJ, stop that! He didn't live here that long.'

'You don't have any idea where he works?' John said, raising his voice over the din.

Two of the kids were tussling over a bright green water gun. She looked at them, opened her mouth as though about to shout and gave up. 'I'm sorry … Who are you?'

John removed a card from his wallet and handed it to her. She read it. 'Oh, you're a detective.'

'Like I say, I was wondering if there was a way I could get in touch with him, perhaps his work—'

'I'm sorry, but the man you're looking for is dead. The house has been rented out again.'

'What?'

'He's dead. He died at the start of last month. I saw the ambulance remove him and everything. It was awful – gave me such a fright.'

'Oh.' John felt the wind slip from his sails. Obviously Alison had not been meeting with Chris Day on the day she had died.

'Poor man.' The woman tightened her cardigan around her. 'He could have been there for a day or more. I do know he was

175

unwell for quite some time. You could tell that by looking at him.'

'What was wrong with him?'

'I don't really know, to tell you the truth. You should speak with his wife about that.'

'He's married?'

'Separated.'

'I don't suppose you know where I could find her?'

'Actually, I can help you there. She owns a florist – Blooming Beautiful or something like that. I used to see her drive the van here with his girls sometimes. Nice-looking family. Makes you wonder, doesn't it? Kept himself to himself he did. My Dean spoke to him a few times, said he was nice, a quiet sort.'

John wondered how a 'quiet sort' coped with the amount of noise he guessed this particular set of neighbours could create. He took out his pen and wrote down the name of the florist. 'Thanks a million for your help.'

She nodded, and glanced towards number eight. 'Poor man, you just never know the minute or the hour, do you? Crowd of foreigners in there now – don't even say hello so they don't.'

John was about to excuse himself when a thought occurred to him. 'Could I ask you to take a look at a photo?'

'Of course.'

He handed her the one of Alison Cooper he had in his inside pocket.

She took it and studied it. 'I think I have seen this woman here, but a good few weeks ago. It wouldn't have been long before he died. She drove a Volvo and I had to ask her to move it because it was blocking me in.'

'Are you sure?'

She handed it back. 'Not a hundred per cent, but I'm pretty certain it was her. She seemed terribly upset about something.'

'Upset?'

'Well, you know. Her eyes were red so she'd definitely been crying. I'm not nosy, but I could tell that much.'

John smiled, 'If you were a betting woman, what per cent are we talking that it was her?'

She frowned. 'Eighty? In the photo you've got she looks real happy, doesn't she?'

John looked at it. 'She does, doesn't she?'

'Exactly, but when people are upset, they don't look anything like themselves.'

John thought of Sarah Kenny. 'No,' he said. 'I suppose they don't.'

30

It took John no time at all to find Blooming Flowers and, as luck would have it, Patricia Day was working.

'He was a good man, you know.' Patricia plucked a long, slender white flower from the bouquet she was working on and set it to one side. She was a small, slight, dark-haired woman. She appeared a little agitated, but that was hardly surprising – the last thing she must have expected that day was a private investigator popping into her shop shortly before closing time, demanding to speak to her about her dead husband.

John stood at the counter watching her nimble hands work. She still wore her wedding band. 'Can you tell me more about him?'

'It's still a bit raw, talking about Chris. He's only been dead a month. Buried February the twelfth.'

'I understand it must be difficult. I'm sorry for your loss.'

She nodded and took a deep breath. 'It's still such a shock. We were separated, and had been for almost a year and a half, but we'd kept in touch and we were trying to work through it. We have the children, three girls.' She yanked a roll of green foil from under the counter, placed the bunch of white flowers and dark green waxy leaves in the centre and began to wrap expertly. When she had shaped the paper into a funnel she used gold damask from a roll on the desk to tie the bottom.

'Those are beautiful,' John said, although he knew bugger-all about plants or flowers.

'Long-stem hydrangeas. Everyone and their mother has a hydrangea in their garden, but these are special.'

'Nice.'

'They're for a wedding. She has good taste.' She put the flowers to one side and rested her hands on the counter.

'Chris's neighbour said your husband had been unwell.'

'Unwell? I suppose you could call it that. It is classed as a disease.'

John's brow furrowed. 'I'm sorry, I don't follow.'

She paused for a moment, as though gathering herself. 'Chris was what people call a high-functioning alcoholic. He got up every day, went to work, came home in the evening and drank until he fell asleep. He was never violent, never abusive, never even cross. I think if maybe he'd been any of those things I'd have left sooner or tried to stop him or got him help before it was too late. But he wasn't. And I didn't.'

'It's hard to help people who don't want your help,' John said.

Her dark eyes searched his. 'You know what it's like?'

'Maybe not what you went through exactly, but I know enough to understand there's little you could have done if he didn't want to take the first step.'

'I've thought about it a lot since he died. I can't help thinking it was like a physical thing – like it had him in an invisible grip. It tightened, but in a gradual way. It's difficult to pinpoint when

Chris stopped being in control of it and it was in control of him. I think it was the weight loss I noticed first. Then he started getting tired earlier in the day. I spoke to him about it, tried to get him to see someone, but he kept saying he was fine. One Saturday after breakfast he just collapsed. I was here, in work, and my eldest daughter called. She was hysterical.'

'It must have been frightening for everyone concerned.'

'It was.' She wrapped her arms around herself.

'They said his liver was all but destroyed. There was talk of him being put on the transplant list, but for that to happen Chris had to be clean and sober for six months. He tried, I know he did – he really tried. But it just wouldn't let him go. It wouldn't release him.'

'So what happened?'

'We waited, and as we waited we just fell apart.' She shrugged and John looked on with sympathy. That involuntary gesture was such a pathetic summation of the devastation alcohol had wrought on her and her children's lives.

'So he never got his transplant.'

'No one was willing to list him if he wasn't going to meet them halfway.'

John removed Alison's photo from his jacket and slid it across the counter to her. 'Do you recognise this woman?'

She looked down. 'Oh, I know her – she's a doctor. She's the one who saw Chris the day he collapsed.'

'She looked after him?'

'Yes. She was very nice, patient, came out to the waiting room to keep us updated on his progress. I remember the way she included the girls too. It helped.'

'That was the only time you met her?'

'No – she championed Chris to go onto the transplant list, but it wasn't up to her. She was terribly upset that they wouldn't put him forward. She really was a lovely woman. She came to his funeral to pay her condolences. Why are you asking about her?'

'She died last Friday.'

'Oh, I didn't know.' She placed a hand at her throat. 'What happened?'

'She killed herself.'

'Oh.' Patricia was shocked. 'Oh, that is truly terrible. Why would she do such a thing? She was so lovely.'

'I don't know,' John said truthfully.

'She cared, that woman, she really cared about her patients. I think it's so easy for people to be cynical about the medical profession, these days, but that woman was a true friend to our family.'

Patricia paused for a long time. 'I think Chris had made peace with himself. In his last few weeks he grew sicker and sicker but he was convinced he was going to be cured. Kept telling me and the girls not to worry.' She glanced up. 'They do that, though, don't they? They know crying is useless. They like to pretend that the answer to all their prayers is right around the corner. Denial. What a waste.'

John asked a few more questions and left her with his card. Outside he paused to look back through the door. Patricia Day was standing behind the counter, staring into space. twisting her wedding band.

She was right, John thought. What a waste.

181

31

Ivan Colbert felt sick. He undid his top button and paced back and forth across his office. He wished he had time to remove his shoes, and that he had cancelled his next appointment. Ever since his meeting that morning he had been beside himself.

He truly wished he had never met Frieda Mayweather. He checked his pulse and was alarmed to find it racing. He went into his private bathroom, swallowed a painkiller and rinsed his wrists under the cold tap.

He kept thinking of Alison and propofol. Propofol? Why would she have taken propofol? It didn't make any sense – but nothing about her death did. He had known she was depressed – but not that she was suicidal: she had so much fight and vigour. She had known life wasn't cheap. In fact, of all people, Alison had understood the true value of living.

He wished it had been him in that bathroom, not her.

He had spent much of the afternoon reading over his notes from years before. He had stared at his handwriting and understood the words, but every time he tried to picture himself performing the surgery his hands shook and his mouth went dry as the desert.

He couldn't do it. As much as he owed Frieda, he would simply have to refuse her. It wasn't fair of her to put him under this kind of pressure. He would have to grow a set and tell her that, no matter what she said, it wasn't going to happen. He would stand his ground. What else could he do?

He looked at his reflection in the mirror over the basin. 'You can do this, Ivan.'

He turned off the tap and returned to his office. The buzzer on his desk sounded. He pressed a button. 'Yes?'

'Sir? Mrs Lambert is here.'

'Lam-*bair*. The *t* is silent, Fiona.'

'I'm so sorry, sir.'

He smoothed his hair and straightened his tie. Deep breath, Ivan, he thought, deep breath. 'Send her in.'

A moment later a woman in her late forties opened his door and glided across the carpet on a cloud of Opium. 'Ivan.'

'Felicity, you're looking stunning as ever.'

'Oh, now, if I was *that* stunning I wouldn't be here.' She threw back her head and laughed as he took her hand in both of his and pressed it softly. 'How *are* you, Ivan?'

'I am very well, thank you. And your family?'

'Everybody's wonderful. Maeve is flourishing – and you know, of course, that Aidan is on his gap year.'

'He's in Thailand, isn't he?'

'Yes!' She batted him on the arm.

She was flattered that he had remembered, flattered that he thought her son dicking around for a year on his father's money was a detail worth retaining. This was his life now, he thought. This was how he functioned. He smiled his fake plastic smile, gave his fake plastic compliments and no one was any the wiser. It was perfect. It was doable.

By the time he had shown Felicity out and made Fiona note down her next appointment – derma peel and vein-threading – Frieda had arrived. She bustled past him and settled herself into the chair before his desk. 'I have spoken with the family of the girl we discussed. We will be all set and ready to go on Sunday. My theatre has been cleared from six until eight. Brendan will assist, as will Elise and I.'

Colbert cleared his throat. He opened his mouth to tell her he could not do it but no sound came out.

'Honestly, some days, Ivan, are too much. I have Hagen hounding me about donations and the new solicitors are more squid than shark. I wish Bolt hadn't retired. He was the sort of man a clinic like ours needs on retainer.'

'Frieda, I have an appointment on the way.'

'You called me – remember? Your message said we needed to talk. I'm here. Talk.'

'Oh, well, it can wait.'

'Just tell me what's going on and quit the drama, Ivan.'

'Well, it's about the surgery, the patient we discussed. The thing is, Frieda, and I've given this a lot of thought, I don't think I can do it.'

'Course you can.'

'Well, no, that's just it, I don't believe I can.'

'Oh, bollocks, Ivan, it's like riding a bike. You did the last one fine, didn't you?'

'Yes, but—'

'Look, Ivan, I told you we've found the perfect candidate to replace Flintov – even better, actually, because we can keep it in-house. But it'll take a few weeks to sort out his work visa. He's coming from bloody Singapore of all places. All I'm asking is that you do this one pretty minor surgery and that's it. We can call it quits after that.'

'Frieda, I don't think you understand—'

'No, *you* don't understand, Ivan. Aidan Corrigan is putting more than a hundred grand into this hospital's coffers in exchange for his daughter's future. I don't have to remind you that the pool of private patients is shrinking, do I?'

'No.'

'I have two patients currently suing us right at this moment, I have staff demanding more money. A place like this costs money to run, Ivan. I'm securing the future, our future, not to mention saving that woman's life.'

'Very altruistic of you.'

'Oh, don't play the wounded victim with me, Ivan. I know you too well.' She stood up. 'This is neither the time nor the place to start developing a conscience.'

'This has nothing to do with conscience. I am not capable of that kind of surgery any longer, Frieda.' He lifted his hands. 'These are not capable.'

Frieda stopped by the door. 'Then they'd better get bloody capable, because on Sunday morning I want to see you scrubbed up and ready to go. End of discussion.'

32

Pavel waited across the street from the house, smoking. It was still dark and the early morning was cold and wet. It was too early for traffic and no one was about. He wondered how many occupants there might be inside. There was only one car parked in the drive, a red Ford Mondeo, but that meant nothing.

There were no toys in the garden and only one set of curtains were pulled upstairs. Of course, that didn't rule out the possibility there was more than one person inside. Either way, it was always better to err on the side of caution.

After a few moments of studying the neighbourhood, he pitched his cigarette away and turned up the collar of his jacket against the cold. He walked across the road, up the short path and vaulted over the side gate of the townhouse. He went to the back and walked across the decked patio. It was greasy and neglected, with patches of green mould growing within the planks. Pavel had to be careful to avoid slipping and banging into the rusted metal furniture.

He glanced up. The light from the alarm box rolled blue, back and forth. He used a bench to climb onto the garden shed's roof and unscrewed the cover from the alarm box. He swore. It was a new model and impossible to deactivate.

He slid back to the ground and hunkered down beside the shed. There was a set of sliding doors to his right. He examined the lock. This he could open, but not without the alarm going off.

He decided distraction was what he needed.

He climbed back over the side gate and returned to the front of the house, where he looked around for something to use. Nothing. He climbed over the low wall separating the house from the one next door and found a cement garden ornament – a duck pulling a small stone cart. It was ridiculous but it amused him. He carried it back over the wall and hurled it through the side window of the car. Then he climbed back and crouched behind the gate to listen.

In a matter of seconds the front door opened and he heard a male voice. 'Oh, what the fuck!'

Pavel hurried to the rear of the house. He worked on the sliding-door lock, keeping his hands steady, trying not to get frustrated. Within two minutes he had slipped inside the house and closed the door. He found himself in a small dining room off an even smaller kitchen. Through the open kitchen door he could make out part of the stairs. He crossed the room and moved behind the door. A light came on and the man came into the kitchen, He began to open and close press doors. Pavel could hear him cursing under his breath. After another few minutes he heard the front door slam, then the alarm being set. The lights went off, leaving him standing in gloom.

Nobody else had appeared. He waited for the man to go back upstairs, heard footsteps overhead, the creak of a bed.

He waited.

Almost a full hour elapsed since Pavel had smashed the car window before he moved again. He climbed the stairs slowly, taking great care to avoid any squeaky boards. As he moved closer to the return he fished a scalpel from his pocket and removed the plastic security case. The man's bedroom was to the front of the house, the last door on the left off the landing. It was closed over, but not shut fully. Here Pavel paused, listening intently. Was he really asleep? How could he not be aware of an intruder in his home? Could he not sense the danger? Could he not hear Pavel's heart beating hard and fast despite his attempts to control his emotions?

Pavel put his hand flat against the door and gave it a gentle shove. It opened silently. He pushed it a little wider and crept into the room.

It was darker than the hall, but he could make out the shape of his target lying on his side. He was facing away from the door.

Pavel listened to the rhythm of the man's breathing. It was deep and even. He stepped across the room and slid the blade over the man's shoulder and flush against his throat. He put his lips close to his ear. 'Wake up.'

The man jerked. 'Huh …'

'There is blade. Feel it.' Pavel pressed harder.

The man stopped moving immediately. 'What do you want?'

'Only name.'

'What?'

'Only name.'

'I don't know what you're talking about.'

'You brought girl to Bosnia three weeks ago. She have kidney from girl called Ana, Ana Sunic. Who is for? Who is girl?'

He felt the man tense under his hand. 'How do you know about that?'

'Travnic.'

188

The man shifted. Pavel pressed the blade tighter. He felt a trickle of hot blood run over his finger.

'Don't do stupid thing. Give name.'

'I think you're going to kill me anyway, no matter what I do.'

'I want only name.'

'I don't know her name.'

'You know name.'

'I don't – look, I just fucking work for her.'

'Her?'

'Frieda. Look, I don't know names, I wouldn't know details like that. It's just case numbers. Frieda would never give out a name. She wouldn't trust anyone with that information.'

Pavel thought about that. 'What is case number?'

'Forty-seven.'

'Forty-seven? Many people.'

'I don't know what this is about but I swear to you – I *swear* – I don't have the girl's name.'

'I believe.'

'Fuck, good. Then you'll let me go?'

'Yes.'

Pavel loosened the blade from his skin. He felt the man's body relax slightly. At that moment, Pavel grabbed his hair, yanked his head back and slit his throat.

Before he left the house he took the man's hospital pass, a set of keys and a remote control. Satisfied, he switched off the alarm and left the house by the front door.

33

When John woke he lay on his back staring at the ceiling. His feet were pinned under Sumo, who was sprawled across the bottom of the bed, asleep. He was exhausted – yet again he had barely slept. He had tried to call the number Jackie had given him before he had gone to bed and, to his surprise, a man – Sid, he presumed – had answered, but as soon as he had heard who John was he had told him to 'do yourself a favour and naff off, son', then hung up. The phone had been off the hook for the rest of the evening.

John kept thinking of Sarah. He wasn't angry any more. He tried to imagine himself in her position. This guy Wright had obviously come with the intention of causing her grief. He had no doubt about that. Sarah had protected her family. She had stood alone.

She had not trusted him – even after everything they had been through together over the last few years.

That burned him.

At eight John got up and made coffee. He put Sarah out of his mind and forced himself to think about Alison Cooper instead. Was it time to roll up the case, offer his condolences and let Rose Butler grieve? What had he learned that might offer her any solace?

He had found out that, by all accounts, Alison Cooper was a dedicated and diligent worker. She loved her children enough to stay with a cheating jackass of a husband and fight for her family. She obviously had a strong affection for her patients and felt for their plight. She had cared deeply for Chris Day and his family. She had been depressed, was secretly on an anti-depressant that might make things worse if mixed with other drugs or alcohol.

John wondered if she was as hands-on with the other names on that list as she had been with Chris Day. Perhaps it was worth checking them out before he gave Rose Butler the old heave-ho.

Just before ten he parked the Manta in the usual space and walked down the street to his office building. He became aware that two men had fallen into step behind him.

John played it cool, keeping his footsteps steady. He paused outside Whelan's to light a cigarette, shaking his lighter repeatedly as though it would not function. The two men had no choice but to walk on by.

John watched as two thick heads in bomber jackets passed him. Neither man spoke or looked at him, but they couldn't have been more obvious if they'd hung neon 'We're following you, John Quigley' signs around their necks.

Where had they picked him up? There was only one place they could have waited comfortably for him to park. John doubled back the way he had come.

'Hey, Rosa,' he said, to the curvy waitress who was setting up tables in the Brazilian café opposite the gates of the private car park.

191

'John, it's too early for lunch but I can rustle you up something.'

'No, thanks, honey, I'm grand. But I was wondering, were there two guys in here a few minutes ago? Big fellows, wearing bomber jackets?'

'Yes, they sat there.' She pointed to the table inside the window.

'They there long?'

'Long enough to drink four coffees between them.'

'Thirsty work, all that sitting around.'

'Is everything okay?' Her brow creased. 'Are they trouble?'

'Don't worry, everything's fine. I'll see you.'

He left and went back to his office. He was at his desk only a few minutes when the door opened and the two lugs entered, followed by a smaller man.

John frowned. What was the point of an intercom if the building was so goddamned easy to access? He'd have to have another word with the ground-floor harridan. 'Can I help you, boys?'

Neither spud-head spoke.

Like cartoon crooks or extras from a Guy Ritchie film, the two bigger men stood to one side allowing the smaller man through. John thought the move clichéd and amusing. They then shut the door.

'So, like, what the fuck were you bothering Suzy about?' The smaller one spoke. He was in his mid-twenties, slim, around five feet six. His clothes were designer and fitted him well. His dark hair was loose, his skin tanned, and he wore a diamond stud in his left ear. Good-looking, if you liked that kind of thing – John could see why Suzy had the hots for him. His eyes had a curious glassiness about them.

'Here, you deaf or something, guy? I assed you a question.'

Assed. His accent put him outside the Pale, but beyond that

John couldn't say. Far as he was concerned, the sticks was nothing more than a big car park waiting to be cemented over.

'Let me guess, you must be Jaffa.'

'See that, boys?' he said. 'My reputation precedes me.'

John's lip curled. He was a cocky wee shit, a mouthpiece on legs. But it was easy to be cocky when you had two man mountains on either side of you.

'So go on, guy, what's the deal with you?'

'I'm a friend of Mike's, that's all. Think you'd be glad folk care enough about your girl to keep an eye out for her.'

'Mike asked you to look in, did he?'

'I didn't say that.'

'Yeah, well, you've got no fucking need to be upsetting her.'

'Upsetting her?'

'Yeah.'

'She didn't look upset when I left her.'

'Listen, I'm doing you a favour here, guy. I'm trying to be reasonable.'

John laughed. 'Look, Biscuit, me and that girl know each other from way back, long before your narrow arse appeared on the scene, so if I want to talk to her I will.'

Jaffa didn't like that too much. John was clearly wrecking whatever gangster film he thought he was starring in.

'You stay the fuck away from Suzy, and don't be telling Mike there's no hassle unless you're looking for hassle. Suzy's taking care of business, like he asked her to. That's all anyone needs to hear.'

'Looking after business involves the payroll. From what I hear, folk haven't been getting paid.'

'Fucking here now. They'll get what's coming to them, don't you be worryin' about that, guy.'

John narowed his eyes. He didn't like this jumped-up grass snake stinking up his office and he sure as hell didn't like his tone. 'You be sure to treat them young lads right.'

'You don't worry about it. It's not your business.'

'I can make it my business, if you want.'

'Ah, would you dry up out of that? Look at him, lads – look at the head on him.'

'Was there anything else?'

'No, head, just wanted to meet and make sure we all know where we stand.'

'I'm pretty sure I've figured that out.'

Jaffa cocked his head. 'Then we got no trouble, guy, tell you that.' He opened the door and walked out, the goons following.

John shook his head. What was it with young men, these days? He glanced over to Sarah's desk. Man, she would have cracked a gut laughing at something like Jaffa clogging up her office.

His hand hovered over the phone, but then he remembered that because some idiot thought taunting a journalist live on air from inside the Mountjoy was a clever thing to do, all cells were regularly checked and mobile phones confiscated.

But then he remembered this was the Joy and a rusted colander had fewer leaks.

He dialled, left a message on an answering machine and sat back to wait.

Mike Brannigan, inmate 194, returned his call exactly twelve minutes later.

'John?'

'Mike.'

'Let's hear it – I don't have a lot of credit left on this one.'

'You spoken with your sister lately?'

'Weekend. Why?'

'I think she's being handled by that gobshite she's been seeing.'

'Handled how?'

'I don't think she's running the show.'

'What have you heard?'

'Boys below haven't been paid, and that's just who I know about. He was here a few minutes ago trying to throw shapes around the office.'

'Why?'

'I went to see Suzy the other day.'

'Oh, yeah? Social visit, was it?'

'Mike, I don't want to be in your business. I'm calling you and telling you what I think you should know. Sorry to have bothered you.'

'Ah, keep your knickers on, John. That culchie prick – sorry I didn't have the chance to run him before I landed in here.'

'Who the hell is he?'

'He's a fucking no-hope flea from Roscommon or some fucking backwater. Owns or part-owns Tobago's nightclub.'

'Tobago's? That still open?'

'Yeah, far's I know. He tried to get me to put on a few gigs there using the station as advertising. I said no. Next thing he's crawling all over Suzy. So you saw her, huh?'

'I did.'

'How'd she look?'

'Like she could do with a good meal. How much longer do the state get to provide your B-and-B?'

'Another four to five weeks at least, depending.'

'So what do you want to do?'

'Get her out from under that muppet for one.'

'Might not be so easy.'

'Shit, John, tell me about it. When it comes to Suzy, nothing ever is.'

34

'Are you not wrecked? You were up and out mad early – I thought you might have gone or something.' Grace handed Pavel a cheese sandwich and a cup of tea. It was late morning. They were sitting on the blue sofa, the television on low in the background. Some balding American talk-show host was giving people advice on how to 'structure their lives'. Rick was not there. Grace had said he was pissed with her. Pavel hadn't asked.

'How's your hand? It still fucked? Looks like it was bleeding again.'

Pavel glanced at it. There was some blood on his shirtsleeve. It wasn't his.

'So, any luck?' Grace persisted.

'Luck?'

'Yeah, this morning. You were looking about for a job, right?'

Pavel chewed his sandwich and swallowed. 'Yes. I had luck.'

'Cool. Anything interesting?

He shrugged.

'Fingers crossed that you get it. It's so hard to find work now. I used to have this gig on a Saturday, sweeping up hair at a salon, but they had to let me go 'cause they were cutting back.'

Pavel glanced at his watch. He wondered how long it would be before she – the woman Frieda – learned of O'Brien's death. He wondered how long it would take her to put the pieces together, to arrive at the conclusion that he wanted her to arrive at.

Not long after midday Rick arrived back at the flat with four other people in tow, two girls and two other guys. The girls wore identical black leggings and identical bored-bitch expressions; the guys looked young and hostile. All the boys were carrying six-packs of Dutch Gold in each hand. Rick was wearing a top hat and a striped scarf so long that, though he had looped it numerous times around his neck, it hung to his knees. Pavel stared at the top hat. He thought Rick looked like a fool.

'Grace?' Rick pulled a face. 'What are you doing here? I told you I had the people coming over today. It's my day off, yeah, hello?'

'It's raining.'

'Yeah, so? Use your room or whatever. We're setting up here.'

Grace looked at Pavel, two bright spots of colour high in her cheeks. 'Do you want to go for a walk or go across to Parnell Street to the cinema, catch an early film? I don't know what's on but we could check it out. I've got some money.'

Pavel gazed at the five interlopers. One by one they looked somewhere else. Rick tried to hold his eyes but eventually his own dropped away too.

'It's okay, no biggie. Pavel, we'll go out for a while. I'll grab my coat.' She looked up at Rick, a half-smile on her face. 'Sorry, Rick, I swear I must have forgot or something.'

'Yeah, whatever.'

Pavel unfurled his body, making sure Rick could see he was

taking his time. He walked to the bathroom and closed the door. He leaned his head against it.

'She's such a loser,' one of the girls was saying.

'Is that the guy she picked up? Oh, my God, he looks fucking wack. Think they're doing it?'

'Ugh.'

'How should I know? Stella, put those in the fucking fridge – they're going to get warm.'

'See the way he was staring at us? You should just put that guy out, man. That shit's bananas and this is your castle, man.'

'Yeah, it's your gaff.'

'Yeah, yeah, I probably will – relax, yeah?'

'Her too.'

'Yeah, right.' The other girl gave a snotty laugh. 'As if Rick's gonna lose his ticket that easy.'

'Shut the fuck up.'

'I'll take care of it, Rick, okay, Rick, want some tea, Rick, can I come to the gig, Rick?'

'I told you to—'

Pavel flushed the lavatory and stepped out of the bathroom.

The group studiously ignored him. Rick hunkered down and put a CD on. Cypress Hill.

Grace came out of her room. She had changed into an unflattering dress and black leggings, like the other girls wore. She had put on lipstick. Pavel felt a flush of anger – that, and a desperate need to grab his holdall and hightail it to a hotel.

'Ready to go, Pavel?'

He put on his coat, grabbed his holdall and opened the door for her.

'Don't forget it's your turn to buy bread and shit,' Rick called after them.

Pavel looked at him for a moment before he closed the door.

'Are you okay?' Grace asked, as they walked along Parnell Street.

'Yes.'

'You're very quiet.'

'I am fine.'

'I should have took the umbrella.'

They walked along a little further. Pavel lit a cigarette and smoked. 'This Rick, how long time you are together?'

'Me and Rick? Well, lessee . . . Like I told you, I used to share with this girl and he was sort of seeing her and all – I told you that, yeah? – but then when she moved out he sort of stayed over more and more often. We never really had any, like, whatchamacallit, formal thing nor nothing, it just sort of, happened, you know? Anyway, my landlord don't give a shit as long as the rent's paid. He don't even fix shit there any more – the heater in my bedroom hasn't worked for months. 'S okay, it's company. I used to get a bit scared there on me own. People round that place can be ... Well, you've seen it. It can be rough.'

'You should go, find place better.'

'Yeah, right. Fuck, Pavel, there is no better place I can afford. I'm barely getting by on the dole as it is.'

'What is dole?'

'Dole, social welfare.'

Pavel looked at her. 'You have home.'

'I don't think so. You never met my old man.'

They arrived at the cinema and Pavel let her choose the film – he didn't care what they saw – but he refused to let her pay for her ticket and he bought her a packet of jelly snakes, although he was disgusted at the price. When the lights went down he felt her head rest on his shoulder. He left it there. The weight was strangely reassuring.

35

John left the office early and went home. He fed Sumo, took him for a walk and was browning some mince in a pan when his phone rang.

''Lo?'

'John, it's me.'

'Hey, Stevie.'

'I went by the office but it was closed up. Where are you?'

'I'm at home.'

'Can I swing by?'

'Sure.'

A few minutes later Sumo charged the door, barking up a storm, and John had to use his leg to wedge his dog's way to it. He opened it a crack. Stevie Magher, resplendent in his blues, was halfway between the gate and the door – just to be on the safe side.

'Grab a hold of that fucker's collar before he tries to eat me.'

'I don't believe it.' John grabbed Sumo's collar and pulled the dog to one side. 'The last time I saw that get-up was that day in court. Looking nice and snug too, it is.'

'You calling me fat?'

'No! Broad and manly, Stevie, broad and manly. I'd say you're a right hit with the old ones in it.'

Stevie rolled his eyes. 'You going to ask me in or what, like?'

John opened the door fully and jerked his head towards the kitchen. 'Kitchen.'

Stevie stepped past but kept a wary eye on Sumo, who was strangling himself trying to get a good whiff of the visitor. 'Keep a hold on that yoke.'

'He's all right, he's met you before. Just keep your hands to yourself and there won't be any hassle.'

'It gets bigger every time I see it.'

'Bejaysus! Now there's the pot calling the kettle black.'

In the kitchen Stevie pulled out a chair and sat at the table while John made him a cup of coffee.

'You mind if I keep cooking?'

'Work away. Smells good.'

'You want some?'

'Nah. Ailbhe will have the dinner on.'

John went back to his pan. He drained the fat off the mince into a tin can and added a finely chopped onion. Sumo sat between John and Stevie, keeping his tawny eyes firmly fixed on the new guy. 'So what's the *craic*, Stevie?'

'I have a name for you on that car – the one that was at the funeral. It's not a private car but part of Express Empire, a high-end rental service.'

'Ah.'

'But your luck is in. The day of the funeral the Merc you clocked was rented by a regular. One Ivan Colbert.'

'I know him, Stevie. I interviewed him the evening of the

funeral. He works out in that big swanky clinic in Lucan, the Alton.'

'He has the car on call on a monthly basis, uses the same driver each time too.'

'That can't be cheap.'

'It isn't, but Colbert's driving licence is suspended.'

'For what?'

'Got caught DUI in 'ninety-seven and again in 'oh-two.'

'Fuck me – a surgeon with a drink problem? Remind me never to sign up for an operation with that guy. Good job he's retired. He told me it was down to arthritis.'

'Could be, but listen up.' Stevie grinned 'You'll never guess who his regular driver is.'

'Hit me.' John stirred the onions to keep them from burning. He added a squirt of tomato purée.

'Shane Breen.'

'Who?' John looked over at his friend. 'Doesn't ring any bells.'

'How about if I said Bullyboy's eldest?'

'*Paul* Bullyboy Breen?'

'Yep.'

John started to laugh, He poured a tin of chopped tomatoes into the pan. 'I don't believe it! Now, there's a blast from the past. Must be ten years or more since I saw him.' He shook his head. 'I thought the kid seemed familiar. Wouldn't have put that together in a million years, though. Tell you what, Stevie, I appreciate this.'

'Not why I'm here, John, though I will hold you to some work for the information.'

'A deal's a deal.' John added salt to a pot of boiling water and added a cup of basmati rice. He glanced at his pal. He had a bad feeling that Stevie was about to darken his day. He knew he wouldn't have dropped by just with the info on the car and driver. 'Spit it out, Stevie, you're making the dog nervous.'

'This didn't come from me.'

'You never have to say that to me, Stevie, you know that.'

'I know, lad, I'm sorry.' Stevie sighed and ran his hand across his strawberry blond crew-cut. 'Floyd, the boyo from England, he's been putting together a pretty comprehensive case against Sarah. Word is, he thinks you know more than you're letting on. He's planning to haul you in tomorrow.'

'Fuck. Who's he been talking to?'

'Detective Jim Stafford.'

'Aw, no. No wonder he's got a bad opinion of me. Stafford? He'd pin Shergar's disappearance on me if he'd thought it might stick.'

'Aye, well, there's more. They've found where Wright was staying and managed to get a hold of some of his gear.'

'Go on.'

'From what I can gather yer man had been stalking Sarah, her sisters and you for a few weeks in October. Floyd's got photos, addresses, the works.'

'Right.'

'He never went back to his hotel room after the eighth of November and the van he had been driving was traced to the pound. It had been crushed but the impound details are all on computer.'

John lowered the heat under the rice.

'John, the van was lifted from Fairview.'

And there it was: the blow he had been waiting for. Funny how it didn't seem to matter what he had begun to wonder privately. Fairview, just a stone's throw from where Sarah had been attacked.

'Shit,' he said.

'Look, there's no evidence to say this guy Wright ever met with Sarah. No witnesses or anything like that.'

'Right.'

'But she needs to tell Floyd that. It looks bad with her gone. If there was some way you could get hold of her, get her to talk to this guy . . .'

'I don't know where she is, Stevie.'

'The longer she's missing, the worse this is going to get. Floyd's angling for a warrant for her arrest and, to be honest, the way he's building his case it won't be long before he gets one. Then there's going to be press interest. I don't need to tell you how that's going to play out.'

John switched off the gas under his food. He found he no longer had much of an appetite. He opened the fridge and pulled out two bottles of Krombacher. He offered one to Stevie, who took it without hesitation. He got a bottle opener from the drawer and sat down at the table. 'You're right I need to get to her before he does. But I'm slap bang in the middle of all sorts of shit right now.'

'You think she offed this guy, Wright?'

'You can't me ask that, Stevie. Don't take me wrong, I know we're friends, but you're a guard at the end of the day.'

Stevie nodded. There were indeed lines that shouldn't be crossed, no matter how close the friendship. 'Well, boyo, here's to ya. And another fine mess you seem to have got yourself into.'

They clinked bottles and Sumo, who hadn't taken his eyes off Stevie for the entire time they had been talking, finally relaxed and lay down at John's feet.

Not long after Stevie had left, John fed Sumo, made a cup of instant coffee and drank it standing at the sink overlooking his scabby garden. He really ought to do something about the meadow out there, he thought briefly. Paul Bullyboy Breen . . .

Tom Cooper. Interesting how the paths merged.

He called Rose Butler to let her know how he was getting on, but she was not at home and didn't have an answering machine. He tried the number Jackie had given him, but it rang out. Just before nine he called his sister, half expecting that to be a bust too. But she answered.

'Hello?'

'Carrie, it's me.'

'Let me guess. You're not coming tomorrow night?'

John blinked, trying to remember where he was supposed to be going in the first place.

'No? I figure if you're calling me this late it means you're crying off dinner, right?'

'Shit, I'd forgotten all about that, sorry.'

'Wow, John, being forgotten about always makes me feel so special.' His sister sighed. 'You remembered it was your birthday, though?'

'Nope, not even that. I'm sorry, Carrie. Honest to God, I've so much shit on my mind this week I don't know if I'm coming or going. Look, I'm going to need to ask you a huge favour.'

'What kind of favour?'

'A Sumo-sized favour.'

'Oh, no.'

'It's just for a few days.'

'Oh, John, I love Sumo, you know I do, but he *hates* being here. He gets so miserable – he barks, he growls and he scares the shit out of James.'

'I know, but I wouldn't ask unless I had another option.'

'What's going on? Are you going out of the country?'

'Worse. I've a feeling I'm going to be hauled into a police station tomorrow and you know what that lot are like – you can't guarantee they'll let you back out.'

'Hauled in? For what? What have you done now?'

'Nothing – it's got nothing to do with me. And, by the way, why would you automatically assume it had?'

'Because it's you! Tell me.'

He paused for a second. There was no one in the world he could be more open with than Carrie, but he didn't want to worry her unduly.

'John, tell me what's going on or I won't mind the beast.'

Then again, she always knew how to get him to talk.

'There's a cop over here from London. He's looking for Sarah and seems to think I know where she is – but I don't. I got word earlier that I'm more than likely going to be hauled in for questioning.'

'Why's this guy looking for her?'

'I can't say.'

'You *can't*?'

'I can't. If I could I'd tell you, you know that.'

'She's in trouble, isn't she? That's why she's gone.'

'Maybe.'

'Oh, great – and knowing how much the boys in blue love you there's no knowing how long they'll hold you.'

'Right.'

'All right, I'll take Sumo, but you call me if they're doing a number on you and I'll phone my solicitor Garvin and get him to light a fire under their arses.'

'Appreciate it, sis.'

'Yeah, yeah. Look after yourself, John. Ring me as soon as you're breathing air again.'

He hung up, feeling a little less anxious.

He poured himself a beer and went into the sitting room, put on an Iron and Wine CD and put his legs up.

Alison Cooper, Sarah Kenny, Suzy Brannigan. He laid his head back on the sofa. Why was Alison at Chris Day's home? What did the inclusion of Bullyboy mean? Maybe he should just concentrate on finding the rest of the people on Alison's list – it couldn't hurt. It wasn't like he was breaking sweat for Rose Butler anyway. Least he could do was cover the bases.

While he was thinking about these things, he closed his eyes and drifted off to sleep.

36

Pavel woke up with a start. For a moment he had no idea where he was. He turned his head. There was a lamp beside the bed. He switched it on and squinted at his watch. It was just after ten p.m. He lay for a while, staring up at the ceiling, letting his eyes make shapes of the spackled plaster. His mouth was dry and his head was pounding. Hung-over. It had been a long time since he had felt like that.

He pushed the covers off his naked body and swung his legs out to the side. His stomach lurched and he groaned softly.

The memories came back hard. After the cinema he and Grace had bought a cheap bottle of Polish vodka and drunk it between them. There had been no one in the flat when they'd got back and he and Grace had sat around smoking and drinking. He had sung songs in his native tongue, she had played guitar. They had kissed, and now here he was.

He looked over his shoulder to where her chubby arm lay resting on the indentation his body had left. He reached out and laid his finger on her skin. It was so pale, so warm. He had never seen skin so white before. He withdrew his hand and sat there rigid, awash with self-loathing. How did this honour his sister?

It was no good. He had to get out of there, no matter what happened – he had to get away from this girl. What the hell was he thinking? She was a stupid child, not even his type. What the hell was wrong with him?

He stood up gingerly and dressed as quietly as he could. He need not have worried about making noise – Grace was dead to the world.

He pulled on his T-shirt and looked for his shoes. There was no sign of them. He tried to remember where he had taken them off but he couldn't even remember getting undressed.

He opened the door leading to the living area. For a moment the light blinded him.

Then he saw something that made his blood run hot.

Rick was sitting sideways on the sofa. Pavel's holdall was before him, unzipped. He stepped into the room.

Rick jumped, embarrassed to be caught snooping. 'Yo, hey, man, I thought – look, I know this looks bad and shit but I wasn't going to take anything. I got a right to know who's staying in my house.'

Pavel walked towards him and boxed him as hard as he could in the side of the head, knocking him to the floor. He snatched up his holdall, checked it and zipped it shut.

Rick rolled on the ground with his hands to his ear. 'Ow, fuck me, what the fuck? Ow. Hey, fuck, you freak. You've got a ton of fucking money in there. Why would a busker be carrying money like that around with him? Huh? And what's with the blood, man? There's fucking blood on your fucking clothes, man, a lot of fucking blood. Yah, ow.'

Pavel shoved the holdall under a chair and looked around for his shoes. He found one, then the other.

'You can do the silent shit all you want. I know you're fucking well dodgy, man – I knew when I saw you with her. You don't know Grace – I bet you're an illegal or some shit. I wouldn't be surprised if the cops were looking for you. Yeah, I bet you're fucking wanted or some shit.'

Pavel sat on the chair and put his shoes on. He tied the laces carefully.

'Hey, I'm talking to you.' Rick got to his feet and stepped towards him. Pavel waited. Then, without any warning, he launched himself up and grabbed him by both ears. He brought Rick's head down while he jerked his knee up, smashing the boy's face as hard as he could.

Rick grunted and fell backwards. He lay on the ground gasping, holding his face as his nose bubbled blood. Pavel knelt down, his legs on either side of Rick's chest. He slapped the boy's hand away and leaned close to his face. 'Stupid fuck.'

'Get the fuck off me.' Rick was still trying to act hard but there was sheer terror in his eyes.

Pavel grasped his smashed nose and twisted it. Rick opened his mouth to scream but Pavel clamped his free hand over it. 'Listen, stupid fuck, I tell you, don't be more stupid. Be like blacks, mind business.'

Rick's head twisted back and forth. Tears of pain streamed down his face.

Pavel spat on him and wiped his hand on his victim's T-shirt. He stood up. As he collected the holdall, the door to the bedroom opened and a sleepy, crumpled Grace squinted out. Pavel put his foot on Rick's chest, warning him to stay out of sight and keep his mouth shut.

'Pavel?'

'Go sleep.'

'Are you going somewhere? I thought I heard something.'

'I go for food. Yes?'

'Okay, cool.' She closed the door.

Pavel looked down at Rick.

Rick stared at him with loathing, which Pavel did not mind, but also with fear, which he felt happier about. He took his foot off the boy's chest and stepped over him. He picked up Grace's keys, put on his coat and left the flat. He made his way down the street. He bought milk and two pastries in the twenty-four-hour Spar shop and carried them across the road to a phone box. He dug out a piece of paper from his pocket and dialled a number.

'The Alton Clinic. Please hold.'

Pavel took a bite of his pastry and listened to the some terrible recording of Vivaldi's *Four Seasons* on Pan pipes.

After thirty seconds, the woman was back on the line. 'Thank you for holding. How may I help you?'

'Frieda Mayweather, she is doctor. I want talk with her.'

'Dr Mayweather has left for the day.'

'Give her number, tell her phone, now.'

'Sir—'

'Is important, tell her Flintov calls.'

'What is this in connection with?'

'Tell her Flintov,' he repeated.

'Flintov. Will she know what that is about?"

'Yes.'

'Very good.' She took his number. He hung up.

More Vivaldi. He took another bite of his pastry. He hadn't even had time to chew before the phone rang and a voice crackled in his ear. 'Frieda Mayweather. Who is this?'

He swallowed and wiped away crumbs with the back of his hand. 'I want name.'

'Who is this?'

'Flintov, he could not give me name I want. But he could give to me your name. So *you* will give me name I want.'

'I don't know what you're talking about.'

'Case forty-seven. You think now.'

There was a considerable gap this time and when she spoke again Pavel could hear the caution in her voice. Caution, and something he could not put his finger on – almost excitement.

'You're the person who brought the flowers. I checked. Mad Flowers never sent anybody and there is no one called Ademi working for them.'

Pavel said nothing.

'You were behind Brendan's death too.'

'I want name of girl.'

'Go to hell.'

'You will give.'

'Who the hell do you think you are to threaten me? Do you have any idea who you're dealing with?'

'I am brother of Ana Sunic.'

'Who?'

Pavel clenched his hand around the receiver and slammed it repeatedly against the phone. Then he took a deep breath and lifted it to his ear again. 'I am Pavel Sunic. I will call you in the morning. You will give me name.'

He hung up and left the phone box.

37

Emma Foster was angry at John's intrusion. She was a tiny, tired-looking woman in her fifties and, as she stood facing him on the worn granite steps of a large house overlooking the Dodder river, she reminded John of an angry hummingbird.

It was ten past ten and she was in a pink quilted dressing-gown with matching slippers. A long-haired tabby cat sat just inside the door glaring at him with cat disapproval. 'I'm sorry,' she said, tightening the dressing-gown around her throat with both hands. 'Who are you again?'

'My name is John Quigley. I'm a private detective.'

'Okay, but what do you want? How did you get my name?'

'Your husband was being treated by Dr Alison Cooper for kidney failure late last year. I was hoping I could speak with him.'

'No, you can't. Not unless you can find him, the rotten lousy – may God forgive me – shit.'

John gaped at her.

'He's gone, isn't he? After all I did for him. I nursed him – he had high blood pressure and diabetes – I looked after him and what does he do? As soon as he gets better he ups and leaves me for some floozy he hardly knows.'

She dug a tissue out of a pocket and blew her nose long and hard. 'And now here you are asking me questions. I don't know anything about that man any more. He's cleaned us out. Twenty years we paid into a pension plan and he closed it out without ever saying a word to me about it. I'm telling you now, as the Lord God is my witness, I'll spit in his eye if I ever set eyes on him again.'

John wished she would stop spitting at him.

She waved her hand. 'So what are you here for? What are you bothering me about? Can't you see I'm not well?'

'I'm investigating the death of Alison Cooper. She died this day last week.'

'Yes, I read it in the papers. It was terrible. She was a very lovely woman.'

'I'm sorry for asking, Mrs Foster, but was your husband on a transplant waiting list for long?'

'Ah, he was. He was supposed to lose weight, you see. The surgeon who assessed him said unless he got his diet in order he would not be accepted for transplant. But Allen loved to eat. He loved his food.' Her eyes filled.

'But he got it in the end?'

'He did. Dr Cooper came by and told him herself he was a candidate. Allen was over the moon about it.' She dabbed at her eyes. 'I never believed he'd leave me like that. What sort of person does that at this time in our lives?'

'I'm sorry. It must be hard.'

'He doesn't like it now but I was on that policy and we were married and that's the end of it. If he wants to go running around acting like an eejit with his floozy I won't stop him, but my health is not for sale. I'm waiting next for a letter or something to say he wants to sell this place. I tell you, I wouldn't put it past him. But this house is a family home. I raised my children here. I'll go out of it feet first – I'll tell him that when I see him.'

'Mrs Foster—'

'I mean, the cheek of him.'

'When did he have his transplant?'

'November.'

'And where was it?'

'Well, this is it,' she said, with a vindictive look on her face. 'No one is supposed to know, but he went abroad for it.'

'Excuse me?'

'He went abroad. Dr Cooper arranged it.'

'Abroad?'

'Yes, to a private clinic – Zürich, I believe it was. Now, I didn't go myself. I wanted to go, of course, but he insisted I stay behind. Dr Cooper said she would look after him.'

'And Mercy Hospital set it up?'

'Oh, I don't know now. Certainly Dr Cooper was involved. She picked him up from here and brought him back. He was gone for just eight days.'

'Only eight days? Is that all?'

'Oh, yes. Mind, it took him a good few weeks before he was back to anything resembling normal.' She sniffed. 'He started going to the gym, getting into shape. Next thing I know he's telling me he doesn't want to regret his remaining years and off he goes, gone, just like that.'

On his way back to the car John thought over everything he had learned. Privately arranged transplants in Zürich? Neither Tom Cooper nor Alison's mother had mentioned anything to him about Alison being missing for eight days at a time.

Coleen Clancy was not in when he got to her stone cottage in

Ringsend. He left a message for her and his card. Next he drove to the pricy cul-de-sac in Dalkey that Tobias Johnson called home. He parked the Manta on a neat grass verge outside a large yellow house surrounded by neatly clipped box hedges. It was a well-maintained split-level house with a wraparound porch set in mature gardens.

The double wooden front gates at the beginning of the curved drive were locked but there was an intercom set into the concrete post to the right. John pressed a button and waited. A moment later it crackled. 'Yes?'

'Er, hello, I'm looking for a Sofia Johnson?'

'My daughter is still at school. Can I help you? I'm her father.'

'Mr Johnson, my name is John Quigley. I'm a private investigator. I was wondering if I could talk to you about Dr Alison Cooper – I believe your daughter was a patient of hers.'

'I'm sorry but I have nothing to say about Dr Cooper, other than it's a terrible tragedy, her passing.'

John noted the lack of emotion in his voice. 'Mr Johnson, is your daughter on a transplant waiting list?'

'No, she's not. Goodbye now.'

The intercom went silent.

John debated about ringing again. He stood outside the gate, his curiosity piqued. Why was the man so reluctant to talk to him? Human nature being what it was, he would have expected people to be keen to find out why he was investigating her death. And if his daughter had been on the list, why wasn't she on it now?

He got behind the steering-wheel and lit a cigarette, rolled down the window and started the engine. Before he could move off his phone rang. The number was blocked, but he answered anyway.

''Lo?'

'John?' It was a woman's voice, high and shaky.

'Who is this?'

'John … you've got to help me.'

'Suzy?'

She said something, but he couldn't make out the words. 'What are you saying, Suzy? You need to slow down.'

'He was screaming at me … I don't know what to do any more …' She was sobbing now.

'Where are you?'

'At the flat – hurry, John, please. I'm afraid he might come back.'

'I'll be right there.'

He hung up and gunned the engine to life, pulled out of the cul-de- sac into the traffic and put his foot down, hoping Suzy was being her usual dramatic self. Hoping but not buying it.

38

BLOOD MONEY

Frieda Mayweather was having trouble containing her irritation. She was facing two uniformed guards, neither of whom she enjoyed talking with. 'I just can't believe anyone would hurt Brendan like that. He was a kind and gracious man. He will be greatly missed.'

'He worked for you for how long?' the guard on the right asked.

'Eight years.'

'And did he often miss days?'

'No – that was why I was so worried. It wasn't like Brendan to miss a day, and certainly unlike him not to call if he had to stay away. Oh, poor Brendan. Do you have any idea what happened?'

'Well, no,' the other guard said. 'His car was broken into but nothing was stolen, as far as we can tell. No sign of disturbance at the house, other than the crime scene and—'

'It's an ongoing investigation,' the guard on the left added, the one with the hound-dog eyes and dark five o'clock shadow – Kinsella, his name was. He looked over the top of his notebook at her. 'You say you don't know much about his private life.'

'Well, no.' Frieda glanced down. 'He was a staff member, very trustworthy, very diligent. I'm not in the habit of socialising with my staff. It can lead to problems.'

'Did you know he liked to gamble?'

'No, I certainly did not.'

Kinsella nodded, his eyes never leaving her face. Frieda waited for him to say something else but he did not. He annoyed her – she couldn't get a read on him.

Her phone rang. She picked it up. 'Hold my calls for the moment, please . . . Who? Tell him I'll call him right back.' She hung up. 'Gentlemen, if there's anything else don't hesitate to ask, but I gave my statement to the guard who came yesterday and I'm not sure what else I can offer you.'

'We're aware you gave a statement,' Kinsella said.

Frieda gave him a tight smile. She didn't like the way he was looking at her. 'We're all deeply shocked at Brendan's passing.'

'You've got interesting security here.'

'Oh?'

'I'm sure I recognise one of them.'

Frieda arched an eyebrow. 'You mean Mr Hannity, of course.'

' Derek Hannity, that's him all right. Interesting choice of protection.'

'Mr Hannity was incarcerated a while ago, yes. However, as far as I am aware he has served his time.'

'Mr Hannity killed one man and cut another so badly his own mother didn't recognise him at the hospital. I'm not sure I'd want him on my staff.'

The first cop looked between them, clearly puzzled.

'Did you hire him personally?'

'I hire everyone here personally, Sergeant. I have also an ex-force member on the books, a Mr Dennis Groves. Perhaps you recognised him also.'

'I don't know him.'

'Well, you can't know everyone.' Frieda glanced at her phone, then her watch.

Kinsella and the other guard exchanged a glance. Evidently the interview was over.

'We'll be in touch if we learn anything.'

'Of course.'

After the guards had left, Frieda picked up her phone and called Tobias Johnson. 'Tobias? I'm sorry about that. I was in a meeting. How can I help you? Is Sofia well?'

'She's fine. Look, Frieda, I've had a detective here earlier, asking about Alison Cooper.'

'A detective?'

'A private detective.'

'Oh, I see.'

'Why would a detective be here asking questions about Alison? Why would he automatically come to my home?'

'I have no idea.'

'Well, goddamn it, Frieda, I think you should find out, don't you?'

'I'll look into it and get back to you.' She hung up and pressed her fingers to her forehead. What the hell was going on? First some lunatic had threatened her, then the cops had turned up and now this.

She picked up the phone and dialled Ivan Colbert.

'Mr Colbert's office, how may I help?'

'Fiona, is he available?'

'I'm sorry, Ms Mayweather, he's with a client.'

'Ask him to call me as soon as he's free. Tell him it's urgent.'

'Yes, of course.'

She made another call. 'Saul? Frieda.'

'Frieda, what can I do for you?'

'Alison Cooper.'

'Oh, God, now what?'

'Is a detective asking questions about her?'

'Some idiot was here the other day – why?'

'You don't sound concerned.'

'It's a nothing investigation. Her mother called him in.'

'Who is he?'

'He left his card here. Hold on.' She could hear him shuffling paper in the background. 'Quigley – John Quigley, from QuicK Investigations.'

'Do we have anything to worry about?'

'No, of course not. It was a fishing expedition. He was asking me if I thought she was having an affair, for Christ's sake.'

'Well, that may be, but he called to Tobias Johnson's house today asking about her.'

'Oh.'

'Yes, oh – you should have bloody called me and let me know there was an investigation.'

'Frieda, I'm sure it's nothing. If the police are happy with the findings I can't imagine what this fellow will dredge up. I'm sure he's just stringing the family along to make a few quid. He'll soon run out of people to pester.'

'I really hope so, Saul. We have a lot of interests that wouldn't hold up to much scrutiny. The last thing we want is a twit causing us trouble.'

She hung up and called Tobias Johnson back.

'Well?'

'Nothing to worry about. He's a low-rent called in by the family to look into Alison's untimely death. I imagine he's just checking with everyone who might have known her.'

'I hope you're right.'

'I am, of course.' Frieda glanced at the clock on her wall. 'Unfortunately I have some other bad news.'

'What?'

'Brendan O'Brien is dead.'

'Brendan? Wasn't he the man who—'

'Yes. Let's not say anything else now, please.'

'What happened?'

'From what I can gather he was killed at his home by an intruder.'

'An intruder?'

'Yes. I hate to speak out of turn, Tobias, but the police believe he may have had considerable gambling debts.'

'My God, that's terrible. And someone *killed* him for that? What the hell is wrong with people?'

Frieda flicked a piece of lint from her skirt. 'Well, you think you know a person . . . May the Good Lord have mercy on his soul.' She spent another moment or two reassuring Tobias that all was well and rang off.

Twenty to two, and still no word from Sunic. Part of her hoped he had been hit by a car or some other tragedy had befallen him. But she knew how unlikely that was. He would have to be taken care of and to do that she needed to locate him.

Frieda drummed her fingers on the desk, thinking, using all of her formidable brain to put together a plan of action. By the time the phone rang at two she was ready.

39

It took John Quigley exactly thirty-four minutes to reach the
South Circular Road. He parked in the old convent grounds,
and after Suzy buzzed him in he took the stairs three at a time.
She opened the door wearing the same see-through nightdress
she had worn the day before but this time she and it were
streaked with blood. She had cuts and bruises to her face and a
split lip. Her mascara ran in tracks to her chin.

'What the hell happened to you?'

Suzy fell back against the wall, crying. 'He came at me, John.
I found out he was lying. He told me he was looking after me,
but he was lying. We had this big fight and then I pushed him
and he totally lost it.'

'Where is the fucker?'

'He's gone. He left an hour ago. I'm sorry. I didn't know who
else to call.'

'We need to get you to a hospital.'

'No, no,' she shook her head, 'I'm not going to any hospital.'

John closed the apartment door. He put his arm around her shoulders and walked her up the hall. He opened the door to the living room. It was in complete disarray, with furniture turned over and glass all over the floor. The mirror over the fireplace was smashed and hanging sideways by one screw.

John put Suzy into the hanging white chair and squatted before her to take a closer look at her injuries. After a moment he went into the galley kitchen, opened the fridge and scooped some ice cubes out into a tea-towel. He thought for a second, then dropped some more into a glass, poured vodka over them and added a splash of lime.

'Here, drink this and put that ice up to your eye. You're going to have a hell of a shiner tomorrow – you know that, right?'

'Yeah, thanks.' She took the drink and the ice.

John swept some broken glass off the sofa and sat down. 'So, what happened here?'

She sniffed loudly and looked past John to the window overlooking the grounds below. 'He kept pushing me. I asked him where the money was, why some of Mike's guys hadn't been paid when he'd said they'd been taken care of. He said they had, then I said, "Okay, let's call them." He accused me of calling him liar, and I said, 'Yeah, well, if the cap fucking fits…" He lost it. Started screaming at me. I got scared. I said I was going to me ma's. He tried to stop me, I shoved him and next thing I knew he was hitting me – he just kept hitting me.'

She raised her head to him, but her gaze went only as far as his chin. Tears streamed down her face.

'Don't cry over that tosser. Suzy, listen to me. We're going to get you dressed and then you're going to go to your mam's house for a few days, okay?'

'Are you barking?' She jerked her shoulders back. 'I can't go to her like this! I can't, John, please.'

'And you *can't* stay here. What if he comes back to finish the job? Suzy, you need to go home for a while, be with your own crowd for a bit. It's not safe for you to be on your own.'

She began to cry. 'I can't. It would destroy me ma if she saw me like this. She'd tell Mike and he'd kill Jaffa.'

'Whatever he gets he deserves.'

'It's not him I'm worried about.' She put down her drink and folded herself onto the arm of her chair, sobbing her heart out.

John sighed. He got up, pulled her to her feet and held her close. 'All right, Suzy, stop crying. It's going to be all right.'

She kept crying.

'Dry up your tears, come on now.' He pushed her away from him and bent his head to look at her. 'I need you to get dressed and pack a bag. You can come and stay in mine for a few days while we work out what to do.'

She wiped her eyes with the heel of her hand, smearing her mascara even further across her blotched skin. He thought she said something but he wasn't sure. 'What? What did you say?'

'I s-said th-th-thank you.' She collapsed against him, weeping like a child.

John held her with one hand and slid his mobile phone out with the other. He dialled his sister's number, all the while trying to remember what his nana used to say – what was it? 'It never rains but it pours.' Right at that second he had to agree. She was right. Damn, was that woman ever wrong about anything.

'Carrie? Have you got Sumo?'

'Of course I have – I picked him up earlier.'

'I'm afraid I need him back.'

'What?'

'I'll explain when I come by. See you in about half an hour.'' He hung up before she could blitz him with questions.

'Go on, Suzy, get a bag ready.'

*

'Your sister seems real nice. Real genuine, like.'

'Thanks.'

'I didn't know it was your birthday. I'm some present for you, aren't I?'

John put his camera down. Despite her protests he had documented every cut, scrape and bruise Suzy had, reminding her that it would not be above Jaffa to try to have her arrested and taken to court for assaulting him or some other bogus crap. The skin on her face was darkening as a selection of bruises developed and her left eye was now swollen shut. John had given her two soluble painkillers, but he was worried about her eye. Unfortunately she still refused to go to the hospital and when he tried to insist she had begun to cry again.

'She is,' he said.

Carrie had been shocked when he had arrived to collect Sumo with Suzy in tow, but she had covered it as best she could. She had given John his dog and some food she had ready for him, but she had been frightened. He had promised to ring her and let her know everything was all right.

'You two close?'

'I suppose so. There's only two years between us, and ever since our folks passed on we've sort of relied on each other. You okay? You want me to make you another cup of tea? How's the pain?'

'I'm okay for the moment. Thanks anyway.'

They were in John's living room with the television on, the volume low. John put the lens cap back on his camera and dropped into the easy chair by the coal fire. Sumo was lying on the floor by his feet and Suzy was sitting on the sofa, her legs pulled tightly up under her. Her hair was wet from the shower she had taken and she was wearing a pale pink tracksuit and fluffy slippers, also pink.

'Me and Mike used to be so close. Back in the day we did loads of shit together. Now I hardly ever see him.'

'He worries about you.'

'He worries about his money.'

'That too.'

'You can't tell him about this, John – he'd go fucking mental. You don't know him like I do. Please, John, don't say anything.'

He sighed. 'Okay.'

'I don't know what to do any more.'

'First things first. We need to take care of that payroll. Not trying to give you a hard time or anything, Suzy, but it's Friday and some of the lads at the station have kids. They're living pretty hand-to-mouth.'

'I know, I know.' She picked at the varnish on her thumbnail. 'I don't know why I fell for Jaffa's bullshit, I really don't. He said he loved me. He was even talking about us getting married next year ... Fuck.' She lowered her head onto her hand. 'I'm so fucking stupid.'

'Suze, come on.'

She wrapped her arms around herself and took a deep breath. 'You didn't see him, John. He was like a demon, kept going on and on about the fucking money I'd loaned him, said he wanted to know what you knew about it. I told him nothing, but that I had to pay my brother's crew, all of them. I told him I needed back some of the money I loaned him before the end of the week. And then, like I already said ... he lost it. Started screaming at me that I was a fucking retard and didn't I know how much I'd hurt him by talking to you. He kept saying I was accusing him of something and he didn't like that. Every time he hit me he was yelling that he wasn't a loser ... Then he said I was only a jumped-up cunt ...' She raised her head and looked at him with anguish in her one open eye. 'Who says shit like that to a person they're supposed to love, right?'

'That fucker doesn't deserve you, Suzy. I'm telling you, stop beating yourself up and let's think of a solution.'

She dropped her head to her knees.

'How much money did you give him?'

'A lot.'

'How much?'

'Mike's going to kill me if he finds out.'

'Suzy, how much did you give him?'

She wouldn't look at him. 'Eighteen thousand.'

'Jesus Christ.'

'I know.' She lit a cigarette and smoked it, her hand trembling wildly. 'It's nearly all of the money Mike left me.'

John's phone rang. He pulled it out of his pocket and looked at the screen. He didn't recognise the number so he put it on silent and shoved it back into his jeans. 'Suzy, you need to talk to Mike about this. Folk have got to be paid.'

'I can't – he left me in charge and I've totally fucked this up.'

'Okay, but pretending it hasn't happened isn't going to make it any better. The longer you leave it the worse it'll get. Plus that little shit owns a nightclub so he must have *some* of the money to hand, enough for the wages to be paid anyway.'

'The nightclub's not doing well. That's why he asked me for a loan. I can't ask him for it now.'

'Want me to do it?'

'*No!*'

Sumo's head rose from the carpet. He bared his upper teeth, then looked at John, who scratched him between the shoulder-blades until he laid his head down again.

'How did I let this happen?'

'You fell for a line,' John said. 'You wouldn't be the first and you can be damn sure you won't be the last.'

'I should have known somebody like Jaffa wouldn't be interested in me for me.'

'Hey, stop that shit. Don't say stuff like that. People like Jaffa are users, pure and simple. It wouldn't matter to him who anyone was or what they were like.'

She wiped a tear away with her thumb. 'Mike's going to freak out.'

'Yeah, well, Mike's not one to talk about making mistakes, now, is he?'

That got him at least the trace of a smile. John felt bad for Suzy, but he was also very worried about her. She was vulnerable, and he doubted that Jaffa would let things go so easily. Suzy was his cash cow. Then there was Mike. When he got wind of what Jaffa had done to his sister there was no telling what might happen.

It was one big, stinking mess.

He felt his phone ring. Again he ignored it. 'Suzy, listen, I've got to go out for a while. I'll try not to be long. Things will work out. You're going to stay here for a few days. I'll make up a bed for you in the spare room when I get back. There's food in the fridge or a couple of takeaway menus by the phone if you're hungry.'

Suzy looked at him. 'You really don't have to do this.'

'Yeah, I do – Mike's a friend. *You*'re a friend.'

'Jaffa's going to be looking for me and I don't want to drag you deeper into the shit, John.'

'Oh, Jaysus, don't be worrying about that. That I can do all by my lonesome.'

'You don't know him. He's a vicious little shit when he wants to be.'

John stood up and patted her shoulder. 'I've run across one or two of those before. Trust me, everything's going to be all right.'

She tried a smile, but couldn't pull it off. John slipped out of the room before she could read the anxiety in his eyes. Truth was, he had to speak to Mike and it wasn't going to be pretty. On top of that, Jaffa was an unknown quantity, John still had a case to close out, a cop gunning for him and a missing Sarah Kenny he wanted to find.

Sumo had followed him out into the hall and was gazing at him with his tawny eyes.

'What are you looking at?' He smoothed the hair on the dog's head.

This was a mess, and everywhere he turned he was sinking deeper into it.

40

Pavel crossed his legs and leaned back in the plush chair. The woman, Frieda, was eyeballing him, with the trace of a smile on her lips. She had offered him a drink, but he refused it. He wondered why she had asked him here. He doubted she would give him the name he wanted, and she couldn't call the police, so how would she try to appease him?

'So, let's cut to the chase, Mr Sunic. I really don't know what to make of you. Part of me thinks I should just call the police in and let them deal with you. You killed Brendan O'Brien and murder is still murder, even in this country.'

He shrugged. 'Call.'

She linked her fingers together. 'It's a fantastical tale, though, isn't it?'

'No.'

She smiled frostily. 'I wonder how it might sell as a story. Here at the Alton Clinic we don't deal in body parts. Ours is a clinic specialising in transformations, not transplants. I don't

231

know what you've heard but you're completely wrong, of course. We did not secure a kidney for anyone here. Why would we?'

Pavel said nothing. She was a better liar than most people, he thought. She must think he was wearing a wire or had a tape-recorder of some description.

'What do you think is the point of all this? Even if you called the police and they combed through our records, they would find nothing. We have nothing to hide.'

Pavel tapped the side of his head. 'I have names – Travnic, Flintov, O'Brien. They will find ... reason to look more.'

She smiled icily. 'Well, of course, there is always that.'

'Give me name, I will leave.'

'Oh, of course!' Frieda Mayweather said, throwing her hand up and leaning back in her chair. 'Assuming for a minute that you're not a deluded crackpot and I believed a word of what you're telling me, let's boil it down to the bare minimum. You would expect me to find some poor kid that you say has your sister's kidney and tell her, 'Sorry about the mix-up', then yank out that kidney and send her on her way. Right? That it?'

'No, I want name.'

'Better yet! You'll do the dirty deed yourself – is that it? Ridiculous.'

Pavel stood up. He was untroubled by her refusal. He had known it would be like this, but he had wanted to see what she would offer and make sure she understood his position as he understood hers.

'Your sister was hardly a victim. I am sure she knew what she was getting herself into.'

'Ana is dead.'

Frieda grimaced. 'I didn't know.'

'Now you do.'

'Like Brendan, like Andrei.'

He wagged a finger at her. 'No, not like them.'

'What do you want? Bottom line, what is it?' Frieda said, her voice raw from barely reined-in anger. 'You know I can't give you what you've asked for so you want something else. What is it? Money? I'm sure you have a price in mind.'

'I want only see who are people who use people like cattle. I want see people who will be God, who will pick lives to live and lives to condemn.'

'You think that's what this is about?' Frieda shot out of her chair. 'You bloody naïve idiot. You think you can come here and threaten me like this?'

'I make no threat.'

'Get the hell out of here before I have you arrested.'

'Give name of person forty-seven I will not come back.' He tapped the side of his head with his forefinger. 'Think.'

'I said, get out.'

Pavel picked up his holdall. He shook his head and left without another word.

Before he had reached the end of the corridor Frieda was on the phone. 'Hannity, where are you? . . . Good. He'll be exiting the building in a moment . . . Yes. He's wearing blue jeans, a navy three-quarter length jacket and carrying a dark grey holdall. I want you to follow him and find out where he's going. Can you do that?' She glanced at the wall clock. 'No, be discreet, but stay with him until you're sure . . . Yes, alive.'

She hung up. A moment later her buzzer sounded.

'What?'

'Ms Mayweather, Mr Colbert is here to see you.'

'Send him in.'

She glanced up as her door opened. She could tell from the set of his jaw that he was working himself up to something.

'Frieda, we need to talk.'

'Ivan, sit down.'

He did as she asked.

'I afraid I can't do the surgery tomorrow.'

'What are you talking about?'

'The Corrigan woman. I can't do it.'

'Ivan, this is really not a good time for you to have one of your episodes.'

'I realise I'm probably leaving you a little in the lurch but, Frieda, you offer me very little choice.'

'Choice? *Choice?*' Frieda exclaimed. 'Don't talk to me about choice, you of all people. Let me tell you something. If it wasn't for me you'd be out of a job. You wouldn't have been allowed cut a toenail if it wasn't for some of the choices I made.'

'Frieda, I know you've done a lot for me and I'm very grateful but—'

'A lot? You mean covering your arse, falsifying reports, *lying* under oath, risking my own licence, not to mention jail, and you're going to sit there and talk to me about choice – about being grateful?'

'Frieda—'

'Fifteen years ago you killed that woman, Ivan. You killed her as if you'd taken a gun in your hand and shot her in the head. You were drunk, you were sloppy, and if it hadn't been for me you'd be broke and doing time for manslaughter through negligence.'

Some of the colour drained from Colbert's face.

'And I covered for you. I've always covered for you. Now, you're going to fix that girl for me and you're going to make her family very happy. I don't want to hear anything more about choices. You made yours a long time ago and I made mine. This is our path.'

Colbert stood up shakily. He turned and walked to the door. 'Propofol.'

'What?'

'They found propofol during Alison's autopsy.'

'I see. Your friend was depressed, Ivan. She had issues.'

'She had issues with you and your business. But I wrote Alison's prescriptions and I never wrote her one for propofol.'

'What the hell are you going on about?' Frieda bristled. 'Why are you bringing this up?'

'You saw Alison the day she died.'

'You think I drugged her with propofol? Have you lost your mind?'

'I know she threatened you, Frieda. And now she's dead.'

'You need to keep your head straight, Ivan, and your imagination under control. There's a lot more at stake than you seem to realise. And, Ivan, keep off the damn sauce for a few days. I need you to have a steady pair of hands. Get out and don't ever mention propofol to me or anyone else again.'

41

Pavel let himself into the flat using the spare key Grace had given him. He found Grace sitting cross-legged on the floor by the sofa. Her hair was down, spilling loose and curly over her shoulders. She was reading a glossy magazine.

She looked up. 'Hey, you're back – you were gone ages. What's all that stuff?'

'Food.'

He passed her the bags of groceries he had picked up in the supermarket. Grace scrambled to her feet and took them from him.

'You didn't have to do that.' She peeked inside and gave a squeal. 'Holy shit, pasta and cheese and all sorts! Wow, thanks, that's way fucking cool of you.'

Pavel did not move from the door. She glanced at him, and something in his expression wiped the smile from her face. 'What is it?'

'I want say goodbye and thank you.'

'Oh. You're leaving?' She sank back down, letting the bags rest by her thigh. 'Well, do you have to go right now?'

'Is better I go.'

'I bet you haven't even eaten anything all day and you've brung all this food. You could stay for a while, have something to eat. Rick's gone to work so we'd have the place to ourselves.'

'Good.'

'I think he had a fight with someone.' Pavel said nothing. 'You should eat something.'

Pavel tried to think of Ana, he tried to think of Stolvat and Ademi, his time in the prison, the blonde woman with the dead eyes he had spoken to earlier. He wanted to turn and go, run down the street, book into a shit-hole and lie down until the night claimed him. 'Okay, I will eat.'

'Cool!' She kissed him impulsively on the cheek and danced off into the kitchen. She began clattering pot and pans around. After a moment she returned. 'You know, I'd like to make you spag bol.'

'Okay.'

'But, here's the thing.' She pulled a face. 'See … this is going to sound really stupid, but, well …'

Pavel tilted his head.

'I actually don't know how to make it.'

Pavel gaped at her in disbelief.

'Don't look at me like that. We normally just eat toast, noodles and sandwiches and chipper food, that sort of thing.'

Pavel removed his jacket and tossed it over the sofa. 'Open beer. I will show how make food.'

'Open beer! Now, *that* I can do.'

Pavel frowned at her giddiness and rolled up his sleeves. What kind of country was this where a woman could not cook? He entered the kitchen, opened the bags and washed a chopping board. He set Grace to peeling onions while he browned the mince.

Grace opened two beers, turned on the radio and sang along to some Stevie Wonder track. Pavel shook his head. She really was a stupid young woman – but she had a hell of a voice.

'Come on, Pavel, let loose for once.' She bounced her hip off his.

Outside Hannity wrote the address of the flat on a scrap of paper. Then he made a phone call. 'Got him.'

'Good,' Frieda Mayweather said. 'Come back now. There is something we need to discuss.'

42

John parked the Manta under a street-light and stuck the disabled sign on the dashboard. He crossed his fingers that the car would be still there and untouched when he returned. When it came to parking he didn't know what he feared most: clampers or car thieves. One crowd was as bad as the other, he figured.

He crossed the road and entered the side of door of a decrepit pub just off Dorset Street. It was a long, narrow building, with a dull copper bar at one end and a scuffed pool table at the other. A group of scobie-looking teenagers played pool and sipped bottles of beer they had no right to be drinking. They cut their eyes when he came in. John reckoned they had ID even if it was never asked for. That was the way kids were, these days.

The bar was half empty, not surprising for a midweek night. A few local heads sat about sipping slow pints. Conversations were sparse and most of the drinkers appeared to be watching a football match on a television bolted to the wall just over the doors to the toilets. Nobody looked at John directly, but he knew everyone watched him as he made his way along the bar. The stools were conspicuously empty. Nobody sat at the bar any more: it was too risky to have your back to the door – you couldn't tell who might come in behind you and your reaction time might be hampered. This had been proven a few years before when two men wearing motorbike helmets had stepped inside and blasted two brothers off their stools, sending one to the great bar in the sky. The other found a different establishment to frequent.

John nodded to the barman. A customer watched him approach with feigned disinterest. John slipped onto the stool beside him. It was Paul Bullyboy Breen, owner of said bar, not that many knew it. 'Hey, Bully, how's tricks?'

Bully glanced at him. 'What tricks?'

John grinned. Bully had always been a burly man, but now he was running to fat. He was pasty-faced and wore his thinning hair slicked at the sides and tied with a piece of rawhide into a ponytail less than an inch long. 'Long time no see. How are you keeping?'

'What do you want?'

'Can I buy you a drink?'

'I got one.'

'All right. How about a word?'

'Take two – fuck off.'

John signalled to the barman, who appeared not to notice. 'Didn't know you were out and about again, Bully.'

Bully snorted. 'You mean didn't get my card, Quigley? Fucking post, these days.'

John was unbothered by his attitude. There had been a time – long before – when he and Bully had got on pretty well, not friends exactly, but well enough to be civil. Bully had drunk in the bar where John had worked and John had often turned a blind eye to his other activities. Back in the day Bully had been a hustler and small-time drug-dealer. He had made all-right money, nothing major, but in his impatience to go up the ladder he had stepped over the wrong line once too many times. When he had tried passing off a brick in the pool hall in Crumlin, despite it being very much a no-go patch, the wrong ears had got to hear of it. On Bully's next visit to the hall he'd been taken out back and had had it explained to him unceremoniously that his presence would be tolerated no longer. To make the point even clearer, a bottle had been smashed over the back of his head, leaving a gash that had needed nearly forty stitches to close it.

Of course, Bully hadn't got his nickname for nothing. The following week he had sent an unknown cousin along in his place. The cousin was treated to much the same lesson as Bully, but unlike Bully, he had tried to save himself from the beating by squealing like a stuck pig. Word got back to Bully that his card was marked.

Rather than get bopped in the raw, Bully enhanced his reputation for stupidity by purchasing a gun to protect himself. The only problem was that when Bully got stopped and searched – as he routinely was – the same gun, newly purchased, was found to have been used in the attempted shooting of another drug-dealer some months earlier. Faced with uneven odds and bemused Gardaí, who knew he was innocent, Bully had two choices: declare where he had got the gun, take a lighter sentence and hang that particular scobie out to dry or, ding ding, keep his big yap shut and take a longer spell inside.

Not much of a choice, really. Bully had kept his yap shut and, stupidity or not, his silence had elevated his worth on the street: the initial contract on his fat head was rescinded.

That had been nearly fifteen years ago, when Bully was a

younger and more amenable person. Now he was a hardened, jail-roasted, street-savvy thug. He didn't have a whole lot of time for private investigators, shared past or not.

'I was looking for your youngest lad. Shane, isn't it?'

'You see him here?'

'No, but I'm guessing you know where to find him.'

'What do you need to talk to him for? That kid's straight. What's your business with him?'

'He's driving someone I'm interested in.'

Bully took a sip of his drink. He made no dramatic movement and gave no outward sign of tension. But John knew he was on alert. 'You still got that tattoo, Bully? The one of the two men standing back to back?'

'What do you want, Quigley?'

'You remember a guy called Tom Cooper?'

'Yeah.'

'His wife killed herself last Friday.'

'I heard.'

'Didn't see you at the funeral.'

'So?'

'So I'm surprised you didn't go to pay your respects. Seeing as how I'm guessing he has *something* to do with your kid having that job.'

'I told you, that kid is clean. Stay the fuck away from him. People like you drag dirt wherever you go. I don't want none on that lad.'

'Must be handy for Tom to keep an eye on Alison's pal Ivan with the kid driving him.'

'I won't tell you again, Quigley. Don't bring shit down on that boy. He's straight.'

'Fair enough. I'll find him through the usual channels. I just thought the polite thing would be to speak with you first. For

old times' sake. Plus I didn't want to run it through his employer
– it makes them nervy, having somebody asking questions.'

'How come you're interested in his passenger?'

'He might have been knocking boots with someone I'm
investigating.'

'Just you looking?'

'Well, the woman's dead, but the cops aren't involved. They
might be interested in the future, they might not.'

Bully glanced at his watch. 'If I get the kid to talk to you, you
keep his name out of any shit you stir up.'

'Do my best.'

'Your *best* means fuck-all to me.'

John sighed. 'We should do this more often.'

'I mean it, Quigley. That kid has a chance at a straight life so
don't fuck with his game plan.'

'Bully, I swear, if it can be done without mentioning him
anywhere I'll make sure it stays that way.'

He left the bar. Outside, he was relieved to see the Manta
remained untouched.

Less than an hour after he had arrived home, a knock at the
door sent Sumo into a barking frenzy. When he opened it, he
found Bully Breen and his son Shane standing on the doorstep.
'Hold on a sec.' He put Sumo into the sitting room with Suzy
and shut the door. He ushered his guests into the kitchen.

'Still got the wolf, then,' Bully said.

'That I do.'

'Shane, this is John Quigley. An old associate of mine.'

The boy nodded to John. He was taller than either man, but
slightly built. He had dark hair and the same pug nose as his
father. He couldn't have been much more than twenty and
seemed nervous, but not overly so. His eyes were hazel and he
looked directly at John when he nodded hello.

'You could have just called, Bully, there was no need to—'

Bully's upper lip curled. 'You wanted to talk to the lad. He's here, so talk.'

John offered them chairs but they both refused. John leaned against the sink and folded his arms across his chest. 'Shane, you're the driver for a man called Ivan Colbert, aren't you?'

'Yes, I am.'

John liked that – 'yes', not 'yeah'.

'What age are you?'

'Nineteen.'

'You're very young to be a professional driver.'

'This lad's been driving since he was old enough to see over a steering-wheel,' Bully said, with undisguised pride. 'Got his full licence the week he turned eighteen, been a full-time driver nearly as long. He's going to own and operate his own fleet one day soon. Aren't you, lad?'

'I hope so,' Shane said, smiling shyly at his father.

'Did your father tell you why I wanted to see you?'

'He said you wanted to talk to me about Mr Colbert.'

'That's right. What can you tell me about him?'

'He's a consultant. He works for the Alton Clinic. He directs surgeries and stuff. You know, he tells people what they need to get done, pulling skin tighter, injecting that stuff into their faces that fills out wrinkles and makes skin smooth – what do you call it? Botox.'

'He does cosmetic surgery?'

'Yes, but not personally as far as I know.'

'How long have you been driving him?'

'Nearly ten months now.'

'What's he like?'

'He's okay, doesn't talk much, but that's fine by me.'

John took out Alison Cooper's photo and passed it to him. 'You recognise this woman?'

'That's Dr Cooper. She died last week.'

'How do you know her?'

'She's a friend of Mr Colbert.'

'What sort of friend?'

'What do you mean?'

'What is the nature of their relationship?'

'I don't know about *nature*, but I think she works with him sometimes.'

'Are you saying she works at the Alton?'

'I'm not sure. I don't think so.'

''So what do you mean?'

'I don't know, they talk medical stuff a lot.'

'Is that all they talk about?'

'Huh?'

John cocked his head. 'I mean, did you ever see her and Colbert get ... cosy?'

'No.' He shook his head. 'Nothing like that.'

'You never got the impression she and Colbert were more than just work colleagues?'

Shane grinned. 'Mr Colbert? No way.'

'Why do you say that?'

Shane looked at his father. 'I don't want to get in any trouble.'

'Why would you be in trouble?'

'I dunno, I just don't feel right talking about this. Mr Colbert is pretty decent to me.'

John felt his curiosity rise. 'Shane, Alison Cooper is dead. I think it's admirable that you are a discreet person, but I need to find out what happened to her. So far the only person she's been linked to other than her husband is this guy Colbert, and if they've been having an affair I need to know.'

'I'm just saying, I only drive for Mr Colbert, I don't know nothing about his private business.'

'He ever make romantic dates with her? Late-night hotel stops, weekends away—'

'Look, I never seen Mr Colbert with any woman – know what I mean?'

'No.'

'He's not into women.'

'He's gay?'

'Yeah.'

'He ever try anything funny with you?' Bully said, sounding aggrieved.

'No, Dad.' Shane rolled his eyes. 'It's not like that.' He turned back to John. 'Look, he's sound. He's never tried anything with me, honest.'

John sighed. Another theory had just gone out of the window.

'Look, mister, this job is deadly – I get paid well and I get to drive top-of-line motors. Please don't cause problems for me.'

'I won't. I already told your dad and now I'm telling you that I'll try my best to keep your name out of anything I turn up.'

Shane looked at Bully, his face a mixture of resentment and resignation.

Bully never took his eyes off John. 'We're even now, right?'

'Sure.'

'I don't want to see you round the bar no more.'

'Scout's honour.' John held up two fingers.

'Fuck you and your honour,' Bully said. 'Come on, son.'

'Who was that?' Suzy asked, when John joined her in the sitting room.

'An old pal.'

'Jesus, John, do all your friends talk to you that way?'

'Just the ones who know me.' He took a seat by the fire and drummed his fingers on the arm of the chair.

'What's eating you?'

'I don't know. Something's staring me right in the face and I can't see it.'

'How do you know?'

'Just a feeling.'

She lit a cigarette. 'Your dog isn't as vicious as I thought he was.'

'He's a good boy, really.' John patted Sumo's head.

'You miss her, don't you?'

'Who?'

'You know who.'

John shrugged. 'I've got to make a phone call or two.'

Suzy curled her feet under her and raised the remote. 'Take your time.'

43

Pavel couldn't sleep. He had an ugly feeling he had made a mistake in meeting with the woman, and now he was making another. He knew he should have left when he'd said he was going to, but once again he had allowed himself the luxury of a warm bed and an eager, soft body. He understood his weakness: after so long in prison it felt good to be with a woman, especially a woman as enthusiastic as Grace. He was a fool, he thought, a stupid fool led by his dick when he should have been following his brain. She was a needy young girl and he had no business messing around with her.

At twenty past eight the next morning he made his way to the end of the street to use the phone box. He called the Alton and asked to speak to Frieda. He didn't really think she would be there, but she surprised him by coming on the line.

'Enough time, I want name,' Pavel said.

'You know that's not going to happen, don't you? I'm very sorry your sister died, but I cannot help you.'

Pavel leaned against the glass. 'This is mistake.'

'I don't know what you think you're going to achieve but you must understand that the people who—'

Pavel hung up. He leaned his head against the phone and exhaled deeply. What had he expected? Had he been stupid enough to think a bitch like that would crumble at the first sign of trouble? Had he really expected her to roll over so easily?

He cursed softly. All the bloodshed, all the hate had brought him to this place and he would not be thwarted now. Not by a soft bed and not by a dead-eyed woman. She thought she had him ringed in. She would soon see how much she had underestimated him.

He stepped out of the phone box and walked to the local shop. He bought cigarettes and a can of Red Bull. He lit one and walked back towards the flat. A light rain had begun to fall when he had been on the phone. He kept his head down and his hands in his pockets. When he reached the block he hurried down the wet metal steps and put Grace's key in the door. As he turned it a hand clamped hard on the back of his neck, a needle was plunged into his upper arm and he was shoved roughly into the flat. He heard a voice say, 'Goddamnit, hold him still.'

He heard doors opening, then Rick yelling, 'What the fuck's going on?"

Pavel managed to shrug off his attacker, but when he tried to take a step away the world tilted at a crazy angle and the next thing he knew the floor came rushing up to meet him.

Before he hit the deck he became aware his hands were numb and he could not form words. Before his eyes closed he saw Rick running, naked. The boy jumped the couch but got his feet tangled in the loose-cover and went down, hard.

The man who had pushed him through the door pulled a gun from his waistband and pointed it. Pavel saw Rick's ruined nose as he turned and put up a hand to shield himself.

The man pulled the trigger. Rick fell back and was still, half of his face gone. The man stepped over him and shoved open the door to Grace's bedroom.

Pavel heard her scream, then two dull popping sounds. After that, Grace was silent. Pavel's eyes closed.

'She said he had a holdall with him,' Derek Hannity barked. 'Find it, Terry.'

Terry went off to search the bedrooms and returned with it a few minutes later. 'Got it.'

'We need to make sure there's nothing else that connects the clinic to here.'

Within minutes they had turned the apartment upside-down professionally. Satisfied, Hannity told his accomplice to bring the car around.

The traffic was barely moving, and people were hurrying to work, umbrellas raised against the downpour. No one took any notice of them carrying the unconscious man to the car and, if they did, they decided it was none of their concern. They laid him on the back seat and Hannity threw a blanket over him.

They climbed into the car. Hannity took the passenger seat. He was tall and broad-shouldered, with little or no excess fat anywhere on his body.

Terry was much the same shape as his boss, but he was shorter and younger. He was also more excitable and nervous, which irked the hell out of Hannity.

He removed a mobile phone from his pocket and keyed in a number. The call was answered immediately. 'We got him,' he said.

'Call me when you're at the gate. I'll meet you downstairs.'

'Right.' Hannity looked over his shoulder at the prone man. He was breathing raggedly and he wondered at the dose he had administered. She wanted him alive, and was not the sort of woman who allowed for cock-ups. That much he knew.

Terry started the engine. He was pale and sweating heavily. As they were driving away he glanced at Hannity. 'I don't like shit like this. It's not what I signed on for, Derek.'

'You don't have to like it.'

'Who the fuck is this guy and how is he any kind of threat to her business anyway?'

'You ask too many questions.'

'I thought she'd be smarter than that.'

'She is smarter than that.'

'Fuck – what if someone saw us going in there? You didn't have to shoot them, Derek, they were just fucking kids.'

'They were witnesses.'

'Still . . . fuck, man.'

Hannity wished he would shut up. Terry was married only a few months and he worried ridiculously over the most mundane things. Hannity disliked him more with each passing day, but Terry was the youngest brother of Ed Loach and Hannity had done time inside with Loach and respected him as much as he respected any man. Which had been enough to give his twerp of a brother a job and enough to keep from throttling him.

'Keep it cool and don't blow through any lights,' he said. 'We're not going anywhere in this traffic anyway so stop revving the fucking engine like you're in Le Mans.'

'What do you think she'll do to him?'

'How should I know?'

'I don't like her, man, she freaks me out.'

'I already told you, you don't have to like shit, just do your job.' Hannity turned his head to cut off any other attempt at conversation and stared out the rain-soaked streets. Clouds hung low over the buildings and the traffic was bumper to bumper by the time they had reached the Quays. Terry whistled through a gap in his teeth until Hannity told him to knock it off.

Hannity put on the radio. He didn't care what Mayweather had in store for Pavel. That wasn't his concern. It wasn't anybody's concern. The sooner Terry accepted that the better.

Neither man spoke until they approached the Alton Clinic. As soon as they pulled through the gates Hannity made a quick call. They drove into the underground car park.

Frieda Mayweather stood waiting by a service lift with a trolley. Unusually she wore a white lab coat. He had never seen her dressed in anything other than a suit. She approached and glanced into the back seat. Terry pulled the blanket down. She grunted her satisfaction upon recognising Pavel. She looked at Hannity and he was struck as always by the strange light in her eyes. He had only known one other person with that kind of intensity and he was long gone from the world, thankfully.

'Was there any trouble when you took him?'

'None.'

'Fallout?'

'Two.'

'Okay, get him out of the car and onto this. Come on, hurry.'

They lifted Pavel out and deposited him on the trolley. Frieda Mayweather folded a white sheet over him, leaving only his head exposed. She put the holdall under the sheet at his feet and, with Terry's help, wheeled him into the lift.

Hannity stepped forward. 'This guy's going to cost you extra. I never agreed to snatch-and-grabs.'

She stared at him. He stopped the door closing with an outstretched hand. She looked at it, and after a moment he removed it. She gave him one last look as the doors closed and she disappeared from view.

44

Suzy called her mother just before John left the house. She said she was fine, but that she was staying with a friend for a while. John wasn't really paying attention to what she was saying or how she said it, but he wasn't surprised to take a call from Mike Brannigan before he had reached Portobello.

'I need you to find out what's going on with Suzy. I've had me ma on the phone freaking out.'

'I know what's going on.'

'Well?'

'She's staying at mine for a few days. Jesus, do you have an office in there as well?'

'Why's she staying with you?'

'She's had a bit of a falling out with the boyfriend.'

'Yeah?'

'Yeah.'

'What sort of a falling out?'

'Mike, I really think you should talk to Suzy—'

'I'm talking to you.'

John sighed. 'He did a number on her.'

'That fucking prick. How bad is it?'

'Nothing major, just a few cuts and bruises and a black eye. I took photos in case she wants to press charges. She'll be okay but she doesn't want your mother to see.'

'Me ma's not stupid, she knows something's up.'

'Suzy'll be fine. Look, Mike, that's only some of it. Yer man has most of her money.'

'Does he, now?'

'Mike, listen. She didn't want to tell you any of this because she doesn't want you doing anything stupid. You're inside, right, but you'll be out in no time. You need to stay out of this.'

'You don't worry about me. Listen, take this number down.' John hastily scribbled it on a notepad he kept in the car. 'That's a friend of mine. I need you to call over to him if you get a chance. He'll cover the lads' wages for this and last week.'

'Okay. What about next week?'

'You don't worry about next week.'

'Mike—'

'Just get that money and dig the lads out.'

'Mike, listen to me—'

Mike hung up. When John redialled he got an electronic voice telling him the number was not in service.

'Shit.' John drummed his fingers on the steering-wheel. He had a bad feeling about that call, a very bad feeling indeed. He checked his watch. What to do? Shit, why was everything so complicated? Well, what could he do? Mike knew now and that was not exactly John's fault – well, it was, but it couldn't be helped. As Mike had said, their mother had known something was up anyway. What was the point in lying?

The traffic inched along. John fumed silently. He needed to start tidying shit up. First this goddamned waste-of-time case.

He would spend the morning chasing down the last two names on the list from Alison Cooper's agenda and speak to them. Then he needed to see Rose Butler and tell her he was sorry but that, as far as he could make out, her daughter had been depressed and had more than likely killed herself. After that he'd go and collect the money for the lads in the radio station, get Suzy sorted, and *then* try once and for all to get the near impossible Sid on the phone. Easy, right?

Yeah, right.

He was in for a more unpleasant surprise when he reached his office. He had just unlocked the street door when a man approached him. 'John Quigley?'

'Yes?'

'Could you come with us, please?'

'Us?'

The man indicated he should look behind him. John did so and found himself staring into a pair of hooded eyes. They belonged to a man with a podgy, pockmarked face and thick, oily dark hair. Indian, John thought, He looks like an Indian – Native American, he corrected himself.

'You're a hard man to get hold of, Mr Quigley.'

English accent.

'Floyd, right?'

'That's right.'

'Caught me at a bad time, I'm afraid.'

Floyd smiled. 'That so?'

'Yep.'

'I'm hoping you'll manage to make time to speak with me today.'

'Boys, come on, it's Saturday.' John looked at the keys in his hand. 'You got a warrant for me?'

'As a matter of fact I do.' Floyd produced it with a rather theatrical flourish and gave it to John to read.

'All right, I'll come in with you, but I'm telling you right now, I have no idea where Sarah Kenny is and I haven't spoken to her in months.'

'Let's go,' Floyd said, leaning close as though he expected John to make a run for it.

Twenty-five minutes later John was sitting on a hard plastic chair in an airless office overlooking the overly neat gardens of Harcourt Terrace. Floyd sat opposite him, the other officer to his right. A tape-recorder lay between them.

'How long have you and Sarah Kenny been partners?'

'You going to read me my rights?'

'Do you think you're under arrest?'

'I hadn't a whole lot of say coming in here.'

'Floyd smirked.'

'You didn't get a warrant for the laugh. I'm here now, let's roll.' John leaned closer to the tape-recorder, 'But I'm glad this is only an *informal* chat.'

'How long did—'

John's mobile rang. He took it out and glanced at the screen. Mike. He pressed end. Mike would get the message. 'What were you saying, Bud?'

'How long did you and Sarah Kenny work together?'

'Five – no, six years now.'

'You two are close, I hear.'

John shrugged. 'I thought so, but you never really know a person, do you, Officer?'

'I don't know. Do you?'

'You ever answer a question?'

'Are you asking me one?'

'Does it sound like I'm asking you a question?'

The corner of Floyd's mouth twitched. He opened a cardboard folder and slid a page across the desk to John. It was an arrest sheet. The photo accompanying it showed a man staring at the camera, good-looking, with ice blue eyes and Slavic cheekbones. His expression suggested he was somewhat displeased with his surroundings.

'That's Victor Wright,' Floyd said.

'And?'

Floyd slid across another piece of paper, a copy of a marriage certificate. John read two names: Sarah Kenny and Victor Wright. They had married on 13 June 1998 in a register office in Slough. 'This man was your partner's husband.'

'Once more for the cheap seats at the back,' John said. '*And?*'

'Your partner's now deceased husband.'

'Where do I send the mass card?'

'Funny guy,' Floyd said, without an ounce of humour in his voice. 'Did you know about this man?'

'Can't say I did.'

'I wonder why that is?'

'No idea. Maybe Sarah thought I wouldn't have much in common with him.'

'You had her in common.'

'I see. So this guy's dead and he was married to my ex-partner. Is that it?'

'Not at all.'

'So why am I here?'

'What can you tell me about Sarah Kenny?'

'She likes cloves.'

'Excuse me?'

'She likes cloves. Not me, they make me want to puke – I think it's like licking the top of a battery. But she likes them. She gets those clove sweets sometimes and eats them in the car and I swear to God they turn my stomach.'

Floyd's smile got a little strained. John liked that.

'You're really not helping matters here, Mr Quigley.'

'No? Didn't find any cloves on the body, I take it.'

'How did Sarah seem the last time you saw her?'

'Tipsy. She'd been to an art sale.'

'That would have been the night of the twentieth of November,' Floyd said. John noticed he brought up the date without having to refer to any notes.

'If you say so. I don't remember.'

'You don't remember the last time you saw your *close* friend and business partner?'

'I didn't place a lot of importance on it at the time.'

'So, on that date did she mention to you she might be leaving Ireland?'

John thought of that last night, how Sarah's dark eyes had searched his face, the feel of her lips on his. 'No. She didn't.'

'Don't you find that a little odd?'

'She's a grown woman. I'm not her keeper.'

'You friend and partner ups and leaves without a word, and you don't find it strange. Weren't you worried something had happened to her?'

'She left me a note.'

'Ah – do you still have it?'

'Nope.'

'Were you and Sarah romantically involved?'

'What business is that of yours?'

Floyd studied him. 'You're angry.'

'I'm hungry, not the same thing – well, maybe a little angry. We'll call it hangry.'

'I believe you. I don't think you had any idea she was leaving.'

'I already told you that, along with the I-don't-know-where-she-is part.'

'Would it surprise you to know Victor was staying here in a bed-and-breakfast back in late October?'

'I didn't know the man. If you'd told me he was a cross-dressing circus midget I wouldn't be surprised.'

Floyd slid another photo across the table, this time of John and Sarah standing outside the hardware shop on Wexford Street.

John felt a little jolt. Sarah had her hands on her hips, a bemused expression on her face. What had we been talking about? he wondered.

'A lot of photos like this were found in Victor Wright's belongings.'

'I'm glad he caught my good side.'

'Want to know what I think?'

'Do I really get a say in that?'

'I think Wright was here because he was stalking his ex-wife. I think he contacted her. Perhaps he wasn't so blasé about her leaving him to rot in a prison cell as you seem to be about her going.' He leaned across the table. 'I think Victor Wright died in this fine city of yours. And I think Sarah Kenny, your good friend, was the one to kill him.'

'You think? You don't know? Why don't you know? You have a body, right?'

'Yes.'

'So where did you find him?'

'Why is that important?' Floyd glanced at the other officer, narrowing his eyes. 'Why did you even ask that?'

'You said you *think* he was killed here. Why don't you *know* he was killed here?'

'His body was found on a beach in Wales.'

'Wales?' John laughed, 'I can tell you now, Sarah didn't pop over to Wales to kill some ex-husband, as far as I know.'

'I don't believe she did either. The costal guard confirms that the channel currents could very easily have carried his body to Wales from Dublin.'

'That's a bit of stretch, isn't it?'

'And then there's the van he was driving. It was impounded from Fairview. Sarah lived in Clontarf in October, didn't she? Pretty close by, wouldn't you say?'

'Her mother lived there.'

'But she was staying with her mother for a spell last year.'

'Yes.'

'Funny he never came and collected his van.'

'Maybe it broke down.'

'I don't think so.' Floyd looked at him for a while, then smiled slyly. 'It gets a little more curious. I spoke to Belinda, the nurse hired to look after Sarah's mother when she was diagnosed with early-onset Alzheimer's. She told me Sarah was acting very strangely around that time, that she insisted Belinda and her mother move in with her sister and her husband for a few days. Now, why do you suppose she would do that?'

'She probably needed a break. She was exhausted and had taken on a hell of a lot of responsibility.'

'I can tell you're very fond of Sarah.'

'So?'

'So if she came to you and said a man was threatening her, you'd feel protective of her, wouldn't you?'

'I suppose I would.'

'Would you kill for her?'

John looked him straight in the eye. 'Yes, I would. But not murder.'

'Did you kill Victor Wright?'

'No, I didn't.'

'Do you think Sarah killed her ex-husband?'

'No, I don't.'

Floyd looked at him for a long time.

John felt a bead of sweat run down between his shoulder-blades. 'Are we done here?'

'I will find her, you know. The longer she stays missing the worse it is for her. You know that.'

John pushed his chair back and stood up. 'We could have had this chat on the street.'

'I suppose we could,' Floyd said.

The muscles in John's jaw bunched, but he opened the door and closed it softly on the way out. He wouldn't give Floyd the satisfaction of slamming it. He wouldn't let him see how rattled he was.

45

Pavel's hearing returned first. He became aware of a beeping sound, and his own breathing. He attempted to open his eyes, but the lids were heavy and his limbs felt weirdly disjointed. He was trembling, the shaking intermittent and painful. He took one breath, then another, pulling air deep into his lungs. He had been doped up before and felt reasonably sure he could control his body. All he needed was a little time.

Finally he managed to force open his eyes. He waited for them to adjust to the light. He was in a room, with curtains pulled across a window and a single light burning over his bed. There was a machine beeping in the background and he had an IV drip in his arm.

He was in a hospital.

He tried to turn his head but couldn't move it. For a while he drifted in and out of consciousness.

He had a bad ache behind his eyes. He blinked, trying to focus on the curtain. He tried to think. He remembered walking, then a man's voice. He remembered being pushed into the flat.

He remembered Grace's terrible scream.

He let his eyes drift shut again.

He thought of her lying sleeping in the early-morning light. He had brought the men there. His actions had caused her death.

He heard the door click. He opened his eyes a fraction and looked through his lashes.

A cool hand pressed against his neck and rested there for a few seconds. He could smell perfume.

'I know you're awake.'

He recognised her voice immediately.

'Can you hear me?'

He pushed his eyes open but when he tried to speak he found he could not.

Frieda Mayweather lifted his eyelid and shone a light into one of his eyes, then the other. She checked his pulse and the IV in his arm. 'I find myself wondering why a man of your obvious intelligence and determination should have let it come to this.'

She rested her hands on the metal guardrail of his bed. Pavel stared at them. Her skin seemed unnaturally smooth. She wore a wedding band and no other jewellery.

'I suspect you probably think me a cruel person – and, looking at things from your perspective, I would probably feel the same.'

Pavel blinked. He wished he could move his arms. If he could he would grab her and wring her neck.

'When Saul and I first spoke about the dire state of transplantation in this country we were just talking, you know. It was a simple conversation over a few glasses of wine. I never dreamed it would come to something like this.'

She glanced at Pavel.

'This is awkward, I know. You're lying there and you're probably thinking that everything I do or say seems self-fulfilling and cheap. Your sister is dead, you feel anger. But you must understand what is at stake here, Pavel. What we do, what we strive to do, is restore life.'

She pulled up a chair, sat down and crossed her legs. She smoothed the sheet where it had come loose.

'When people come to me they are already dead. Not literally, of course – I'm sure you know that – but for most of them death is waiting in the wings. They are face to face with finality. They sense their time running out in days, hours, minutes. They've tried everything but to no avail. The lucky ones are waiting on lists for donors, trying to hang on, but every day is one day closer to the grave and they know that. The unlucky ones have been told "No, I'm sorry, no life for you, no hope. Go home, be with your family." You would need a heart of stone not to feel for them. They have children and loved ones, commitments, and they're *afraid*. They're afraid they won't make it another day, they're afraid they won't be around long enough to receive our call and be saved. They live every day knowing their future is hanging on charity, on the goodwill of the grieving. Can you imagine living that life? Living with a hammer poised over your head? Knowing that every breath you draw feeds your destruction and takes you one step closer to death?'

She looked away for a moment, apparently choked with emotion. Pavel's fingers twitched.

'You must think us monsters, but we're not. What happened to your sister was unfortunate and I grieve for your loss – I do. But you must understand, what we give is life. Life for life. It's biblical in a way.'

Pavel closed his eyes again. It was easier that way.

'I understand you, though. In fact, I rather admire you. You see things in black and white. You have a single purpose in life. I knew when you walked into my office there could be only one outcome. I think you knew that too. I was surprised how easy you made it. I thought after Flintov and O'Brien you would be difficult to … well, you know what I mean.'

Pavel opened his eyes and looked directly at her.

She tilted her head, trying to read his expression. 'You're upset, angry, no doubt. I know. I understand your frustration. I want you to hear me when I tell you – I mean really hear me – I'm sorry it had to end this way. I became a doctor to save lives, not to take them, but if it's any consolation your death will mean life to several others. How many of us can be that special?'

Pavel opened his mouth. 'You,' he finally managed to whisper, ' will …'

Frieda looked startled. She stared at Pavel for a long time, then smiled sadly and shook her head. 'You don't understand. I haven't convinced you. For that I'm sorry.'

She stood and took another needle from her lab coat. 'This is propofol. Try not to worry, it's a sedative and will help you relax. I'm waiting for your blood samples to come back. I hope you believe me when I say I'm truly sorry for all the inconvenience I have caused you, Pavel. It was never our intention for you to suffer as you have.'

Pavel tried to move his hands, but only his thumb and index finger would respond.

'Oh, don't worry, you won't feel a thing,' Frieda said. She removed the drip line and injected the solution directly into his hand. 'And you can go knowing that whatever wrongs you have done, whatever evil you have committed, you will, in one way or another, have atoned for them.'

Pavel tried to stay awake, but before Frieda had crossed the room he was out for the count. Gone into the twilight.

46

John was just coming back from picking up the radio-station staff's wages, a strange journey that had led him to a garage in Stonybatter, when he decided to call Suzy. He called her mobile but it rang out. He tried his own landline but that rang out too. He walked on, saying hi to a few of the flower-stall workers. She was probably in the shower or had gone to the shop for something. He tried that line, but it didn't fit. He'd ring her again in a few minutes.

He hurried down Wexford Street and let himself into his building. He dropped off the money in his office and went down to the station to see when Clique would be there – he was the only one John could trust. On the way back up he paused at Rodney's floor. A light was burning in his office. After a moment's hesitation he tapped on the solicitor's door and poked his head inside. 'Rod?'

Rodney was leaning back in his chair with his hands folded

on hs stomach, dozing. He opened his eyes blearily. 'John.'

'Catching forty winks, Big Man? Can't say I blame you – feel like a bag of bones myself today. What are you doing here on a Saturday?' He dropped into the chair before Rodney's desk.

Rodney straightened slowly. He rubbed his hands over his face and smoothed his hair down. 'I had a few things to see to. You?'

'I got hauled in for questioning. You eaten anything today, Rod?'

'Are you concerned?'

Rodney was sore with him and John knew why. 'Don't be like that.'

'What can I do for you?'

'I wanted to say I'm sorry about the other day. I was upset and I acted like a complete bollocks. I'm sorry.'

Rodney sighed. He sat forward and linked his hands together on the desk. 'It's all right, I deserved it.'

'No, you didn't. See, the thing is I've been thinking about this and I'm not angry with you. Hell, I'm not even angry with her. I'm more pissed off with myself than anyone.'

'With yourself?'

'Oh, yeah. Here I am, the great detective, and I can't even see what's under my bloody nose. Course I'm pissed off. I should have known something was wrong. No … that's crap. I *did* know something was wrong but I didn't push to find out what it was. I worked with her every day. I should have known she was afraid. I should have known she needed help, but I didn't help her and instead of manning up I yelled at you. So I'm sorry.'

Rodney nodded slowly. 'Okay then.'

They sat for a moment.

'How's the new case? Trouble? Is that why you were questioned?'

'Not the case so much, just about everything else. I tell you,

Rod, I don't know. I've so much shit rolling around my head right now I can't think straight. I think I did something wrong earlier, betrayed a trust, and now I've just come from a talk with Floyd, the cop looking for Sarah.'

'What did he say?'

John recounted the interview.

Rod listened, his face serious. 'From what you say everything he has is pretty circumstantial.'

'I worry about her.'

'I know you do.'

'Floyd bothers me. He's a gundog with a scent in his nostrils.'

Rodney shrugged. 'A scent it just that, though, ephemeral.'

'What now?'

'It doesn't last, John. Unless he has something concrete to prosecute Sarah with, he's just chasing a ghost.'

'I hope you're right, Rod, I really do.'

After he'd left Rodney, John drove back to Ranelagh. He parked outside his house and went in. Sumo met him at the door.

'Suzy?'

He poked his head into the living room, then checked the rest of the house. She was nowhere to be found and there was no note.

He tried her phone again. It went unanswered.

Now he was worried.

He grabbed his keys and went out again, leaving a puzzled Sumo standing in the hall.

On the drive to Suzy's apartment he tried not to let himself get into a flap. She could be anywhere – she might have decided his house was too small and boring to spend another minute cooped up there. She might have gone to her mother's.

He pulled into the yard and parked under the steps leading to the front door. He tried her apartment. No answer. He looked across the car park. Suzy's car was under the car port.

She could still be anywhere.

He stood around on the steps until a couple came out. He pretended he was looking for his keys, thanked the guy for holding the door open and ran up the internal stairs to Suzy's apartment.

Outside her door he called her phone again and pressed his ear to the door. He could hear it ringing faintly in the distance.

Okay.

Now he was beyond worried.

He took a step back, raised his foot and kicked the door as hard as he could just above the lock. He did it again, then again. The lock held, but the interior frame splintered. He kicked the remaining section to pieces and ran into the apartment.

The door to the bedroom on his right opened and a startled semi-naked Jaffa stepped out and regarded the wreckage. 'What the fuck are you at?'

John grabbed him by both ears and yanked him into the hall. 'Where is she, you fucker? I swear to God I'll wring your fucking scrawny neck if you've laid a—'

'*John, stop!*'

He glanced to his right.

Suzy was kneeling in the middle of a double bed, naked but for a hastily pulled-up sheet. 'What are you doing here?'

'What the fuck does it look like, you stupid prick?' Jaffa yelled, holding his fingers to his ears.

'John, I'm sorry – I was going to call you, I was going to—'

'You were going to call me?' John said, in a low voice. 'You were going to call me and tell me what exactly?'

'John, please, I'm sorry. I appreciate you taking care of me, but it's all right now, everything's been sorted. It was all a mistake. Jaffa's sorry – tell him, honey.'

Jaffa looked at John. 'You're going to pay for that fucking door, guy.'

John grabbed him by the throat and pinned him to the wall. 'You ever talk to me again you'll be lucky I don't put you through the fucking window.'

'*John!*'

John tightened his grip until Jaffa was going puce.

'John, please, don't hurt him – John, *please*.'

Jaffa tried to prise John's fingers loose and made a strangled whistling sound, but in the end John released him. He stepped over the splintered door and walked away.

47

Ivan Colbert removed his shoes and socks and paced his office. He was agitated and feeling a little sick. In less than twenty-four hours he was supposed to perform an operation he was in no condition to attempt. Even thinking about it made his knees feel weak and his hands shake.

He walked to the press containing his drink. He laid his hands on the door but did not open it. No, he would not drink. He still had patients to see.

Patients. His lip curled. He walked away and sank into his chair. Rich, over-plucked, under-stimulated housewives with nothing to do but carve up their bodies in the wild pursuit of lost youth. He was reduced to drawing on skin with felt tip. This was what he had reduced himself to.

He closed his eyes, thinking back to the halcyon days when he had worked in Canada, his prestigious position, his stellar reputation. Some men did it for money, but not he. Oh, it would be folly to say that money had not been a factor, of course it had

– it had afforded him a lifestyle of great comfort and security. But he had always thought of himself as a man of simple needs. Once you'd bought an apartment, a car and a wardrobe, what else was there?

No, money had not been his reason to get out of bed, to push himself so hard. He had revelled in one thing: the certainty that he was one of the best surgeons in all of Canada, and very possibly the northern United States.

Was that ego? He didn't think so. It wasn't hubris either, or vanity. He had been simply gifted. He could do things that others could not do – or were afraid to do. He did not panic under fire. When hearts stopped, he could coax them back to life. When others sweated, he had remained calm, cool and collected. He had excelled. He had been driven and he had been focused. He had been godlike.

Colbert dug his toes into the carpet.

He had let it slip away. Some days his descent into shame haunted him, stalking his thoughts and dreams. It had happened so quickly, one malpractice suit, then another on the heels of it. He had been unlucky with that one: unfortunately it had resulted in an ambulance-chasing bottom-feeder who liked to dig and had found some discontented family members easily swayed by greed. Everything, his life's work, had come crashing down around him. If it had not been for Frieda, he might have lost his licence in its entirety. She had lied about his patient, falsified a blood-pressure report, paid off a theatre nurse, threatened another with deportation of a family member.

She had saved him.

So he owed her. She owned him. He was in league with the devil and he had no one to blame but himself.

He glanced towards the drinks cabinet again and licked his lips.

Maybe just a quick one, to take the edge off.

His intercom buzzed.

'Yes?'

'Sir, Ms Mayweather is here to see you.'

Shit. How did she do that? Could she smell his fear through the air-conditioning?

'Send her in.'

Frieda came in and closed the door. 'You look like hell, Ivan.'

'And hello to you too.'

She glanced at his shoes and socks. 'I have him.'

'Excuse me?'

'Him – the man who killed Flintov.'

Colbert blinked. 'I don't know what you mean.'

'I said I have him. The same bastard killed Brendan.'

'Brendan O'Brien?'

'Yes. He killed him and he killed Andrei and, by God, it wouldn't surprise me if I wasn't on his list too.'

'What did you mean when you say you have him?'

'He's downstairs, unconscious.'

'But you've got to get the police.'

Frieda looked at him as though he was barking mad. 'Don't be so stupid. Get the Gardaí and do what? Hand him over? Let him talk? Tell his sob story about his dead sister and her missing kidney? Are you serious, Ivan, or have you just unmoored yourself from reality for the hell of it?'

'What sister? What are you talking about?'

'He claims his sister was a donor. He claims she died. That's why he murdered Andrei and Brendan. He's a monster.'

'Where did you say he was?'

'Downstairs. My suite. He won't be going anywhere in a hurry.'

Colbert sagged. 'Frieda, what the hell have you done?'

'I told you I'd take care of things and I have. Don't look at me like that. I couldn't have him running loose. He made his choice.'

Colbert couldn't believe what he was hearing. 'But what now? You can't keep the man indefinitely. What are you planning to do with him?'

'We're going to dispatch him. I'm drawing up paperwork now to cover our arses and you're going to operate on him later today.'

'*Dispatch* him?'

'Ivan, this man knows about us. He knows about our operation. He has *killed* innocent people. Are you prepared to have someone like that out there?' She threw her hand up towards his window.

Innocent, Colbert thought. He wondered how she didn't choke on the word. 'Frieda, we are not murderers.'

'No, but he is. He killed Flintov, his wife and their staff. People like him can't be stopped. They can't be bought off. They cannot be reasoned with. He wanted me to do the impossible, knowing full well I couldn't. And now I've taken steps to make sure we're all protected and you're giving me stink eye like I have any other choice. I don't. He made his decision to come here, to threaten me. He killed Brendan to get to me. I've made my decision. You need to make yours.'

'Frieda, have you lost your mind?'

'No, I have not. Nor any other part of me.'

She stood up and smoothed her skirt. 'Look, I understand this is hard for you. But we made a deal, Ivan. I have covered your arse and you have covered mine. Now I can feel a draught. You need to re-evaluate your current thinking. If we let someone like this *thug* dictate terms to us we might as well throw in the towel and hand ourselves over to the police. Now I don't know about you, but I like my life the way it is.'

'What do you expect me to do?'

'I'll organise the paperwork, make it seem as though he signed himself in. Lucky for us he has a broken nose, which we can say he wanted us to repair. You're going to operate on him, but you're going to make sure he never comes out of surgery.'

'Frieda—'

'I'll make sure he has signed off all the appropriate paperwork stating he knows the dangers and there will be, of course, no one to sue us. I understand it might be a little difficult for you, but within a few months you'll be vindicated and we'll be free to carry on our work.'

Colbert stared at her. 'So, not only do you expect me to murder this man, you're throwing me to the wolves as well?'

'Ivan, it's either the wolves or the sharks.' Her eyes seemed strangely serene behind her glasses. 'You take your pick and let me know what you decide. Now, are you ready for tomorrow?'

'What?'

'Corrigan. Don't tell me you'd forgotten.'

'No, I had not.'

'Good.' She strode out of the room and did not close the door behind her.

48

John drove to the back of Wexford Street, parked and walked to the office. He was fuming and felt a fool. He had gone out on a limb for that girl and what had she done? Run back to the arms of the fuckwit who had screwed her over and beaten her senseless. What was wrong with her?

Just outside Devitt's pub he saw Clique walking towards him. The young man had his iPod on and his computer bag hanging low on his hip. He smiled when he saw John and switched off his music. 'Hey.'

'Hey yourself.'

'You talk to Suzy about the wage bill?'

John hooked his fingers into his back pockets. 'I spoke to Mike. No point with her, she's wound tight with this loser. I picked up enough money earlier to cover the last two weeks. Next week is still up in the air.'

Clique pushed his hair back from his forehead and looked at

John, his gaze calm and thoughtful. 'That's great, man. The guys'll really appreciate it. I'll swing by shortly and pick it up.'

'If I'm not there I'll leave it with Rod.'

'Are you okay, John?'

'Me? Yeah, of course, why wouldn't I be?'

'Dunno, man – because it's you? You take things too much to heart.'

'Click, don't worry about me. Okay? Take it handy.' He patted Clique on the shoulder and walked on. He felt sick.

He let himself into his office, closed the door and locked it. He let out a huge breath he hadn't realised he was holding. He didn't bother switching on the light. Last thing he wanted to do was advertise where he was. The answering machine on his desk blinked in the gathering gloom.

He lit a cigarette and slumped into his chair. After a moment he hit play.

There were two hang-ups and two messages. One from Patricia Day and one from Coleen Clancy.

He called Patricia Day at her shop. 'Hey, it's John Quigley. You were looking for me earlier?'

'Mr Quigley, thank you for getting back to me.' She sounded tired and sad.

'No problem, what can I do for you?'

'You asked me to contact you if there was anything out of the ordinary concerning Chris.'

'Yes?'

'After we spoke I went through some of his things. They're all boxed up here – I kept meaning to sort everything out but … I haven't been able to since the funeral. I'd been putting it off, I suppose.'

She paused for a moment.

'Anyway, I was looking through his more recent bank statements, and I found numerous loan applications. He'd been trying to get a personal loan in the weeks running up to his death.'

'How much are we talking about here?'

'Twenty-five thousand euros.'

'That's a lot of money.'

'It is.'

'And you've no idea what he wanted it for?'

'No. He was so ill – I can't imagine he'd have wanted to saddle us with a debt like that.'

'Perhaps he was desperate.'

'Please, Mr Quigley, he even tried to take one out using my shop as guarantee. I just – I just can't believe he would do something like that behind my back. I know it might seem like we're doing okay but I have a huge mortgage, three growing girls and a business that's going slower every day. Chris knew all this, he knew it.'

'I'm sure he had his reasons.'

'You know something – what is it? What do you think that money was for?'

'Mrs Day, I'll be honest, I don't have any answer for you.'

'How could he have wanted to do this to us?' She began to cry. 'How could he have put our home at risk? What was he going to do with this money? Blow it on some last-gasp holiday or something? I don't understand how he could have been so – so thoughtless.'

John had no answer. But his interest in the case and in contacting the other people on Alison Cooper's list had revived.

After he had hung up he called a woman he knew. Edel worked for a major credit company and knew more about money and money problems than John knew about cars. She was a buxom fifty-five-year-old grandmother with a filthy laugh and the patience of a saint. She had been a client of John's once, and he had saved her a whole lot of money and heartache when

278

she had finally plucked up the courage to leave the cheating scumbag who had fathered her six children and two of her sister's.

'Well, John Quigley, your ears must be burning. I was just saying to my Lucy she ought to think about settling down and getting married. You still single?'

John laughed. 'Yes, I surely am.'

'Nice boy like you? I can't believe you haven't been snatched off the market before now.'

'I'm not exactly beating them away with a stick, Edel.'

'So I can tell Lucy you're free?'

'You can tell her whatever takes your fancy but, for the record, I'm pretty sure that gorgeous girl of yours can dig up her own man.'

'Humph – that's exactly what she says. See? You're perfect for each other.' She sighed. 'Now, I know you didn't ring me for my matchmaking skills, so what can I do for you?'

John explained his case and the suspicions he was developing. 'What I really want to know is this. Is there any way you can find out if Alison Cooper had been depositing large chunks of cash into accounts her family might not know about?'

'Leave it with me, John. I'll chase her money down. If she was making that kind of money it'll turn up somewhere.'

'I appreciate it, Edel.'

'That's all right, son.'

'So tell me,' John said, 'any budding romance on the horizon with you?'

Edel laughed her dirty laugh. 'No, John. Why? Are you offering?'

John Quigley laughed for the second time that day and it felt good.

49

After he had left Edel, John went home and let Sumo out. While the big dog sprayed his favourite bush in the garden, he sat at his kitchen table and called the English number Jackie had given him.

After a few rings, the man he had spoken to the first time he had called, the mysterious Sid, picked up. John could hear loud dance music in the background. 'Yeah?'

'Sid?'

'Who's askin'?'

'John Quigley.'

'What? Speak up – the line's a piece of shit. Who is it?'

'John Quigley,' he bawled.

The music grew muffled, then a door closed and John could no longer hear it.

'You're the geezer that's been ringin'.' He sounded old and gnarly, with an accent that wouldn't have been out of place in an English soap opera.

'Yes – I'm looking for Sarah.'

'I'm gonna tell you what I told her sister, and what I told anyone else. I ain't seen her, she ain't here, and I don't want nothing to do with her business, you understand me?'

'You have an idea how to contact her, though, right?'

'Which part of "I don't want nothing to do with her business" did you not understand, mate?'

Before John could reply the line went dead and when he tried to call back it was engaged. 'Son of a bitch!'

He fed Sumo, then tried the number again. Still engaged. Rather than sit about the house fuming, he decided to pay a visit to Coleen Clancy's home. He could have telephoned, of course, but, as Sarah always said, face-to-face made lying a whole lot more interesting. The irony nearly choked him.

It was pitch black when he parked outside Coleen's cottage and walked up a red and black tiled footpath. Her doorbell made him smile. It was an art-deco cat holding a beach ball – the bell-push.

He rang and waited. After a few moments a hall light came on and a woman opened the door. She was about his age, tall, with short brown hair. She wore a loose brown linen shift over cream trousers, and silver sandals. A silver ring glinted on the second toe of her right foot.

'Yes?'

'Coleen Clancy?'

'Yes.'

'My name is John Quigley.'

'You're the detective who's been calling me.' She looked at him with a curious open expression.

'Yes.'

'I called *you* earlier.'

'I know – that's why I'm here.'

'I called you to find out why you'd called me and now you're here to see why I called. It's all very circular.' She smiled in confusion.

John returned her smile. She had a nice voice and a pleasant manner. After the last few days, he found that comforting for some reason.

'I called before because I'm investigating the death of Dr Alison Cooper.'

She didn't say anything, but from the expression that flitted across her face at the name he understood that she had known the dead woman and was now wary of him. That disappointed him. 'You knew her, I believe.'

She hesitated. 'I did.'

'Did you know she died?'

'I read about it in the papers.'

'Can you—'

'I'm sorry, Mr Quigley, I really don't see what this has to do with me.'

John leaned a shoulder against the wall. 'Miss Clancy, I understand. It's late, you're tired and I'm some weirdo calling to your house. Truth is, I'd rather be sitting at home eating oven chips than knocking on strangers' doors and bothering them. But Alison Cooper is dead, her children are missing their mother, her mother is missing her daughter and I promised I would do what I could to get to the bottom of her death or even why she might have taken her own life. So far I've been faffing about like an idiot, but I'm currently growing a theory, and even if it's only a half-baked one, if there's anything, *anything* at all, you could tell me about Alison Cooper I would really appreciate it.'

She studied him. He could see her weighing him up with her grey eyes, coolly deciding what to do with him.

She opened the door wider. 'I think you'd better come in.'

He stepped past her into a short, dark hall. She closed the

door and asked him to follow her. She led him down a short flight of steps and into a large, warm kitchen. The air smelled of homemade bread. A glass of wine stood on the counter.

'This is really nice,' John said. 'I didn't realise these houses went back so far.'

'They are a bit Tardis-like, all right.' She waved a hand towards a large beech table.

He took a seat and watched as she walked to a double oven and checked inside. 'Whatever that is, it smells amazing.'

'It's only bread. My sister got me hooked on home-baking recently.' She took out a brown loaf and set it on a wire tray to cool.

She picked up her glass and sat at the table across from him. She linked her hands before her. John studied her. She had a nice face, but under the kitchen light he noticed a few things he hadn't seen at the door. Coleen Clancy's skin was pale, yellowish and her eyes a little sunken. She did not look well.

'What happened to her – to Alison?'

'Suicide, apparently.'

She pressed her fingers to her chin. 'Poor woman.'

John took out his notebook. 'Miss Clancy—'

'You can call me Coleen.'

'Okay, Coleen, I don't want to appear rude or anything, but are you . . .' He shook his head. 'I'm really sorry for asking this, but are you sick?'

She tilted her head. 'Is that any of your business?'

'It might be, in a related way. I suppose what I'm really asking is, are you on a transplant list?'

She took a sip of her wine. 'I'm on it somewhere, I'm sure.'

'What is your condition?'

'I have hepatitis B.'

'I see.'

'I can tell by your face that you don't. I've had it for quite a while. It's a blood disease – did you know that?'

'I think I did,' John said, embarrassed to admit he knew bugger-all about hepatitis other than there was an A and a B.

'I didn't know I had it until last year. I noticed I was tired all the time, but I worked as a fashion co-ordinator – and who the hell isn't tired in that business, right?'

'Right.' John did not tell her he knew even less about what a fashion co-ordinator might do than he did about hepatitis.

'So I'm tired and trying all these tonics and berries and new-age crap.' She rolled her eyes. 'By the time I'd dragged my arse to the doctors, they reckoned it had been swirling around my system for any number of years.'

'I'm sorry to hear that.'

'I'm sorry too. I thought I might have done a whole lot more with this life than I have done so far.' She smiled. 'Like got married, maybe had a kid or two, or done more travelling. Something tangible.'

'You talk like you already have one foot in the grave,' John said.

'Well, the hep B was bad news, but finding out I had cancer on top of it really sealed the deal, so to speak.'

'Oh.'

'What can you do?' She shrugged. 'Double whammy. At this stage I've come to accept that there is really nothing more anyone can do for me.'

'That can't be true, surely. You're only a young woman.'

'Thanks. You're sweet to say so, but the truth is I'm a woman with an incurable disease, a definite time limit and very few options left open to me.'

John was impressed that she could be so matter-of-fact. 'Surely something can be done?'

'I can wait and hope for a miracle. I can make myself sick

with chemo, swell up like a balloon and let all my hair fall out for an extra few months, or I can spend whatever time I have left doing some of the things I always wanted to do. Like baking bread, it seems.' She laughed, stood up and got a bottle of wine from a built-in wine rack. She opened it and took another glass from a press by the sink. 'Drink?'

'Sure, I'll have a small one. Thanks.'

She poured, passed him the glass, raised hers in a mock-toast and took a sip. 'No need to look so uncomfortable.'

'I'm very sorry,' John said. 'I just can't imagine what you're going through.'

'Thanks, but it's okay. Really. I was afraid at first – terrified, to be honest. But now … now I'm . . . I want to say at peace with it, but that would be a lie. I'm very fucking angry, really, but I suppose I'm just resigned to dying.'

'I don't know how you're so calm about it. If that was me I'd be freaking out.'

'I did freak out for a while, but what good is that? Even when I thought it was just my liver that was shot I was out on a limb. Things have got a lot better in the last few years – there's been an increase in liver transplants, between fifty and sixty a year now, but demand is up too and there's no guarantee I'll get one in time, especially with an existing condition like hep B. I live in a country where we're dependent on goodwill from families to donate after a loved one dies. I can't make people donate organs. I can't make myself the most valuable person on the list.'

'I didn't realise that was the situation.'

'People don't.' She swirled her wine. 'Ever read Douglas Adams?'

John shook his head. 'I'm afraid I'm not much of a reader.'

'He wrote a book called *The Hitch-Hiker's Guide to the Galaxy*.'

'Oh, I know it.'

'Well, in it he described a physical sort of force field, only he called it an SEP field. Know what that is?'

John shook his head. He wondered how much wine she'd had before he arrived.

'SEP stands for Somebody Else's Problem.' She took another mouthful of wine. 'That's what the transplant situation is in this country, an SEP. Do you carry a card?'

'No.'

'Why not?'

'I'd never even thought of it.'

'Exactly. There you go. SEP.'

'Why were you reluctant to talk about Alison when I arrived?'

'Complicated woman, Alison. But she was a friend to me when I needed one. I didn't want to betray her.'

'Betray her how?'

'By talking ill of the dead.' She shrugged. 'But then she *is* dead and the dead hold no secrets.'

'What secrets did Alison hold?'

'What do you think?' She put her glass down and folded her arms. 'Alison cared, really cared, for her patients. I think she would have gone out of her way to help any of us. She was so frustrated by the system, by the red tape, the refusal of doctors to let us get the help we needed if we didn't fit the criteria.'

'I don't understand.'

'There's a free market out there where people want to sell and people want to buy. Doesn't it seem fucked up that people can't decide for themselves how they want to live?'

'You mean an organ-donor market.'

'Yes. So what?'

'So what? It's illegal for a start.'

'Lots of things are. Just because something is illegal doesn't mean it's bad or morally wrong.'

'Are you telling me that Alison Cooper was involved in organ smuggling?'

'I don't believe she was. But I'm telling you, Alison Cooper genuinely tried to help people and didn't rely on taking pot shots at the sick and the desperate from the higher fucking moral ground.' She sat back in her chair, looked down at her hands.

'I'm sorry.'

'I'm sorry too. I'm sorry I ever let myself get infected with hep B. I'm sorry I ever smoked. I'm sorry this is all I have to show for my time on this earth.' She looked up. 'I'm sorry I didn't meet Alison Cooper a whole lot sooner in life. If I had there's a strong possibility we wouldn't be having this conversation.'

'So what happened with you?'

'I was sick, and she said if I was willing to pay she'd introduce me to someone who would help me.'

'If you were willing to pay her.'

'No, it wasn't like that. Alison wasn't making money from it. She wasn't doing it for financial gain.'

John was sceptical. 'Really?'

'Really.'

'So who did you discuss your new liver with?'

'That I can't say.'

'You can't?'

'I won't. You asked me about Alison. I told you about Alison. But I won't drop another name into whatever soup you're cooking up.'

'Why would you protect someone involved in something illegal?'

'What have I got to gain from doing so? They were willing to help me before I was diagnosed with cancer, why would I repay them in such a manner?'

'They were willing to help you for a fee.'

'Nothing is life is ever free.'

John sat back and tried to think. Of the people on the list Chris Day was dead, Coleen Clancy was dying, Allen Foster had had a transplant and what of Sofia Johnson? Tobias Johnson wouldn't even speak to him. Why not? Why had he sounded so cagey the day John had called? Then he thought of what Shane Breen had told him, of Alison and Ivan Colbert's medical conversations. What if Alison hadn't simply been chatting with an old friend? Colbert had been a surgeon, hadn't he? Was it possible he was involved in something more covert?

John thought about Beth Gold's reaction to Colbert at the funeral. She was Alison's closest friend. She had to have known Alison was involved in something shady.

Across the table Coleen Clancy poured herself another glass of red wine. She drained it to the last drop, and tossed the empty bottle into the sink, apparently uncaring whether it smashed or not.

50

Ivan Colbert woke up stiff and cold on the sofa in his office. He sat up and as he did so a heavy-bottomed glass tumbler rolled from his chest and fell to the floor. It didn't break – the thick carpet saw to that. He reached for it and set it upright on the table by his elbow, then rubbed his hands across his face, surprised to feel stubble on his cheeks. He didn't think it had been there when he lay down. Or maybe it had. Had he shaved that morning? It was so hard to be sure.

What time was it?

He checked his watch. It read 20:15.

His last patient had been in at five. It seemed a few hours were missing from his day.

He got up and wandered out to Reception, but the desk was empty. He leaned heavily against the door, thinking that the computer on Fiona's desk looked strangely menacing.

He went back to his office and used his private bathroom. He washed his hands under the hot water and stared at his face in the mirror. He looked terrible – crumpled, uncared-for, like an old cashmere jumper that'd been flung in the back of a wardrobe. There seemed to be a lot of grey in his stubble. He turned his head to catch the light. Time was etched on his face.

How could she want him to start again?

He splashed water on his face and patted it dry with a paper towel.

He went back to the sofa and sat down again.

Where were his shoes?

Ah, there they were, under the desk. He didn't remember taking them off. Wasn't that funny?

In his sleep he had enjoyed silence and a dreamless floating that made the now all the more painful. He thought again of Frieda. He thought of everything she had said, of her expectations, her ultimatums, of starting anew. When he thought of this he remembered what her words had actually meant, understood the weight of what she demanded of him. He thought of the cost of starting again, of faces glancing surreptitiously, mumbled complaints, questions and accusations.

Doubt.

Frieda was right. She had defended him before and they had won, but it had not been without great personal cost. Not to Frieda, of course, never to Frieda. Frieda did not make mistakes. Frieda did not shoulder blame.

Start again.

But it had been a long time ago – he had been younger, stronger. Before, his arrogance had been a living thing. Before, he had not known how hard the fall could be. Now he did.

He was not that man any more. He was not up to the fight.

His thoughts turned to Alison, as they had more and more often these last few days. She had been a true friend to him, a woman of incalculable compassion. If the system had broken her, what had it in store for him?

He bent forward and put on his socks and shoes. He wouldn't be a part of it. He wouldn't be Frieda's bait. None of this had been his doing. None of it was his creation. Oh, he had accepted his fair share of reward, but what good was that – what did it afford him? More sleepless nights and long tedious bouts of self-justification, all of which sat high in his throat because he could not swallow it.

It had been easier when Alison was alive, of course it had. Her passion – her *compassion* was true and it was honest and it had kept him grounded. She cared what happened: she made it seem like it made sense. She had a way of paring back the world to its essential truth. She had been truly altruistic. But she was gone. She had been his compass and now he was adrift in a sea of self-hatred and powerlessness.

He missed her terribly: he missed her smiles, her outlook. He missed his friend.

Oh, God. He felt ashamed of himself. Look at him – so maudlin. Was this what he was reduced to now? Sitting in his office with a fuzzy head and tears in his eyes, bemoaning his path in life?

Well, what had he to be joyous about anyway? He thought of how glibly Frieda had announced she was going to offer him up, how secure she had been in her plan of action, her control of him. He wondered if his well-being featured in her thoughts – if, in fact, it ever had. Yes, she had saved him once but, by God, she had taken her pound of flesh from him. And now here she was, looking for another.

He drew himself to his full height and flattened his tie. After a moment he left his office and walked to the end of the corridor.

On the third floor, in a private suite, he found Pavel. He studied the younger man's unconscious face. Was it the face of a killer? How would one know? He read the chart at the end of the bed.

Ridiculous. Frieda already had him down as a donor. Colbert checked Pavel's chart. Ah. That was why. He was AB negative. No wonder she was eager to keep him in status.

How high a price could she put on him with that coursing through his veins? Matches with that blood type were extremely difficult to find. Frieda must have been delighted when she learned what his body contained – a double prize for her.

Colbert leaned on the bed frame. Sleeping, the man looked no more dangerous than a cat, yet he had killed Brendan, he had killed Andrei and he would kill again, no doubt. But here, now, he was the victim, toothless. To carve him up like an animal was immoral.

They were doctors: their job was to prolong life, heal the ill, to do no harm.

The real monster was somewhere in the hospital, stalking the corridors in six-inch heels and a pencil skirt.

He straightened up. He said it again under his breath. It was something of a relief for him to think that – to admit finally that it was so.

Frieda Mayweather was a monster. Some neuron had fired too closely to another and the semblance of humanity had burned too brightly and extinguished her. He had known it all along – he had seen for himself her calculating eyes, her disregard for anything other than what she alone deemed *worthy*.

Colbert left the room and went next door to the drugs cupboard. He unlocked it with his own key and rummaged through it until he found what he was looking for.

He checked the landing for Elise, Frieda's head of nursing

and second skin. She was nowhere to be seen. He returned to Pavel's side and stood looking down on the young man with the sallow skin and dark hair. If he did this there was no way back.

After a moment he unhitched the drip and injected the solution he carried into the tube in Pavel's hand. As he had expected, Pavel came round within seconds. His eyes were rolling and confused but after a few moments they focused. He looked at Colbert and opened his mouth to speak but no sound came out.

'Wait.' He fetched him a paper cup of water from the bathroom next door. 'Drink this, slowly.'

Pavel drank until it was gone, then wiped his mouth with the back of his hand.

'Do you know why you are here?' Colbert asked.

'Who you are?'

'My name is Ivan. But that is not important. You need to get up and you need to get out of here. I don't know where your clothes are, but that is probably the least of your concerns right now. You've got to get up and get out.'

Pavel looked at him suspiciously.

'Listen to me carefully,' Colbert said. 'Shortly a nurse will stop by to do checks. When she sees you're awake she will call Frieda. When she does that Frieda will make damn sure you go back to sleep again. You will never wake from that sleep. Do you understand what I'm saying?'

Pavel nodded.

'Then you need to get going.'

Pavel pushed the covers back, slid out of the bed and got to his feet shakily. He gripped the railing, clearly feeling weak and nauseous.

Colbert took out his wallet and handed him two fifty-euro notes. 'That should be enough to get you back to town. I assume you have someone you can call on. If anyone tries to stop you downstairs just tell them you're going for a cigarette. If you make it to the road you can flag a taxi down.'

Pavel pulled his hospital gown tighter around his body. He looked at Colbert. 'Why you help?'

'I'm beginning to see things in a different light.'

'My sister is dead.'

'I understand so.'

'Is not over.'

'No, I can't imagine it is. At least for you.' Colbert stood back and let him pass. 'For me, though, it's time to bow out of the show.'

Pavel frowned. He nodded to Colbert, walked out into the corridor and, after a quick look left and right, shuffled quickly away.

Colbert took a deep breath. It was done. He had made his decision, and it felt fine.

He pulled air deep into his lungs and it tasted good.

For the first time in almost a decade Ivan Colbert was free.

51

After a few attempts Pavel had managed to flag down a taxi and even then he'd had to show the driver the money before he would agree to take him to town. He got out on the corner of Gardiner Street. People stared at him in amazement as he scuttled past them.

He knew it was a terrible risk returning to the apartment, but he was running low on options. He stood across the street from it, shivering in the cold. He was relieved to see no sign of activity at the building and no evidence that anyone had been down there.

Finally satisfied, and growing too cold to care, he loped across the street and down the metal steps. He tried the door. It was shut and the Yale lock had snapped into place. He wrapped his gown around his elbow and used it to smash the small glass centre of the door. He pulled the jagged pieces of glass free, snaked his arm through and slipped the lock open.

The air inside smelt foul. Pavel looked at Rick's pale body

lying in a patch of light from the streetlamp. That was where the smell was coming from: Rick had soiled himself as he died.

Pavel glanced once at Grace's door, but instead he stepped over Rick and made his way to the boy's bedroom. It was as small as Grace's. He pulled the curtains and switched on the light. The air was musty and damp, and there was a filthy mess. Pavel began to search for clothes. He found a pair of clean underpants, some black jeans that were too tight at the waist, a T-shirt, a pair of socks and a jumper. He pulled open the wardrobe and yanked out a few pairs of runners, finally settling on a pair of Converse that didn't look too battered. He looked inside them. They were a size too small, but they would have to do for the time being.

He dressed quickly. Then he searched the room. He flipped the mattress up and found an envelope containing a wrap of cocaine and a hundred and twenty euros. He pocketed the money. Next he emptied an old gym bag of magazines and stuffed as many clean clothes as he could find inside it.

When he was sure he had taken anything of use from Rick's room he switched off the lights and returned to the living room. He walked past the body and into the kitchen. He opened the drawers and removed two of the sharper knives. He also took some canned food, a loaf of bread and two beers from the fridge. He put them into the gym bag too.

He stood in the doorway of the kitchen, thinking. He glanced towards Grace's door again. She had some money squared away in a floral china pig by her bed. It would be foolish not to take it.

He opened her door and pushed it wide. The curtains were already closed, just as they had been that morning. He flipped the light switch.

She lay on the corner of her bed, her body twisted in an unnatural position, her eyes staring towards the door. One bullet had struck her in the chest, the other had snaked through her scalp. Pieces of her hair and skin were on the wall behind her. Her naked breasts were dark and mottled with congealed blood.

Her eyes seemed fixed on his. He thought he would like to close them but he could not bring himself to touch her.

He should not have gone with her that first day. He had been soft and stupid. He had fucked up spectacularly, and had it not been for the sad doctor he would now be a cadaver.

But he had survived, just as he always had. And now he had a target, a single unifying reason to stay away from people like Grace or anyone who might soften or distract him from his mission. The woman with the dead eyes. Mayweather. He would make her suffer like she had never suffered before. He would extract from her every ounce of revenge he could.

He lifted Grace's pig – Aubrey, she had called him, he remembered – and turned him upside-down. He removed the black plug that sealed him and shook free the contents. Eighty-five euros and some change. He stared at it: the sum of Grace's life.

He pocketed that, and the half-pack of cigarettes from the bedside locker. Before he left the apartment he wrapped Grace's scarf around his neck and pulled her beanie cap low on his head. The scarf smelt strongly of her and he almost put it back, but the night was cold and he had to be practical. Now was not the time for sentiment.

He left the apartment, closed the door behind him and hit the streets.

On Cathedral Street he hung a right and before long stepped onto the busy paving stones of O'Connell Street. He moved on, crossing the Luas lines. He walked quickly but kept his eyes peeled in case he was being followed. He would not make that mistake again.

By the time he had reached the Quays he was sure he was safe. He walked over the Ha'penny Bridge and disappeared into the crowded narrow streets of Temple Bar.

52

Frieda Mayweather stared at the empty bed for a long moment, then turned to the nurse who stood anxiously to her right. 'I don't understand what you're telling me, Elise. What do you mean he's gone? Gone where?'

The nurse blanched under her withering gaze. 'Well, that's just it. I don't know where he is – nobody does. Nobody has spotted him anywhere. I've personally searched every inch of the hospital, and I can't find him. I have security searching the grounds right now.'

'Elise, the man was comatose. Would you mind explaining to me how could he just get up and *leave*?'

'I don't have any answers, Doctor. He was here when I came around earlier and his vital signs were static. But when I came back to change his IV he was gone.'

'Where are his clothes?'

'They're still bagged in the locker.'

'So you're saying my patient woke up from a coma, and

walked out of the hospital without his clothes?'

'I don't know.'

'That is simply not good enough.' Frieda looked at the bed again. There was no way Pavel could have woken up naturally. Someone had brought him around and the only person she could think of who would do something so stupid was Ivan.

She hurried out of the room and went straight to his suite, but when she tried the door it was locked.

She glanced at her watch: 21:10. He should have been there: the Corrigan surgery was scheduled for eleven p.m.

She returned to her office, lifted the phone and called Hannity.

'Yeah?'

'It's me. He's gone.'

'Who's gone?'

'Sunic.'

'What do you mean, gone?'

'I mean gone. You need to find him.'

'I did find him. I brought him to you.'

Frieda clutched the phone a little tighter. Things like this did not happen to her. It was ... unprecedented.

'Find him. He can't have got far – he wasn't even dressed.'

'He was in the nip?'

'Just find him.'

She slammed the phone down and chewed her lip.

She picked up the receiver again and dialled. When he did not answer she tried again, drumming her fingers on her desk as the phone burred. Only the white knuckles of the hand holding the phone betrayed her fury. 'Ivan,' she said, when the answering machine picked up, "this is Frieda. Look, Ivan, I feel fairly certain you know why I'm calling you. What I don't know is why I *need* to call you or why I'm missing a patient. What I don't know is why you're not here right now. I need you to call me ASAP.'

She hung up and walked to the window overlooking the

back-lit fountain in the courtyard below. She stood by the glass, unseeing, thinking over possibilities. Ever since Frieda had refused Alison Cooper's demand that she do Chris Day's transplant *pro bono*, Ivan Colbert had been acting strangely. Whenever Frieda thought of the day Alison had cornered her and told her she knew of Sofia Johnson's transplant, Frieda had known she would try to use it as a trump card against her. Stupid Ivan and his big mouth. If he had only kept it shut, Alison's suspicions would have remained just that: suspicions. But in confirming his role and, *ergo*, the Alton's role, he had forced Frieda to take matters into her own hands.

She looked out into the darkness, thinking of Alison's ludicrous threat: that she would turn a blind eye to Frieda's lucrative sideline if Frieda in turn helped those who had no hope of being able to afford her services.

Frieda despised people like Alison Cooper. Always with a bleeding-heart agenda, always with an angle, a bottom-feeder, ready to scrape from the jaws of those who were pioneers.

But since Alison's death, Ivan had been slowly disintegrating. Did he know? Did he suspect she had organised Alison's demise? It had been ridiculously easy. She had been so trusting. That, too, had been a flaw in her make-up and only confirmed to Frieda how right she had been to remove her from the equation.

Frieda thought about Colbert for a while, her face slowly tightening as her mind ran through a set of possibilities. Pavel would really want her dead now.

She went back to her desk, picked up the phone again and made another call. Her husband answered on the third ring.

'Gerald, it's Frieda.'

'Hello.' He sounded surprised to hear from her.

'Gerald, listen to me. This weekend I want you to take the boys down to the summer house.'

'What?'

'Yes, the summer house.'

'Why on earth would I do that? Rory has a match tomorrow afternoon. He can't miss that.'

'Perhaps after the match.'

'Why? I have a clinic on Monday. Why would I drive all the way to Kerry for a day?'

Frieda closed her eyes. 'I . . . can't talk about it right now, but I'll explain as much as I can when I get home.'

'Frieda, what is going on?'

'It's nothing, just a precaution.'

'A precaution against what?'

Frieda frowned. This had been a mistake: she should have waited until she had a story ready before she called. 'Don't worry, darling, I'll explain when I get home.'

'Frieda—'

'Talk soon.'

The Mercedes moved through the light M50 traffic easily. Shane Breen glanced in the rear-view mirror. Mr Colbert seemed unusually quiet and rather out of sorts. His phone had rung a number of times and he had ignored it, finally opening his briefcase and tossing it inside. That was unprecedented in the whole time he had been driving for the man.

'Is the temperature all right for you, sir?'

'Yes, Shane, it's perfect.'

'Are you tired, sir? Long day?'

'Yes, a long day, and a long day coming.'

Shane drove along for a while. He wanted to say something else, to offer some joke or make some reference to the news, anything to lighten the air. In the end, though, he remained silent, and when he dropped Mr Colbert off at his townhouse he felt a strange sense of disquiet. 'Will you need me any more tonight, sir? You mentioned you might have late surgery?'

'No, that's fine, Shane. You can take off.' Colbert climbed out of the car and came around to the driver's door. Shane buzzed down the window. Colbert looked down the street and smiled. 'Quiet, isn't it?'

'You should go inside, sir. It's very cold out.'

Colbert looked down. Shane couldn't make out the expression on his face. 'Sir? Is everything all right?'

Colbert patted his young driver on the shoulder. 'Keep it simple, Shane. If you try to keep it simple you'll get there in the end. I want you to remember that.'

'Sir?'

But Colbert was already moving towards the steps of his house, his breath swirling around his head and through the frigid air like tendrils of smoke.

Shane waited for him to open the front door. When the hall light came on, he tooted his horn once and drove off down the street.

Less than half an hour later another car pulled up outside. Derek Hannity climbed out and told Terry to park around the corner out of view.

He trotted up the steps and rang the doorbell. When no one answered he came back down and gazed up at the windows. He dropped his eyes and spotted a black wheelie-bin in a space under the step. He went to it, dragged it out and climbed on it to get over the spiked side gate. He jumped down and slipped around the back of the house.

Using his sleeve he smashed a pane of glass in the downstairs laundry room and opened the window. No alarm sounded, and when he checked to see if a silent alarm had been activated he was surprised to find it had not.

He left the front door on the latch and searched the rooms downstairs before moving up to the next floor.

As soon as he rounded the return he heard music. He could see light from under the door of a room towards the front of the house. He crept quietly along the landing, his ear tuned for any movement. He paused briefly outside the door then pushed it open and looked inside.

'Stupid fuck,' he said, looking at the body of Ivan Colbert. The surgeon was still wearing his suit, though his feet were bare. He had fashioned a noose from a bright silk tie and now hung from the curtain rail that ran over the bay window where his bed stood, fully made.

Terry arrived at his shoulder. 'Oh, shit. It's him.'

'Course it's fucking him, you twat.' Hannity glanced around the bedroom. Two manila envelopes lay on the dressing-table. He opened the first and read it. It was a letter to Colbert's sister outlining his burial wishes and naming the solicitor handling his estate.

He opened the second and scanned the fine copperplate handwriting.

'Fuck me,' he said, when he got to the end.

'What's it say?'

'Never mind what it says.' Hannity folded the letter and put it in his pocket. He looked at the darkening face of Ivan Colbert and spat. 'Fucking stupid old queer.'

'Now what?' Terry said.

'Now we go through this place.'

'What are you looking for?'

'Anything about the hospital or patients, anything like that.'

The two men did a thorough search of the home until they were satisfied that Colbert had left nothing more to incriminate the clinic. Forty-five minutes later they left through the front door and drove away into the night.

53

'Are you all right?'

John glanced up. 'Huh?'

'I asked if you were all right.' Carrie was looking across the kitchen table at him with a slight smile on her lips.

John figured it might not have been the first time she'd asked. 'I'm a bit preoccupied.'

'You look tired. Were you out on the town last night? Making up for your birthday?'

'No, I was here – I just didn't sleep so well.'

'You worried about her?'

'Who?'

'Suzy.'

'To be honest, I'm not. She's made her decision.' John stood up and scraped the remains of his uneaten breakfast into Sumo's bowl. 'I'm thinking about the case I've been working on – or, rather, the case I haven't been working on.'

'The dead doctor?'

'Yes. I should have been paying more attention to it, but between Suzy and whatnot, I've been off my game.'

Carrie poured more coffee into her cup. 'Well, I can't believe she went back to that man after everything he did to her. What was she thinking?'

'Women.'

'Don't give me that guff. And don't tar all of us with the one brush, if you don't mind. Have you spoken to Mike about what's going on?'

'No, but I missed a few calls yesterday and reckon I'll hear from him today.'

'What are you going to tell him?'

'I don't know yet.'

'He won't like it that she's gone back.'

'It's not really my problem any more.'

She put down her cup. 'So why does it look as though you think it is?'

'Because I have a bad feeling my telling Mike the truth about her getting a hiding is going to start something I can't control. I wouldn't have told him about Jaffa doing a number on his sister if I'd guessed she'd go running back to him. What the hell am I supposed to think? He's going to do his nut.'

'None of this is your fault. He ought to know his own sister by now.'

'Yeah, there is that.'

'And Floyd?'

'What about him?'

She raised an eyebrow. 'You're not worried?'

'Oh, that. I don't know, Carrie, everything he has is circumstantial.'

'But you have questions?'

'Yes, I do.'

'Such as?'

'Just questions.'

She drained her coffee and carried her cup to the sink. She put it in and rested her hand on his shoulder. 'Everything will work out, you'll see.'

He gave her a twisted smile. 'I hope so.'

Later that morning he drove to Tobias Johnson's house and rang the intercom on the gatepost, but no one answered. He stood there for a moment, feeling frustrated. He debated climbing over the fence and checking the property out for himself, but in the end he took out a business card, wrote 'Please contact me about Alison Cooper' and pushed it through the letterbox.

He went back to the office. On his way upstairs he called in at the pirate radio station. 'Clique here?'

'Nah, man, he's not on until two,' the youth who opened the door said.

'Ask him to come up to me when he gets a chance.'

The youth nodded and closed the door.

John carried on upstairs. When he rounded the return to his landing he was alarmed to see a shape standing to the side of his door in the shadows.

He stopped. 'Come out of there – come out where I can see you.'

Shane Breen stepped from the gloom. He was in his uniform, a black suit, white shirt and black tie.

'Shit, you scared the crap out of me, Shane,' John said, leaning on the banisters. 'You shouldn't be lurking about like that. Jesus.'

'Sorry – I needed to see you.'

'Next time ring first. I could have hurt you.'

'Sorry,' Shane repeated.

John came up the rest of the stairs and unlocked his door. 'Come on in. You want a cup of coffee?"

'No, thank you.'

'Take a seat.'

John folded himself into his own chair and lit a cigarette. He was relieved and surprised to find his hand was not shaking like a paint-mixer. 'So, what gives? I think it's only fair to warn you that I'm going to see your boss Colbert today. Not sure about shit yet, but I've got a feeling he's involved with Alison Cooper in more than just a friendly way and, yeah, I know he's gay – that's not what I mean. I think—'

'You won't be seeing Mr Cooper today. He's dead.'

'Excuse me?'

'He's dead.'

'What the hell do you mean, he's dead? What happened?'

'He killed himself last night.'

'Oh.'

Shane leaned forward in his chair, and John could have kicked himself. How could he not have noticed the kid was upset? Jesus, he thought, maybe he ought to go back to bar work because he really sucked the big one as a detective.

'You okay there, Shane?'

'I knew something was wrong last night. I knew it.'

'Hey, it's okay.'

'I called to his house this morning and he didn't come down. So I called his phone. No answer. I rang the hospital and he wasn't there.' Shane shook his head. 'I just knew straight away something was wrong. Shit, I knew last night he was out of sorts, but I didn't know he was going to do that. I had no idea. I didn't know.'

He looked at John and tears stood in his eyes. He seemed startlingly young.

'The guards wouldn't come, so I called the fire brigade and said I thought there was a fire inside. They broke the door down and that's when they found him. He'd hung himself.'

'I'm sorry.'

'He was real nice to me, I swear, no funny shit. My old man's been asking and I keep telling him he was a gentleman, you know? Real sound.'

John nodded. The young man's genuine grief was touching.

'Anyway.' Shane rubbed his hand over his eyes hard. 'I was cleaning out the car and shit and I found this.'

He removed an envelope from inside his jacket. 'He must have wrote it before he left his office or something. I found it in the sleeve behind the passenger seat.'

'What is it?'

'You need to read it.'

John took the envelope and opened it. There were two pages of carefully crafted copperplate handwriting inside, beginning with what looked like a poem.

An echo fades into the night,
an eerie mournful sound.
A shooting star disappears from sight,
and I crumble to the ground.
There is no life within this garden;
my sobs are the only sound.
I have poisoned the honeyed fountain
where your love could be found.

'What's this?' John looked up.

'Keep reading.'

John read on.

Shane, there is a detective looking into Dr Cooper's death. His name is John Quigley and his card is within the envelope. I want you to give this to him. I would also take the time to say farewell to you. You have been an exemplary driver and I wish you all the best in your future endeavours. Stay on the path, accept no quick fix.

Mr Quigley, I have been a fool. I thought I could leave behind the world as it was, little realising that fear and shame are more than just emotions. They are like living entities. You cannot leave them behind. They are yours and you must see to them. Lately they have grown so strong I can no longer control them, their hunger is too great. Alive they devour me.

I have always thought when the time came, I would stand and be counted, but I know now I am a coward and I will always seek the coward's way out. I have neither the fortitude to start again nor the will to carry on pretending that the life I am living is without cost.

Alison Cooper was my friend. I stood by and let her make a mistake – one that I knew deep in my heart would be costly. I spoke out of turn, I got her hopes up and I let her walk into the viper's pit.

I see her face when I close my eyes. I hear her voice on the line when no one calls. With my cowardice I know I signed her fate, even if I did not seal it.

Even now I come clean not out of loyalty but out of vanity. Frieda Mayweather would throw me to the wolves, given the chance. I am the useful fool, ready to be cast aside at any given moment. I will not allow her to do any more damage to me or my reputation, such as it is. I release myself, even if I do not forgive. I am sorry for Alison. Tell them I am so desperately sorry. John Quigley, the day you came to see me, you said Alison had Propofol in her system – I wrote Alison's prescriptions, and I never wrote one for this drug. She would have taken it willingly. I believe Frieda Mayweather met Alison the *day she died. I believe it was she who drugged her with propofol. She and Saul Elliot, her partner in all things, had decided that Alison was proving too risky for them and their business interests. Which, despite Frieda's protestations to the contrary, are solely money-based. I may be entirely wrong, but I feel no guilt in pointing a finger, especially at Frieda Mayweather. She is a monster, and she will do whatever she sees fit to protect her own interests.*

I cannot prove Frieda was behind Alison's death but if you do a little research it will not take you long to find out the type of person you are dealing with.

Alison Cooper would never have abandoned her children: she loved them with all her heart.

Ivan Frederick Colbert

John read it again. 'Jesus Christ. What the hell are this crowd involved in?'

'I don't know,' Shane said. 'I thought you'd understand it.'

John glanced up.

'Well, you're the detective, aren't you?'

John put the letter down. He was, wasn't he?

What would Sarah do?

He read the letter again. Met Alison the day she died.

'Hold on.'

He switched on his computer and waited for it to boot up. When it did so, he typed the words from the poem into Google and pressed send.

He got a hit immediately. 'The poem is call "Betrayal", by some dude called Dan McDonald.'

'"Betrayal"?'

'That's what it says.' John looked at the letter some more. 'I am a fucking idiot. Shane, who is this Frieda Colbert was talking about?'

'That's his boss, Frieda Mayweather.'

John Googled the name but drew a blank. He Googled it in conjunction with 'Ivan Colbert' and found a press shot of her on the steps to a courthouse, standing behind Colbert during a trial in which he was accused of malpractice. 'Gotcha.'

'What is it?' Shane said, leaning over the desk.

John spun the screen towards him. 'Is that her?'

'Yes.'

John hooked up the printer and pressed print. The image was grainy but it might be enough. 'I've got to go.'

'Where?'

'There's a girl I want to talk to.'

'What about the letter? What are you going to do?'

'Make a few connections first before I go forward.'

Shane stood and looked down at his hands. 'I should have done something last night. I knew he was acting strangely.'

John picked up his car keys and slipped the letter into his pocket. 'Hindsight, Shane. Believe me, we all wish we could see the shit before it hit the fan.'

54

John drove to the Alton Clinic and parked the Manta in a space just outside the main doors. He got out and looked up at the building. Maybe he was too gauche or uneducated or something, but the smoked glass and smooth concrete did nothing for him, although he recognised it had been expensive. It was soulless – cold, even.

He walked across the gravel and through the large swing doors.

At the reception desk two hotties were talking quietly. One, an attractive blonde, dabbed her eyes with a handkerchief. The other patted her shoulder in a conciliatory fashion. The blonde looked up when John approached. She took a deep breath and visibly attempted to rein in her emotions. 'Can I help you?'

'I'm looking for Frieda Mayweather. Is she around?'

Maybe it was his tone, or maybe it was the jeans and scuffed boots but neither hottie looked at him with too much by way of charm and affection.

'Do you have an appointment, *sir*?'

'I don't.'

'I'm sorry, but Ms Mayweather is extremely busy. If you would like to make an appointment I'm sure she will accommodate you.'

'Yeah, okay.' John leaned on the smoked-glass desk. 'Only, see, I'm a pretty busy guy myself. I don't have time to call back, so if you could just tell her John Quigley wants to talk to her maybe it could shake loose some of her time.'

The blonde narrowed her eyes. 'I can assure you, Mr Quigley, Ms Mayweather does not have time to shake loose, certainly not today. So if you don't mind—'

'I do mind. Tell her I'm here to talk about Ivan Colbert.'

The blonde glared at him. The other receptionist sniffed and looked ready to bawl at any second.

'One moment, please,' the blonde said, in a tone so icy it was a wonder the words left her mouth.

She made a call, spoke briefly and hung up. 'Third floor.' She jerked her head towards a set of lifts.

'Thanks.'

He rode the lift to the third flour, and as the door opened he found himself staring into a pair of grey eyes so devoid of emotion they reminded him of the concrete he'd been scowling at minutes earlier. In person Frieda Mayweather was tiny, like a doll, in a pencil skirt and killer heels.

'You're Quigley?'

'Yes, John Quigley.'

'What can I do for you, Mr Quigley?'

'I wanted to talk to you about the late Ivan Colbert, and the even later Alison Cooper.'

'Oh?'

She was smooth, he had to give her that. But tension radiated from her.

'Sure, I wanted to run an idea by you.'

'Follow me, please.' She led him down a short corridor to a walnut set of double doors, which had her name printed on them in gold letters. She used a swipe card to gain entrance and John followed her past a busy reception area where a secretary worked and two women sat reading glossy magazines.

'Celia, can you hold my calls for a few moments?' she said, as she strode past.

'Yes, Ms Mayweather.' The secretary flicked her eyes to John and then back to her screen.

'Nice place you have,' John said, when she had closed the interior door of her office. 'Very … What's the word? Understated. Guess that means it cost a fortune, right?'

'Please take a seat.'

'Busy for a Sunday, too. I'm guessing you'll have to do a helluva reshuffle now that you're short-staffed, right?'

She waved a hand at a chair and sat behind her desk.

John sat.

'Mr Quigley, Ivan Colbert was my friend and, as you seem to have heard, he died yesterday. So you will forgive me if I'm not in any mood for games of any kind. What can I do for you?'

'Dr Alison Cooper. Did you know her?'

'Not really, she was a friend of Ivan's. I knew of her rather than the woman in person.'

'She was a doctor at the Mercy. She treated a number of patients who required transplants.'

'And?'

'Well, I'm beginning to think she and Ivan might have had an arrangement.'

'An arrangement?'

'Yes.'

'What sort of arrangement?'

'Well, I've been talking with some of the people Alison treated, and by all accounts she seemed very certain she could get them help . . . help that involved skipping ahead of the transplant list.'

'I see, and you think Ivan was involved in some way?'

'It's possible. I don't believe Alison had the technical skills to perform a transplant of any kind, but I believe Ivan Colbert was a surgeon of great renown at one point in his career.'

'He was.'

'He must have been, or why would you have hired him?'

'I hired Ivan as a consultant.' She leaned back in her chair. 'So you think Ivan and Alison were – what? Operating on patients? For money?'

'Yes, it's a possibility.'

'You've obviously spoken to the alleged recipients. These people are willing to go to court to say that they received these organs?'

John smiled. 'Actually I haven't found a single one yet.'

'Oh?' She tilted her head. 'I'm confused. Alison Cooper worked for the Mercy, Ivan worked here. Neither would have had the opportunity to use equipment or theatres in this clinic without my knowledge.'

'This is true,' John said.

'Well, Mr Quigley, I can assure you I did not authorise any member of staff to carry out illegal procedures in this clinic. What an absurd suggestion.' She narrowed her eyes. 'Where would you get such a notion?'

'From Ivan Colbert, actually. I'm guessing he was more than a little upset over the death of his friend. Tell me something, how did you feel when Alison Cooper turned up dead?'

'You are a crass and vulgar man. You should go.'

'Why do you think Ivan took his own life?'

'He was an alcoholic – a great man, but prone to depression. It was no secret that he felt a little adrift in the world.

'How do you think he betrayed Alison Cooper?'

'What are you talking about?'

John removed Ivan's letter from his jacket and opened it. '"Poor Alison. With my cowardice I know I signed her fate, even if I did not seal it." I'm just curious, what fate was he talking about?'

'Where did you get that?'

'Never mind where I got it. What do you think it means?'

'How should I know?'

'Did Alison mention being depressed the day you met her? The day she died?'

Frieda did not reply, but her eyes never left John's face.

'I showed your photo to a waitress at the fancy restaurant where you both had lunch. Smart girl, that waitress, she recognised you.'

'I met a friend for lunch – so what?'

'She's a friend now?'

'I really think you should go.'

'You said that already.' John studied her. 'You know, I've been distracted from the moment Rose Butler – that's Alison's mother in case you're interested – came to see me. I had too much going on, too many plates spinning in the air.' He wiggled his finger beside his head. 'But I'm interested in you now. I will figure this one out and if I discover you had anything to do with Alison Cooper's death you'd better believe me when I say I'll be dogging you like a bad smell.'

Frieda Mayweather stood. 'My advice to you, Mr Quigley, would be to take your active imagination and put it to good use. Maybe you're in the wrong profession. Have you ever considered writing novels?'

John let her show him out. He was not interested in sparring verbally with her. He wanted to talk to two people. He wanted to talk to Beth Gold and he wanted very much to talk to Tobias Johnson.

55

Having spent the night sleeping fitfully on a narrow bed in a hostel at the top of Dame Street, Pavel was tired and muzzy-headed, but at least the last of the drugs seemed to have left his system and he was ready for action. He walked down the street and called into a hardware shop opposite the George's Street Arcade. He bought some duct tape, a roll of garden wire and a pair of needle-nose pliers, then went to catch the DART. He took it to Sandymount, alighted, then bought a bagel and a bottle of water from the local shop.

He walked down Frieda's street, then waited for half an hour at the top of the road, sitting on a low wall, smoking Grace's cigarettes. When the Range Rover passed him, he looped around to the street behind Frieda's. There, he walked straight into the grounds of the run-down house he had scoped out before.

He moved quickly down the side entrance and hurried to the rear of the overgrown garden. Making sure he was not overlooked, he scaled the wall bordering both properties and dropped down on the other side among trees, the pine needles breaking his fall.

He remained crouched for a moment, listening. There was a dog here – he had seen it earlier lying by the front gate in a patch of sunshine, a golden retriever. That complicated things slightly, but the man who had left in the Range Rover – he assumed Frieda's husband – appeared to have locked the animal into the house when he left.

He watched the house for a while, but there was no sign of movement in any of the windows and no other car in the drive. When he was sure that no one else was in, Pavel moved softly through the evergreens and exited on the south side of the garden.

From there he could see into a large, sunny conservatory. It was connected to a kitchen by a large arch. Pavel skirted the property, taking careful note of the double locks, thick glazing and top-of-the-range alarm system.

It was as tight as a fortress. There would be no breaking and waiting with this house. He would have to strike when the people were at home. He retreated to the trees and slipped away to wait.

He did not have to wait long. Shortly after three, the electric gates swung open and the Range Rover drove in. Form his vantage-point Pavel watched as the man and two children alighted, the boys dragging matching sports bags, laughing and jostling each other.

'Come on, guys,' the man called. 'A quick bite and then we need to hit the road.'

Pavel guessed their ages to be roughly eight and twelve. He was not unduly worried about the eight-year-old, but the twelve-year-old was tall and looked as if he might be a handful. He would have to incapacitate him if he couldn't control him.

Pavel watched the side of the house and was rewarded when

both children made appearances in the kitchen. They dumped their bags and immediately went to check the contents of the fridge. The dog trailed after the younger one, wagging its tail.

Excellent.

He moved back into the trees and worked his way along the perimeter again as he tracked the boys' movements through the house. The sitting room was directly across the hall from the kitchen. The boys took their snack inside and began watching a cartoon on a large plasma screen television.

The dog remained with them.

The dog was loyal. Pavel knew he would need to take it out of the equation first. It was a simple decision.

He moved back to the kitchen side of the house, entered the trees once more and sat down to wait. Surely the animal would need to urinate at some point.

At half past three he had his opportunity. The man came out to the car carrying two suitcases, which he put in the boot, and the retriever came with him. Pavel climbed up into the branches of the tree he had earlier sheltered under.

It did not take the dog long to come across his scent. It began to investigate, crossing the yard with its nose to the ground, tail up, but not waving. It moved faster as it approached the trees.

Pavel waited. When the dog came under the branches it stopped to sniff the bagel bag Pavel had purposely left beneath him. As it nosed for morsels, Pavel dropped the loop of wire over its head and jerked tight.

The dog thrashed hard, flinging its body backwards, scrabbling with its hind legs. But Pavel dragged it up close to his chest, never loosening his grip. In less than a minute the dog lay limp and bleeding against him.

Pavel let it fall to the ground and rolled his neck. He grabbed his bag, slung it on and moved towards the house. He slipped behind an ornamental bush that was one of a pair on either side of the front door and waited. In the gathering dusk he was virtually invisible.

After a short while the door opened and the man came out to the step. 'Barney?'

Pavel could smell his aftershave on the air, something dense and smoky. A masculine scent.

The man came out a little further.' Barney! Barney – come on now.'

Pavel stepped out in front of him.

The man looked at him, surprised, but not particularly frightened. It was as though he had no idea what he was looking at. 'Hey, who are you? What are you doing there?'

Pavel stepped forward and drove the knife deep into his chest. The man's eyes widened in shock. He grabbed at Pavel, raking his nails down his cheek. Pavel moved his head backwards out of range. He felt blood, hot and fast, run over his hand.

'I don't …' the man said, before he sank slowly to the ground. He was dead before he was down.

Pavel grabbed him by the ankles and dragged him into the bushes, then kicked leaves over him. There were not enough to cover him entirely.

Fuck.

He grabbed the man again and began to haul him across the gravel towards the trees. He glanced towards the house but no one had noticed.

He was sweating and his arms were trembling with exertion by the time he made it back to the house. He used the heel of his borrowed runners to scuff up the gravel and the bloodstains, scattering some of the leaves over the path to hide the traces.

When he was finished he went inside and closed the front door.

He stood in the hall, immobile. There was another suitcase here, larger than the others, with a waxed jacket draped over it.

To his right there was a large family portrait photograph, obviously taken in a studio. The man he had just killed stood beaming at the camera, one boy in his arms. Frieda was seated, with the younger child, only a baby, on her lap. Pavel studied the picture. She looked happy – at least, her smile did. Her eyes remained as cold and impassive as they had been at the hospital.

A monster, Pavel thought.

Just like him.

56

John caught Beth Gold as she was about to climb into her car in the staff car park. 'Hey, hold up there.'

She looked around, startled.

'Remember me?'

She nodded. 'Yes. How did you know where to find me?'

'I asked at the desk and they said you'd just left. I need to talk to you about Alison.'

'I've already told you everything I know about her.'

'Oh, I don't think so.'

'This is really not a good time.'

John stopped by the rear bumper. 'Ivan Colbert is dead. He killed himself last night.'

She took a deep breath and looked down. 'Yes, I'm aware of that. Bad news travels very quickly.'

'I know it's got something to do with Alison's death.'

'What makes you think that?'

'Guilt. He more or less said so in a letter he left. He said he had betrayed her. He said he was haunted by her.'

Beth Gold closed her car door softly. 'What do you want, Mr Quigley?'

'He said Alison would never have taken propofol. And I found no trace of it at her home or in work. He also said Alison was not the type of woman to admit defeat.'

'What do you mean?'

'When she found out Tom was having an affair, she called Karen Deloitte and got her to split. She fought for her patients tooth and nail – she became involved. She was not a person to give up.'

'I know that.'

'So don't you think it's strange that she checks into a grubby hotel and takes a knife to her wrists? Don't you think it's odd that a woman who will fight for her family so hard one year would leave them the next? Everyone – and I mean *everyone* – I have spoken to about her talks of her deep commitment to her children. Why would she hurt them like that?'

Beth's lower lip trembled slightly. 'I don't know.'

'Alison met Frieda Mayweather the same afternoon she died. They had lunch together.'

'Frieda Mayweather?'

'You know her?'

'Yes, she's a friend of Saul Elliot. Wait, you think Frieda had something to do with Alison's death?'

'Ivan Colbert said she and Saul Elliot were partners in everything. I think it possible Saul Elliot has been sending wealthier patients to Frieda's private clinic.'

'For what?'

'For whatever they need . . . for under-the-counter organ transplants.'

'Oh. for goodness' sake, that's ridiculous!'

'What's ridiculous about it? They come off the transplant list and no one asks why, do they?'

She opened her mouth then closed it again. 'No, I don't suppose they do.'

'Beth, listen to me now. Do you know the name Tobias Johnson?'

She squinted. 'I don't know . . . I'm not sure.'

'His daughter's Sofia was in Alison's book. She was down for a kidney transplant, but her father won't let me talk to her. Also there's another man, Allen Foster. He got a transplant back in November. Alison arranged that one. According to his wife, Alison and he travelled outside the country for it, but I checked with Alison's husband and she never left the country at any point, certainly not for a week.'

'So Alison, Saul and Frieda were working together? I still don't see how any of this is connected to Alison killing herself.'

'It's more complicated than that. See, I don't think they were working together. Not in the sense you mean. I think Alison found out that Saul was shifting patients and used that as leverage to get Frieda Mayweather to help *her* sickest patients.'

'As in blackmail?' Beth thought for a moment, then shook her head slowly. 'I don't believe it. Alison Cooper was as straight a person as you could meet.'

'Alison Cooper was watching people she cared about die because, for one reason or another, they were rejected for surgery. Or because they couldn't afford what it would take to get better. She was a hell of a doctor, and from everything I've heard about her I think she'd take the risk to help. She would have tried to level the playing field.'

'How can you prove any of this?'

'I'm not sure. I need to know what that girl Sofia was in for. I need you to find out what happened to her.'

'I can't do that. It's confidential information.'

'Jesus Christ, I don't want to know her blood type or any personal details, I just want to know why she was here and what was the outcome. Did she get surgery? Can you do that for me?'

'Why? Why should I?'

'Because I think you know Alison Cooper was not the type of woman to kill herself in a shit-hole. I think you have doubts too. You don't know what those doubts are or the nature of your unease, but it's there, right?'

'I don't know.'

'Coleen Clancy told me Alison was prepared to help her, even when others were not.. Chris Day tried to raise a ton of money before he passed away, even risking his family home. I think he was trying to fund a new liver. I think he died before he could make it and that that's why Alison was at his funeral, why she was so depressed after his death. She was trying to make a difference – rightly or wrongly The only link I have at the moment to any wrongdoing is Tobias Johnson and his daughter. I need to know what happened with that child. I need to look Alison's mother in the face and tell her I did everything I could to answer her questions.'

Beth chewed her bottom lip. 'All right. I'll go upstairs and check the computers for her name. But nobody can find out I did this for you – it can get me fired.'

John nodded. 'Call me the second you find out. And thank you.'

He went to walk away but she grabbed his forearm. 'Just so we're clear, I'm doing this for her, not you and not anyone else either. For her. She was my friend.'

'I know that.'

Beth released him. 'What are you going to do?'

'I'm going to set the cat among the pigeons,' John said.

57

John went directly from the hospital to Dalkey. He drove along the neat tree-lined avenue and parked in much the same place as he had the last time he had come to see Tobias Johnson. It seemed that an age had gone by since that day. He pulled in and shut off the engine with one hand, holding his mobile pressed against his ear with the other. He was listening to Beth Gold's voice. He took out his notebook and wrote down what she had to say in his usual almost illegible shorthand.

'Thank you for this,' he said, when she had finished speaking.

He pressed end and put the phone on his lap. He gazed out of the window at the cheery yellow house with the nice garden and the wraparound balcony.

Maybe he was chasing shadows, maybe he was barking up the wrong tree.

Maybe he was using too many clichés.

He got out of the car and walked to the gate. He pressed the intercom. He waited.

'Yes?'

'Mr Tobias Johnson?'

'Who is this?'

'John Quigley, the detective. I don't know if you remember me or not, but I was here before.'

'Yes, I know, and I told you then what I'm about to tell you now. I have nothing to say to you.'

'I'm sorry, but you can either talk to me or to the Gardaí.'

'What are you talking about? Why would I need to talk to anyone?'

'It's about Sofia, your daughter.'

'Get away from my gate.'

'I have their number up on my screen. If I'm wrong I'm wrong – I'm used to the cops being pissed off with me. How about you?'

There was nothing but silence from the intercom.

'You still there?' John asked.

'Why are you doing this?' The voice no longer sounded angry, just frightened and helpless.

'You going to talk to me or not?'

The gates opened. John stepped through them and walked along a cobbled drive until he reached a set of wooden steps leading to the front door on the second level.

He waited at the door, and after a moment, a short middle-aged man wearing chinos and a lemon jumper came along the hall and opened it. He was deeply tanned, with silver hair, silver eyebrows and no real chin to speak of. 'Come in.'

John did as he was directed. He closed the door over. The man looked up at him. He radiated fear.

'You're Tobias Johnson?'

'You know I am.'

John took out his notebook and flicked it open. 'Your daughter Sofia was brought into the Mercy Hospital early last year. She had fainted in school and was suffering from extreme anaemia. She was released but fainted again two days later and was brought back to the Mercy by ambulance. She was subsequently found to be suffering from kidney failure.'

The man looked up at John with loathing and fear. 'How do you know this? My daughter's illness is none of your concern.'

'She was fifteen, right?'

'You have no right to question me.'

'Initial hospital report says she weighed less than seven stone when she was admitted.' John looked up. 'That's pretty light for a fifteen-year-old.'

'You insensitive bastard.' Johnson grabbed John and shoved him hard against the wall. 'Why are you *doing* this to us?'

John pushed him away. Tobias Johnson clenched his hands and held them stiffly by his sides. 'Must be hard to watch someone you love kill themselves.'

'Do you have children, Mr Quigley?'

'No, I do not.'

'Then what the hell do you know about how hard anything is?'

John shrugged. 'Maybe I don't fully, but I can imagine—'

'Imagine? You can imagine? How dare you? Tell me, Quigley, can you imagine sitting at a table day after day and watching your child hide their food? Can you imagine having to police the bathroom after every meal? Can you imagine the screaming fits because you put your foot down and insist your child eat a small potato? Or a yoghurt? Can you imagine searching through bins for food that you hope you won't find? Can you imagine hearing your dentist tell you that your child's teeth are falling out of her head? Can you imagine watching your child's hair fall out?

Seeing her cry because a glass of water makes her feel bloated? Can you imagine all that, Mr Quigley?'

'Your daughter's got anorexia?'

'She has a complicated ED. Anorexia doesn't even begin to cover it.'

'Is that why she was a poor candidate for the transplant list?'

'The *list*.' Johnson's lip curled.

'Yes, the list. She was on it and then you took her off. What did you do?'

'I did what any father would do. I helped my daughter stay alive.'

'You paid for an organ?'

Johnson glared at him. 'Why do you need to know any of this? What has this got to do with anything?'

'It's got to do with Alison Cooper. She was the doctor who admitted your daughter initially.'

'Yes – so?'

'She knew what you did.'

'That woman was a menace. A self-important, puffed-up fool.'

John was surprised. This was the first time he had heard anyone say a bad word about her. 'She was against a transplant?'

'She said Sofia was not mentally stable enough. She would not recommend her for surgery. She condemned my daughter to die. So no, Mr Quigley, when you came here the other day asking after her, I had nothing to say. She's dead. So what?'

'She wouldn't help you so you went to Frieda Mayweather.'

He looked away, but not before John had spotted the recognition in his eyes.

'You did – I know you did.'

'If you know it, why are you asking me?'

'I want to know how you found her. I want you to confirm that she was the one.'

'I won't help you destroy people who helped me when I needed them most. My wife is dead and my daughter is all I have.'

John stepped forward. 'You will help me or I'll call a friend of mine in a newspaper and give him a goddamned exclusive he'll find very interesting. Sofia's sixteen now, right? You want her to read about herself, see her father dragged through the mud?'

'You can't do that – you don't understand. That sort of attention could set her back months! Please, for God's sake, don't do this to her.'

'I'm sorry, I need answers.'

'You bastard. I did what I had to do to save her.'

'This isn't about her. People are dead. Alison Cooper is dead. Ivan Colbert is dead. Something is going on and I will get to the bottom of it. Now, you either help me or I'll bury you.'

Tobias Johnson looked sick to his stomach. He grabbed John's hands in his. 'Please, I'm begging you, don't do this.'

'I'm sorry,' John said, 'but I promised another parent I would find out what happened to her child. I have to do this. I have no choice.'

'Please.'

'I'm sorry,' John said. He opened the door and walked down the steps. Behind him he could hear Tobias Johnson crying like a broken man.

58

'Mr Corrigan, I can assure we will find another surgeon.' Frieda turned off the main road and drove towards Sandymount. 'Of course you're upset. I understand how devastated Ann-Marie must be. But I assure you I will rectify the situation. You have my absolute word on it. Hello?'

She glanced at her phone. He had hung up on her.

Frieda replaced the phone in the car set. Bloody Ivan. He had left her high and dry. His death meant she had no choice but to cancel the surgery and now Aidan Corrigan was livid and threatening to withdraw his donation to the clinic. 'Fuck,' she said, an uncharacteristic swear-word escaping her lips.

At the next set of traffic-lights Frieda tried Gerald's mobile. She was surprised when no one picked up. She glanced at the clock on the dash. Twenty to seven? He was probably driving through an area with poor coverage. She sighed. It had been a hard-won battle to convince him to take the boys to the summer house. Unfortunately she had had little option but to tell him a man had made a threat to her life and it had taken every ounce of her persuasive skill to make him believe she had already put the matter in the hands of the Gardaí. Now it was up to Hannity to locate the threat and deal with it. There would be no taking him to the hospital this time. Hannity had orders to take out Pavel Sunic on sight.

Twenty minutes later she turned into her street and pulled up to her gateway. Her stomach dropped when she noticed her husband's Range Rover parked in its usual spot. She hit the remote locking system and drove in. She was aware that the security light did not come on and there appeared to be no lights on anywhere in the lower level of the house.

She sat in the car for a moment, looking at her home. She took up her mobile and rang the house phone. Nobody answered.

She looked at Gerald's car again. Small hairs prickled on the back of her neck.

She switched the engine off but remained seated, her hands resting on the steering-wheel. No sound from Barney and he normally barked when she came home.

No dog, no light, nobody answering the phone. She dialled another number.

'Yes?'

'Mr Hannity, I want you to come by my house as soon as you get an opportunity.'

'What's wrong?'

'I don't know yet, but something is. The back door will be unlocked. You know the code to the gate?'

'I do. If something's wrong you should wait until I get there.'

'I need to make sure my children are okay. Be here as soon as possible.'

Frieda got out of the car and closed the door softly. She moved quickly to the rear of her car, opened the boot and took out the tyre iron. Without a moment's hesitation she removed her shoes and walked around to the back of the house. She used her keys to open the back door and slipped into the laundry room off the kitchen.

She stood in the shadows, thinking. She tried not to imagine what she feared most. But she was no fool and she wouldn't wallow in uncertainty.

She needed a weapon.

She felt along the shelves over the washing-machine for the toolbox. Her fingers found it and she opened it as quietly as she could. She pulled out a screwdriver. She found the box cutter, too, and stuck it into the waistband of her skirt.

When she was sure she had all she could carry, she stepped lightly into the back corridor and padded along the tiles until she reached the main front hall.

Here she waited. She had lived in this house almost ten years: she knew every nook and cranny of it, every creak of a board. She was on home turf. Surely that gave her the advantage.

She wondered if her children were still alive.

Was this it?

Keeping as close to the wall as she could, she slid around the corner and out into the hallway. She waited. Where was he likely to be? She peered across the hall into the family room. She thought she could just make out the TV and the ugly lamp Gerald's sister had given them the year before.

She tiptoed across the hall and looked in. Nothing. Gerald's office was further along, after the door to the guest WC.

She glanced up the wood-panelled staircase. Above her were four bedrooms and the master bathroom. He was most likely up there.

But she checked the office anyway. She was nothing if not methodical.

By now her hands were slick with sweat and her shirt was stuck to her back. It cost her a lot not to run out of the front door and wait for help. What if he killed her children while she sat outside?

They might already be dead.

She squeezed her eyes shut until her hands stopped shaking. She had to keep a clear head.

She moved up the stairs quickly and with almost no sound, stepping over the third stair from the top, the one that squeaked no matter how many times it was nailed down.

Her elder son's room was first. Gerry was still only a child but already as tall as she was. He was like his father, athletic, sure-footed, a real little heartbreaker.

Stop.

She tightened her grip on the hammer and used it to push open his door. By the light from the window she could see the room was empty.

She checked the bathroom next. Empty.

She checked her younger son's room. Rory was her baby, her little lamb. She held her breath as she pushed open his door.

Empty.

Despite herself she sagged against the wall. Only one room remained. She wiped the sweat from her eye and tried to slow her breathing. He would hear her heart beating, surely.

She looked at her door. Focus. She pushed a strand of hair off her forehead with the heel of the hand that was gripping the tyre iron. She tried to visualise the layout of her bedroom.

The door opened from left to right. If she pushed it all the way it should lie flush against the wall. Then there was the bed – a massive oak sleigh-bed – facing the door at an angle. To the right of that there was a wall of floor-to-ceiling wardrobes, mirrored. To the left of them was the door to the en-suite. Her dressing-table was to the right of the door, a French reproduction piece she had brought from Canada. There was nowhere to hide there.

She took another breath. She wished she had a gun in her hand instead of a tyre iron. If she made it out of this alive, she would see to it that she always had one in the future. She had learned to shoot in Canada and was very proficient.

She took another breath, and this one seemed to steady her somewhat.

Using the hand with the screwdriver she opened the door and shoved it hard. It swung all the way around and bounced off the wall. He was not hiding there.

She hit the light switch. If it was to be this way, so be it. She'd take her chances.

The bedroom was empty. She blinked rapidly, forcing her eyes to adjust to the light.

She yanked open the wardrobes one by one. Nothing.

Damnit, where was he?'

She heard the sound of running water.

The en-suite.

She tightened her grip on the hammer, strangely furious now. To hell with him and his games, this was too much. He was toying with her.

She kicked the bathroom door open and stood splayed against it. The room was filled with steam from the running shower.

The curtain was pulled across the bath.

Frieda knew then, with absolute certainty, that her boys were dead. He had killed them and left their bodies for her to find. She lowered her arms and took one slow step, then another towards the bath. With a trembling hand she reached for the curtain and snatched it back.

Pavel Sunic stood there, soaked to the skin. He drew back his hand and punched Frieda straight in the mouth before she could even scream.

59

John left Tobias Johnson's home and drove back to his office. It was late, almost half seven, and he felt dispirited, hungry, and sick and tired of the world.

The truth was he *did* understand people like Tobias Johnson. He had done what he was supposed to do as a father: he had used everything at his disposal to help his child. In the same situation John could not honestly say he wouldn't have done exactly the same. Tobias Johnson wasn't the bad guy. He was a flawed man, sure, but one who loved his child and did not want her to die. How the hell was that wrong? No, the bad guys were people like Frieda Mayweather and Saul Elliot, vultures, happy to profit off the misery of others. Or maybe that was just the way the world worked, a market for everyone and everything.

He called Beth Gold as soon as he was behind his desk. She had obviously been waiting for his call because she picked up on the second ring.

'Well?'

'I was right about the girl.'

'He went off the grid to get her help?'

'Yep.'

'Jesus. Alison organised it?'

'No, Alison did not help him. She was against his daughter getting surgery – she thought the kid was nowhere near emotionally ready.'

'So it was through Saul, like you thought.'

'Saul Elliot introduced him to Frieda Mayweather. After that it was all down to money.'

'My God, I can hardly believe this.'

'Believe it. His kid is now starving herself to death with a perfectly healthy kidney to support her.'

'Does he know where the organ came from?'

'No, we didn't get into the details. I didn't want to push him any more than I already had done. The man's pretty fucking crushed.'

'So what do you do now?'

'Now I type up what I think and what I know and pass the information to Rose Butler. It will be up to her what she does with it.'

Beth Gold sighed heavily. 'She won't be able to do anything. Alison is dead, Ivan is dead. And if you've ever met Frieda, you know she won't break easy. Neither will Saul.'

'I don't need to break her. I *know* she helped Tobias Johnson's daughter.'

'Did he write that down for you?'

'No.'

'Right – so by now he's been on to his solicitor, and on to Frieda and on to Saul, and they will have spoken to whomever they need to speak to to shut this down.'

'They can try, but I know what I know. And if the cops start digging around they'll find what they need to put a stronger case together.'

'None of it really explains why Alison is dead.'

'I'm telling you, the more I think about this the less I believe she did kill herself. I think she might have been drugged first, then had her wrists cut.'

'You need to get Frieda Mayweather on tape saying she did something, or at the very least confirming some of what you believe to be true.'

'Then that's what I'll do.'

'Good luck, Mr Quigley. You're going to need it.'

John hung up and scowled at the phone. She was right, of course, and that pissed him off.

He called Shane Breen.

'Hello?'

'Shane?'

'Yes?'

'John Quigley here. Tell me something, you don't happen to have the address of Frieda Mayweather, do you?' He wrote it down. As he was leaving, his mobile rang.

He checked the number and grimaced.

Suzy.

No, he had no time to be dealing with her shit. As far he was concerned she had made her bed, and if it was getting messy, too bad. It was no longer his problem.

Ten minutes later John Quigley was back in his car and on his way to Sandymount.

60

Frieda fell backwards. She tasted blood in her mouth. She tried to scrabble away across the tiles but her co-ordination was skewed and her legs refused to obey even the simplest demand.

Pavel Sunic pushed the curtain away and stepped soaking from the claw-foot bath. He looked down at the fallen tyre iron, smiled and kicked it away. Then he grabbed her wrist and twisted the screwdriver from her hand.

He held it out before him. Frieda lunged for it, but he flung it aside and dragged her to her feet. Even as she tried to gouge at his face he swung her up and deposited her in the bath, which contained about a foot of water.

Frieda tried to keep her feet under her.

He struck her again and she stopped trying.

Pavel leaned across her and switched off the shower. He turned on the taps instead. The bath began to fill more quickly.

'Where are my children?' Frieda jerked away from the scalding water pouring out of the hot tap. She had lost the screwdriver in the fall too, but she felt the box cutter in the waistband of her skirt. Pavel had not noticed it.

He rested his hand on the ledge of the tub. 'I do not kill children.'

'You're a liar.'

He shrugged.

'Where is my husband?'

'This one is not alive.'

Frieda closed her eyes.

'You are crying?'

She opened her eyes. He was watching her closely. He shook his head. 'No, you do not cry. You are like Ademi.'

'I don't know what you're talking about.'

'Is man I know. Like you, no heart.'

'That's ridiculous.' Frieda wiped at the blood on her mouth. 'Of course I have a heart, you have me all wrong. Can't you see that?'

'No.' Pavel touched his chest with his thumb. 'You have not. I can see.'

'What do you want?'

'Name of person who is case forty-seven.'

'Then you'll let me go?'

'No.'

'Why should I tell you?'

'Then I don't kill boys.'

She clenched her teeth, her eyes blazing with hatred.

'How do I know they're alive now?'

They waited. Pavel watched her, she watched him. Neither moved and the water got deeper.

'Please, listen to me. If what you're saying is true and their father is dead, don't do this – don't orphan my children.' Frieda began to shake with emotion. She slid her right hand down by

340

her side. 'Your sister is dead. You can't bring her back. Nothing can bring her back. I beg you, don't do this.'

'Yes, Ana is dead.'

'So what's the point of all this?'

'People like you,' Pavel's lip curled slightly, 'think always you are important. Always you have the reasons to do only what you want. My kind are … like shit to you.'

'You're wrong. We're trying to help people. It's not wrong to help people in their time of need.'

'Who is person who is case forty-seven?'

'I won't help you destroy more lives.'

Pavel grabbed her ankles and dragged her towards him. But before he could pull her under the water Frieda's fingers had closed around the box cutter. She pushed the blade forward and swung it hard.

Pavel saw its trajectory at the last second and managed to get his arm up. It skittered down his sleeve, raked his face and embedded itself in his collarbone. He screamed. He flung Frieda back into the bath, but she scrambled out. She tried to run past him, but he managed to snag one of her bare ankles. She fell and smashed into the laundry basket by the sink. She was on her feet almost immediately. Before Pavel could grab her again she lifted a heavy porcelain jug from the antique nightstand and brought it down on his head.

He went down.

Frieda fled, slipping on the water as she skidded out of the bathroom.

She ran out onto the landing and jumped up to catch the cord of the trapdoor leading to the attic. She was pulling it down when Pavel, still with the blade dug into his shoulder, charged her from the bedroom.

He hit her hard. Frieda tumbled over the side of the banister.

Somehow she managed to catch hold of the railing. The drop was almost twenty-five feet onto hard tiles.

'Help me, please.' Frieda said, trying to swing her legs up. But the pencil skirt she wore was too fitted to allow her to gain purchase. Her hands were slick with blood and she ripped numerous fingernails free in her desperate attempt to catch her fall.

Pavel sank down. He looked at her through the wooden banisters. Frieda gritted her teeth and swung her legs again. A stocking-clad foot hooked through one of the spindles. Pavel pulled the blade from his shoulder.

'*Akana mukav tut le Devlesa*,' he said, panting with pain. I leave you know with God. He stabbed Frieda's fingers, using the bloodied box cutter, and Frieda Mayweather fell silently to the floor.

By the time John Quigley reached Frieda Mayweather's home, an ambulance and three squad cars with flashing lights had surrounded it.

John parked the Manta and hurried down the street. He approached a set of neighbours who were standing by the first police car. 'What's going on?'

A woman turned to him. 'We don't know. Intruders, we think.'

As John watched he saw a grim-faced man walk two boys to a waiting ambulance. The children looked scared and confused. A man from the ambulance service draped a silver-foil blanket around both of them and helped them into the back.

John approached one of the guards standing by the gate. 'What's happening?'

'Are you a friend of the family?'

'No, but—'

'Sir, you need to step away.'

'But—'

'Step away,' the guard said.

John moved back to the grass verge. As he did so, the coroner's van arrived.

He watched as two body bags were loaded into it. He glanced at the ambulance. Only one door was open but through it he could see the traumatised face of the smaller boy. He was not crying or making any sound, just sat and stared, his small hands balled into fists.

61

John stayed up late that night and did something Sarah Kenny used to break his balls about constantly: he created a coherent report.

He typed up everything he had, highlighted every note, every detail he could think of, every conversation he had had, all the speculation, all the guesswork, and everything he believed. When he was finished it still looked pretty slim, but he hoped it would be enough.

Early the next morning he got out of bed, had a slice of toast and went to the corner shop with Sumo to pick up the papers.

Back at the house he stood at the sink and read about the intrusion into Frieda Mayweather's home. Gerald Mayweather, a well-respected nutritionist, had been attacked and killed in an apparent robbery gone horribly wrong. Initial reports suggested Frieda Mayweather, his wife, might have disturbed the intruder and bravely fought him. She was described as being found dead at the scene, the result of either being pushed or jumping from the second floor.

The police were looking for a suspect, whom they also believed was involved in the killing of Brendan O'Brien, an anaesthetist at the hospital where Frieda had worked as a surgeon and administrator. One possible theory being put forward was that the intruder had been searching for drugs.

'We are at an early stage in the investigation,' Detective Inspector Jim Stafford was quoted as saying. 'If I knew anything else I'd tell you.'

John smiled when he saw Jim Stafford's name. Though there had been little love lost between the two men since the David Reid case a few years before, he liked the stubby little detective with the caterpillar eyebrows and hair-trigger temper, and knew he would be a thorough and implacable investigator.

John drove to Rose Butler's neat Glasnevin home. On the way there his phone rang twice. One call was a blocked number, so he ignored it. The second was from a friend of his who was able to add an address to the phone number Jackie had given him for the mysterious phone-shy Sid.

Rose was still in her dressing-gown when she answered the door. 'Oh, Mr Quigley, I wasn't expecting anyone. I'm not even dressed yet.'

'I'm sorry to call over like this.'

She studied his face. 'You look tired.'

John gave her a half-smile. 'If I look half as bad as I feel, I must be truly frightening.'

She bade him come in and led him into a small kitchen to the rear of the house. There was a gas fire on and the radio playing softly in the background. Her home reminded John of his parents' place, old fashioned, cluttered, cosy. There were photos of Alison and her family dotted everywhere.

'Will you have a cup of tea?

'I will, thanks.'

'You must think I'm a holy show.' She patted at her uncombed hair.

'It's not even nine. I had no business calling unannounced.'

She made them tea and sat across from him at the table. She looked at the file he had placed before him.

'What's all that?'

'I'm hoping it's enough evidence for the Gardaí to look at Alison's death again.'

She lowered her gaze and let out a long, slow breath. 'So you don't think Alison killed herself?'

'No. I don't know – I don't know what I think, but I don't have the resources or the capability to prove anything one way or the other. Ask me to follow someone and I can follow them. Ask me to look into finances and I know people who can help. But this is out of my league. You need the cops for this line of work and probably a court order or two. Hopefully there's enough here to get the ball rolling. There are two people the guards absolutely must talk to – Tobias Johnson and Allen Foster. These people are the key to why Alison might have died.'

'I appreciate everything you've done.' She reached across the table and placed her hand over his. 'How much do I owe you?'

'Nothing.'

'Ah, now, come on.'

'I mean it. I didn't do a whole lot, really, and I've solved nothing. Mrs Butler, I won't take a penny off you.'

'You did what I asked.'

He slid the file across the table to her. 'You need to put this into the hands of someone on the force who will rattle a few cages. There's a cop called Stafford working another case right now, but that case is connected to your daughter. I've cut out the article from the paper this morning – it's in here.' John tapped the file. 'Stafford's mobile number is in here too. You tell him I gave it to you, and tell him I'm available after he reads that file.'

She took the file from him. 'Thank you.'

'There's one other thing. Alison's husband, Tom.'

'What about him?'

'Mrs Cooper, I hope I'm not overstepping the mark here, but while I have no doubt Tom Cooper is a difficult man to love, Alison did love him.'

She nodded. 'I suppose she did.'

'It's going to be hard on those children without their mother and they'll need all the support they can get. They're going to need you. You've got to find a way to work with him. For their sakes.'

'I miss her.' A single tear rolled down her cheek. 'I just miss her so much.'

John held her hand in his, and long after he left he could feel the soft touch of her skin.

He was back home by eleven.

He found Suzy Brannigan sitting huddled in a long quilted coat on his doorstep. She stared up at him when he opened the gate. Her face was terrible: bruised, white, feral-looking.

'What are you doing here?'

'You fucking bastard.' She got up and walked towards him. She struck him across the face with an open palm. '*You told him.*'

John put his hand to his cheek. It stung.

'You *told* him what Jaffa done.'

'I assume you're talking about your brother?'

'I asked you to keep him out of it.'

'You asked me to help you. I did, and then you went running back to the man who did this –' John grabbed her chin '– to your face.'

'This –' she bared her teeth and jabbed him in the chest with

347

her index finger '– is fucking nothing compared to what Mike had someone do to Jaffa last night.'

'What are you talking about?'

'Jaffa,' she said. 'He was beaten black and blue, and I know, I *fucking* know, it was Mike. I know you told him. Don't try deny it.'

'I did tell him. I'm not going to deny it.'

'I thought I could trust you – I thought you were different. But you're not, John Quigley. You're just another fucking wanker.'

'Suzy—' He reached for her but she slapped his hand away and ran past him up the street.

He let her go. What was the point in stopping her? She would do what she would do and that was how the world worked.

Now he would do what he needed to do.

He needed to find Sarah Kenny.

He let himself into the house. Sumo was waiting just inside the door to greet him. He squatted and patted the big dog's head. After a moment he stood and went to the kitchen.

He called Shane first.

'Shane, it's me, John Quigley.'

'Did you use the letter?'

'I had to include it in a file.'

'So my name's going to the guards.'

'They'll probably want to question you, yes. I'm sorry.'

'My old man's going to be very angry.'

'I know. I'm sorry.'

'I'm sure you did what you had to do.' He hung up.

John pinched the top of his nose. Jesus, was there anyone else he could fuck up? He called his sister. 'Sis? Can you take Sumo for a few days?'

'You've been arrested again?'

'No.' John took out a cigarette and lit it. 'I'm going to need you watch him while I go to England.'

'Why are you going to England? Have you a case?'

'Yeah,' John said, opening the note Sarah Kenny had left for him those months before. 'A missing-person case.'

'You're going after Sarah.' It wasn't a question.'

'I need her, Carrie,' he said. 'I miss her.'

Carrie sighed. 'My neighbours are going to be delighted.'

John smiled. 'He does have a way with people, there's no denying that.' He told her what time he'd drop Sumo over and hung up. He went to his room and began to pack an overnight bag. As he threw socks and T-shirts into it, he thought of the small boy sitting in the back of the ambulance and wondered why people thought dancing with the devil was ever worth it.

Epilogue

Savo Ademi stared at the small screen in disgust. 'Ah!' he said, when the final whistle was blown. He threw his hands into the air. 'Rubbish, rubbish. They should sell this useless bastard. Sell or shoot him, one or the other. This shit does not belong in FC Borac.' He spat on the floor and jammed the butt of his cigar back into his mouth.

'Cough up, Ademi. You lost.' Karadzic, his friend, was grinning at him.

Right at that moment, Ademi hated his smug face. He reached into his pocket, counted out a few bills and tossed them on the table. Without saying goodbye, he rose, drained his drink, replaced his cigar and left the bar.

As he walked along the small street back to his place he grumbled under his breath. Football! It was a terrible thing to be passionate about. It treated a man worse than a cheap whore with one eye on the clock. He hated to lose at anything, but to lose money over football gave him a stomach-ache.

He turned the corner and walked down the single entry lane that led to his home. Misha, his wife, would have food waiting for him. His stomach rumbled as he thought of it. He hoped she had remembered to starch his shirt: there was an inspection in the new barracks the following day and he did not want to have to remind her again.

He walked past the new block of apartments that was being built a few doors from his house. It was part of the rejuvenation of the area. He sneered, thinking of the waves of yuppy shits eating up the neighbourhood, making it impossible for good, hard-working people to find homes where they had grown up.

As he walked past he heard clanging from within.

He stopped and squinted into the darkness. The block was not nearly finished and the workmen – whom he had argued with many times – usually boarded up the windows at night. One of the boards had been removed.

Ademi reached for the gun he carried under his coat. He stepped around the metal crash barrier and approached the window slowly. He looked in. By the light of the street he could see almost to the rear of the apartment. The walls were exposed brick, not even plastered yet, and electrical cables hung down from the ceilings, ready to be hooked up to the main supply. He cocked his head.

There: the sound again.

Kids, he thought, or junkies.

He put the gun back into its holster, placed both hands on the window-ledge and boosted himself inside. He paused to listen, then went to investigate.

He was walking down the unfinished hallway when he felt something slip by his ears.

He flinched, but before he could work out what it was somebody dropped to the floor in front of him. A noose tightened around his neck so hard and tight that it yanked him off his feet.

'*Eog*,' he said, desperately trying to stand on his toes to relieve the pressure.

The figure moved out of the gloom. Ademi's eyes widened as he recognised Pavel Sunic. Pavel had a belt fastened around his chest and attached to it was the wire he had suspended over a beam in the ceiling before he had lassoed Ademi.

Ademi tried to get his fingers under the wire. The closer Pavel was, the looser it seemed. He tried to take a step forward.

Pavel shook his head. He spat in Ademi's face, then turned and sprinted to the end of the hall.

He did not quite manage to decapitate the man Ana had paid to release her brother.

Not quite. But he was satisfied with the result.

LONGFORD LIBRARY

3 0015 00348089 6